Loving
the
Mysterious
Texan

Loving
the
Mysterious
Texan

Mary Connealy

CHAPTER ONE

May – Devereau Island off the coast of Gull Cove, Texas

A n explosion shook her awake.
Her eyes shot open.

On her left a window lit up. Thunder rumbled across the sky growing in speed like an incoming missile. Lightning turned the night to day.

The thunder exploded. A scream tore from her throat. Still half asleep, she tried to fight her way out of a nightmare.

Or was it real?

Windows rattled and the wind howled. She felt moisture on her face and dashed tears away.

Every instinct told her to get up, run, save herself. But from what? Her mind was muddled with fear and pain.

With fumbling hands, she realized she lay on a mattress and swung her legs out of bed.

Lightning-sharp pain jagged through her head.

A cry escaped but she gritted her teeth and shoved at the pillow to sit upright. Thunder roared across the sky, building force. It came for her like a soaring, diving predator. She fought to stay sitting as if she fought for her very life.

The window lit up.

It arched at the top. Huge, stretching from the floor to a cathedral ceiling fifteen feet high, it glowed in the flashing light. The window and ceiling were magnificent, ornate—she'd never seen them before. Her vision worked, but a fog seemed to envelope her brain and she couldn't reason out what was going on.

The window lit up.

"Where am I?" Before the thunder hit, she stumbled to her feet.

The thunder struck. She teetered back. Her thighs hit the bed, but she stayed upright. Distant thunder rolled steadily beneath the rage of the storm, adding strength to the explosions.

The window lit up. It was coming, coming, another deafening assault of thunder.

Where was this place? Glancing frantically around sent fresh torment lacing through her head. A whimper ripped loose from her throat. The salty sting of tears blinded her, even though she wasn't aware of crying. The thunder raged toward her like an incoming bomb.

Roughly she wiped tears away with both hands. When she jostled her head, she set off sickening pain. Her hands were so wet and sticky with tears she ran her wrists and forearms over her cheeks to rid herself of the salt that cut like acid into her eyes. She wiped her tear soaked hands on her nightgown and touched heavy, soft fabric.

Strange clothes, strange room, strange window. She had no idea what had brought her to this place and time.

She looked again at herself but the flickering lightning died and plunged her into darkness. She touched the unfamiliar cloth. Slid her hands down it, knowing she'd never seen the robe before.

The window lit up.

She looked at the white robe she wore and saw black stripes. Like jail cell bars. The stripes glistened wet. Her fingers were tipped in black. She spread them wide and looked at her palms.

Both hands smeared with black. Both wrists. Both arms.

The thunder rolling across the sky. It seized the house, shook it in its teeth. She staggered under the violence.

The window lit up. The black stripes became red. Bright, wet, warm, crimson.

Blood.

She shook her head to rid it of this insanity and the hurt finally made sense as it slashed through her skull.

Not tears. Blood.

She wiped at her head again and felt the source of her pain in a gash.

The thunder exploded. Stunned from the vivid blood, the vicious pain, she stumbled and fell on the bed. Her head twisted away from the ugliness of her fear.

The fixed eyes of a man glared at her. A gaping slash crossed his throat. His blood mingled with her own until the bed was slick. She'd never seen him before in her life.

Sliding and shoving away from his corpse, she got to her feet and ran. And the thunder slammed her bodily and imprisoned her in stormy arms. She screamed.

The window lit up.

The thunder smothered her cries. The storm lifted her. Wind swept her away against her will.

Fighting to get free, she couldn't escape. A blinding light pushed away some of the madness. Not lightning this time, light.

"You're covered in blood!" The thunder rumbled words. Nothing made sense.

She was held fast and moved so quickly she had no idea where they were going. The sky opened up and rain gushed over her and her eyes closed against it. Strong arms ran over her body. The blast of wet cold cleared her mind enough she lifted her head and looked into eyes hotter than blazing lightning. Dangerous eyes. Thunderous eyes. She opened her mouth.

"Shut up." He spoke in a brutal whisper. He carried the violence of the thunder with him, and it still rolled and crashed outside. His hands stroked. Guttural words she couldn't understand washed over her like the pulsating water.

He growled, "Do as I say—only as I say."

And because he seemed to have complete power over her, a raging storm become man, she murmured. "I will."

He looked fully into her eyes and the rage in him burned her to her soul. But the fire and water cleared her head. Until this moment she'd been so overwhelmed, her grip on reality so tenuous, she only now realized the thunder hadn't taken human form. No attacking storm had dragged her into its belly and poured rain down on her head.

This man, this dark stranger, was very real. She tried to regain her grip on sanity and move away from him.

Pressing her against the tiled shower wall, his hands moved through her hair again and she flinched from the pain. He eased his grip. Her eyes flickered open to see him study her scalp. Eyes flashed with a gray blue as fiery as the lightning, then darkened until they were as violent as the thunder. His head and arms were soaked from leaning into the shower, holding her still. He swept blue-black hair off his forehead with one impatient hand.

His jaw tensed, square with the strength of his character. His nose straight and prominent as if he'd been etched from granite. Zeus, the Greek god of thunder come to life. His high cheekbones were taut under the lash of anger. She got only a glimpse as he examined her head, then his eyes went to hers and she saw, beneath the iron will and the rage, compassion.

With a quick look at her wound, he whispered in a voice so rough it sanded against her ears, "If you want to get through the next hour, be quiet."

In her terror, she believed him. His will took complete control of her.

"Did you hear me?" he hissed.

She nodded as she became aware of a pounding that was separate from the pounding storm.

For a long moment, he studied her, then gave a satisfied jerk of his chin. "Absolute silence."

He released her and jerked the shower curtain closed. Once he let go, her knees gave out and she sank to the floor.

Seconds passed, or maybe minutes. The water beat on her head. The door outside opened and she heard another voice. Someone else had come into the bathroom. The pounding had been someone wanting in. She would have called out for help if the man hadn't been so brutal in his order to remain silent.

The same guttural voice that had demanded her obedience said with an authority that few could deny, "Get out of here, Allen."

A hand reached for the shower curtain. She saw the cuff of a red satin robe. The man who'd held her wore black.

She pressed herself into the corner of the shower.

Another hand caught the curtain and held it in place.

There was an instant's hesitation.

Allen spoke from behind the curtain. "Grey, Victor's dead."

Who was Victor? The man she'd been in bed with, surely, there couldn't be two dead men. Who was Grey? The man she'd been in the shower with, surely. She wondered if her life could get more completely out of hand. That left Allen, who was seconds from shoving back the curtain and seeing her, crouched on the floor.

With admirable shock, considering he already knew, Grey said, "Victor? Victor's dead?"

"Yes, his throat's been cut, and we heard Lanny scream."

"Lanny and I will be right out."

Lanny and I will be right out. On a shuddering breath, Lanny knew they were talking about her but the name. Lanny. No. It wasn't right.

But what *was* right then?

"She's the only woman in this part of the house."

"You think she killed him?" Grey sounded incredulous.

"She's the only one in the house," Allen insisted.

"With the thunder screaming away are you sure you heard a woman?"

There was a moment of silence before Allen said, "It...it sounded like a woman to Mother."

"Aunt Estella? On the ground floor? On the other side of the house?"

"No one else heard it," Allen admitted. "We were all awake from the storm but no one else heard a thing. Mother heard a scream. She came up to investigate and found Victor."

"So, you came charging into my private bathroom?" Grey snarled.

She jumped from the malignant anger in Grey's voice and cowered, her knees drawn up, the water pouring down. She realized as she sat there that the blood had been thoroughly washed from her robe. Grey had done it as he held her under the water.

"I...I'm sorry, Grey, I didn't know you'd gotten home. I didn't know you and Lanny had ever met."

"We met tonight," Grey said coldly.

"She wasn't in her room. I heard your water running. I came in expecting to find...find..."

"A murderess coolly taking a shower?" Grey asked with no attempt at veiling his contempt.

Silence reigned in the room.

At last, Grey spoke again. "It's not her. I got home late. Found her in the library reading. We...found our way up here. She's been with me for hours." Grey's voice carried explicit meaning. "We haven't slept. Not for an instant. Though as I recall, I did make you scream more than once, didn't I, darling?"

She thought that required an answer, but he'd said to be silent so she didn't reply.

"Yes," Grey went on, "maybe that's what Estella heard."

"She said it came from Victor's room. Grey, there's no one else."

"Get out," Grey ordered.

"Grey," the voice protested.

"Go, Allen, now. We'll be out in a minute."

A long silence stretched. She waited, forcing her breath in and out, trying even in her breathing to be obediently silent. Finally, she heard the soft click of the bathroom door closing.

The curtain was shoved aside. He turned the shower off with a hard twist. Reaching down, he caught her under the arms and dragged her upright. Once on her feet, he roughly grabbed her shoulders, hauled her out of the shower and pinned her against the tile, water from her sodden gown streamed to the floor. Her eyes didn't want to focus but she forced herself to look at him.

She wished she hadn't. She had to ask, "Who are you? What happened?"

Grey released her, and she stood on her own. His voice rumbled like thunder. "Does it matter who I am? It's obvious from the way you came straight from Victor's bed to climb into the shower with me that any man will do."

She couldn't respond to that ridiculously unfair statement. She trembled deep inside, trying to figure out how it had all happened. The bed, the shower, nothing was clear except the thunder that rolled outside and in Grey's eyes.

He grabbed a black towel, hung with painful neatness on the bathroom wall and with economic movements, made short work of drying his head. With his wet hair, he looked for all the world like he'd just gotten out of the shower—with her. It gave Allen exactly the impression he'd wanted.

Grey tossed his towel at her and she caught it to her chest. "Who I am is Devereau Grey. And what happened is, I just gave you an alibi."

"An...an alibi?" The word didn't even make sense.

"Yes, you did just kill Victor, didn't you?"

Her arms tightened on the towel, already soaked from her thick robe. She was incapable of speech. She didn't know Grey. She didn't know Victor. She didn't know where she was. Her knees sagged as she realized she didn't know *who* she was.

Lanny.

They'd called her Lanny. Her mind was blank and the name didn't touch a chord. She groped for something solid to hold on to.

Grey cut through the wild scrambling of her thoughts. "Whatever you do, don't let anyone know you've been hurt. No one will believe you spent the night in bed with a man when you have that cut on your head. Even with me swearing we were together." Grey studied her for a moment and something feral and hungry shone in his eyes.

"I...I didn't kill anyone!"

"Shut up!" She saw Grey extinguish the fire in his eyes with ruthless self-control. "Do you want the whole house to hear you? I don't care if you're guilty."

"Then why did you do it?" Lanny wailed.

"Do what?" Grey asked with cold amusement. "I've done so many things to you."

"G...give me an alibi," she stammered.

"Simple," Grey shrugged with a bitter smile. "I gave you an alibi because you saved me the trouble of killing my cousin myself."

Grey slammed the bathroom door as he left.

CHAPTER TWO

L anny.

He...Grey...had called her Lanny. Or more accurately Allen had, whoever Allen was. She wanted to sink down to the floor and bury her face in her hands. She wanted to lock the bathroom door and never come out.

There was too much terror outside this room. Then she remembered Grey and she knew she didn't want to be cowering in here when he came back. It was the impetus she needed to dry herself with trembling hands. She ran the towel over her head. It hurt and she thought of Grey's insistence that she conceal her injury. Why? So everyone would believe they'd been together. They wouldn't have been in here...in the way Grey implied they were...if she'd been hurt.

Did he know her? Or. . .he said he'd come home late. But did he know her before he'd gotten home? Before he'd pulled her out of another man's bedroom?

She'd killed his cousin! Her knees collapsed under her and she sank to the cold, wet tile of the bathroom floor.

Her head pounded as she tried to gather the bits and pieces she'd learned. It was all muddled by the thunder and her fear.

A strand of blonde hair drooped over her eye. She was blonde. With a start she realized she had no idea what she looked like. She was overwhelmed with a need to see her own face. Her blank mind clamored for information to fill the void. She found the strength to catch the edge of the vanity and pull herself to her feet. The room seemed to fade and twirl slowly around. She leaned heavily against the sink until her vision cleared. Then slowly, inch by inch, she lifted her face to the mirror. Steam, condensed on the mirror, shrouded her face just as a fog shrouded her mind. She reached her shaking hand forward and swept away the fog.

It was a face she'd never seen before.

Her first impression was of blue eyes so wide with panic the white was visible all around.

Blonde hair, reaching nearly to her waist, so light it disappeared against her scalp when it was wet.

It clung to lips that looked swollen, and to high, ashen cheekbones and long, white eyelashes. Strands of hair concealed half her unfamiliar face. It was a ghostly face. There was no color except for the pale blue of her eyes and the bloody gash on the right side of her head, just visible above the hair line of her temple. The only reality she saw in herself was soul deep horror.

Her whole body trembled with the need to scream and cry and run for...who? Was there anyone other than Grey who would protect her? Where was she?

A tremor shook her and she looked again in the mirror. Her skin was stark white. Another stark white face seemed to overlay her own.

Victor.

Frozen in death. She closed her eyes with a sharp gasp and shoved the towel she still clung to against the mirror as if she could wipe away the memory like she could block a reflection.

She covered her view of her own face but the memory of how Victor looked wouldn't go away. She stood there, stiff with fear until the bathroom door was wrenched open. She whirled to face a fully dressed Grey.

"You can't hide in here." He tossed her a dry robe. "I'm opening this door again in ten seconds, whether you've changed or not." The door snapped shut.

Lanny quickly shed her soaking garb and replaced it with a heavy silk robe, blood red, obviously a man's. True to his word, Grey swung the door open within seconds of her being decently covered. He grasped her arm and pulled her out of the bathroom. Leading her to the bed, he forced her to sit. He stepped back from her, studying her for a long moment then, with a sharp shake of his head, he disappeared into an adjoining room and reappeared with clothing in his hands.

"Here, you need to get dressed. We need to go out and face them together."

She clutched the clothing to her chest.

"Can you dress yourself or do you need help?"

"D...do I get ten seconds again?"

A fleeting smile escaped from those grim lips. "I'll step into your room next door while you change, but make it quick."

He vanished and Lanny tugged the clothes on, sure he'd come charging back in, or Allen would return with his accusations, or Victor would appear to haunt her. He'd picked a dark blouse and a pair of black slacks for her. No undergarments. She couldn't decide if she was offended he'd left those out or relieved he hadn't pawed through her personal items—assuming she had more personal items.

Ready swiftly, she tried to stand and go to him, but her knees trembled and she sank back onto the bed.

A soft knock at the door was her only warning, then Grey was back.

When he stepped in, he studied her for a long moment and the fire faded from his eyes as he stepped toward her.

The silence stretched between them, pulling Lanny's nerves taut. At last, all the rage gone from his voice, he said, "You couldn't kill anyone, could you?" He jerked a shoulder. "Well, except maybe Victor. Everyone who knew him eventually wanted him dead."

Her chest heaved and her head spun. Her hand came out to grope for the bed so she wouldn't fall back onto the mattress.

Grey moved close enough to catch her hand and steady her. "It would be nice if it was you."

A whimper escaped her lips.

"I mean if you didn't do it, somebody else in this house did. And everyone else in this house is my family."

Lanny lifted her eyes to his and saw that compassion she'd glimpsed earlier. She couldn't stop herself from saying, "I don't remember anything. I didn't know my name until you said it."

Grey's gaze sharpened and he looked again at the injury on her head. He parted the hair with utmost care and still his touch was agony. "It looks like blunt force trauma. Not a knife like Victor got. With your fair hair we have to conceal it somehow. No one can know you were hurt or lost your memory. It will shred the alibi."

"I can't stop seeing him, dead." She buried her face in her hands. "I can't pretend anything." She started weeping softly, trying to keep hysteria at bay.

Grey wrapped both arms around her and pulled her against him. After the tears abated, he murmured against her hair, "You really can't remember anything?"

She shook her head.

Grey sighed deeply. "You should be taken to a hospital, but I'm afraid that's impossible if you want your alibi to hold. In fact, I'd say a hospital would be only a stopover on your way to jail."

Lanny turned her face into his chest with a soft moan of fear.

"Your name is Lana, Lana Cole. Everyone calls you Lanny. We've never met. I only know your name because I've had a few phone conversations with Estella that included mention of you, and because I have to make out checks on the Trust."

"Trust?" Lanny lifted her eyes to his.

"The Grey Trust. You're here at the request of Estella Devereau, going over my family's historical records, crates of them in the attic, to preserve them and get them in order. I'm away from the mausoleum every chance I get. But of course, as executor of the estate and head of this household, I had to approve your hiring."

"Hiring? I have a job here?" Lanny couldn't follow what he was telling her because Victor's bleeding throat overruled everything else.

"You were working for the state historical museum but Aunt Estella lured you away from them. You've been living here for a month now, I believe. Lucky girl."

Lanny shuddered.

"I've assumed I'd come home to find you tucked into bed with Victor because my cousin has never met a woman he couldn't seduce. Seems I found that and a bit more. I heard you scream and ran in. When I saw you in there, covered in his blood with him grinning from his throat, I assumed he'd driven you mad as he does everyone sooner or later and you'd done away with him. Someone was bound to. Why not you?"

"So, you decided to provide me with an alibi?" Lanny asked weakly.

"Put simply, yes. What I'd heard of you sounded decent and yet there you stood, soaked in my cousin's blood," Grey said it as if he was discussing the weather. "I got in late tonight and had just gotten into bed when you screamed. I dragged you out. Then I saw the extent of Victor's blood on your hands and tossed you into the shower, your bloody state being a monstrous clue, I'm afraid. Bright boy that I am, since you were in my shower, my head was wet and Allen was at the door, I came up with the little story that covered your tracks. An unsavory story about us spending the evening together."

Lanny felt as if the whole night was descending further into madness. Where one cousin discussed another's death with sneering humor. Where a stranger accused her of murder at the same moment he treated her with kindness.

A hard knocking on the door startled Lanny into clinging to Grey.

Grey said loudly, "I'm getting dressed."

"Be quick about it, Grey," an imperious female voice said. "We hardly expected you to finish what you'd started once you heard of Victor's murder."

"Have you called the police, Estella?"

Estella sounded elderly but there was no feebleness in her, "They're on their way."

"Then stay out of Victor's room, and I'll be out directly."

"She did it, Grey." The dead seriousness of Estella's voice chilled Lanny. She looked desperately at Grey.

Estella continued, "Don't waste your pity on a girl who's been throwing herself shamelessly at your cousin."

"I've been with her ever since I got home. Now please give us a minute. We'll be out shortly."

Grey looked down at Lanny. She wanted to deny it. She wanted to defend herself. She hadn't been in bed with Victor, not in the sense Estella meant. She knew that and yet she knew nothing. She could remember nothing. With brutal honesty she knew she couldn't even be absolutely sure she hadn't killed Victor. She had no alibi save the artificial one concocted by Grey.

Another thought occurred to her. If Grey was her alibi then she was his. She couldn't be sure Grey hadn't killed Victor.

Grey leaned down and whispered, "You didn't do it. I didn't do it either."

"I didn't say you had." Lanny was startled to have her mind read so easily.

"And I now see you can't possibly go out there and lie to the police. Your face reflects every thought that passes through your head." Grey stood from the bed and with gentle urging, forced her to lie down. "I'll tell them you are shocked by Victor's death and I gave you a sedative, then I'll stand guard in front of the door so no one can bother you. I saw some of Meredith's sleeping pills in my bathroom. She's probably hiding them from Allen."

"So, you'll truly give me one or do I pretend to sleep?" She sounded like a child, asking for directions.

Grey smiled. "I believe I'll really give you one. I shouldn't. With the head injury I shouldn't even let you sleep." Grey looked at the door, where Estella no doubt stood waiting to swoop down and accuse Lanny. After a long hesitation, he went to the bathroom and returned with a glass of water and gave her a pill.

He sat beside her studying her. Just as she relaxed into his bed her eyes suddenly flew open.

"I can't sleep in here! This is your room!"

"Hush. Go to sleep, now."

She obeyed him, not sure what choice she had at this point. The night, and maybe already the medicine were taking their toll.

Her heavy lids obediently fluttered shut. She felt his hand brush her hair away from her face. As soon as her eyes were closed Victor's face loomed in front of her and she quickly opened them.

Grey hushed her and held her when she tried to sit up. "Just give the medicine a chance to work."

He stayed with her until a drug enhanced detachment took hold.

As sleep claimed her, he murmured, "Under the circumstances, people would think it odd if you slept anywhere else."

"Yes, Grey," she whispered as the whole nightmarish evening faded. As she sank into sleep, she heard the distant, fading rumble of thunder.

CHAPTER THREE

Grey turned Lanny's limp form onto her side so the head wound was covered. His hands manipulating her body brought back the feel of washing the blood away. She was delicate and battered, yet with the strength to fight against him when he'd grabbed her.

He sat beside her studying her straight blonde hair and her translucent skin. She looked like a woman who'd never been in the sun. Though her eyes were closed, the terror in their blue depth haunted him.

"God protect her." He whispered the prayer and waited in silence urging the petition to the Almighty. "And protect us both from the evil in this house."

He turned from her, and went to face a nightmare. Either the woman in his bed was a murderer, or someone in his family was. Worse yet, if anyone in his family gave it clear thought, they'd know he was lying. Grey's faith wasn't such that he'd bring a woman up to his room. And well they knew of his beliefs because he'd told them often enough that they needed to embrace his faith and give up the family's dark history.

He'd seen no sign that any of them had ever heard a word he'd said. And they were all so twisted, they didn't know what it meant to be a Christian. They'd take his actions at face value because it was something any of them would have done.

Grey pulled open his bedroom door, stepped into the hallway and shut Lanny away from the Devereaus, leaving her deeply asleep.

He stepped out into grim company.

"Get that woman out here now." Estella turned on Grey and attacked even before the door clicked shut. Grey had expected nothing less.

"I heard her in Victor's room. I know she did it." Estella was fully dressed. She had her white hair twisted neatly into a chignon and she'd even applied her usual thick layer of make-up.

Why, at this late hour, did she look like she'd never been to bed?

Grey realized for the first time Estella was getting old. Despite her rigidly proper appearance, she looked every one of her eighty-four years. She breathed hard, partly with anger but also from the effort of climbing the stairs. Her thin lips turned harshly downward. Much of what Victor was could be laid at Estella's doorstep. She'd pampered Victor and battled Grey in some twisted effort to control them both.

Grey ignored the question. Speaking to no one in particular he said, "You're sure he's dead? I'd better have a look."

Grey had already seen Victor and knew there was no possibility his cousin was still alive.

"There's no doubt. Oh, no doubt at all." Allen came up the stairs. "The police should be here soon."

Grey was keenly aware of the differences between Allen and his brother Victor. Allen was nearly six inches shorter, he had thinning brown hair, was fifty pounds overweight, and had washed-out brown eyes hidden behind wire rim glasses. He always had a harried look. His weak chin matched his weak will.

Estella never had to exert herself to control him. Allen was happiest with his nose in an account book. Grey hadn't spent much time with Allen as an adult, his wife Meredith had managed to drive most people away from them both. But Grey had come to depend on him as Grey contrived to spend more and more time away from the windswept isolation of this mansion on its own private island off the coast of Texas.

Grey went into Victor's bedroom and nothing had changed since he dragged Lanny out except now the lights blazed. There was indeed no doubt. Victor lay staring at the ceiling. His throat slashed and no longer bleeding.

Grey studied the room from the doorway. He looked for some answer to what had gone on here tonight and found nothing. Grey itched to be allowed some time in the room before the police got here. To search for stray blonde hairs or suspiciously placed drops of blood. He knew the family, bunched behind him in the doorway, would watch every move he made.

He couldn't do anything that would draw suspicion on himself or Lanny, so he looked at the gruesome remains of his cousin and tried to find the tiniest sliver of familial, or even Christian love.

He came up empty and asked God's forgiveness for that.

Victor had lived an empty life. No career. No wife. No children—well, no legitimate children. Grey thought of the trusting women Victor had betrayed and the family money that went to support Victor's lecherous habits. It amounted to empty.

Grey was inclined to carve that word alone on Victor's tombstone. And in that one tiny way, to face the afterlife with such a legacy, Grey could be sorry for Victor's death. Beyond that Grey just chafed under the coming tumult.

He stepped back knowing the police wouldn't want the crime scene disturbed.

"Are you satisfied?" Meredith wore a long ivory silk robe. She held a highball glass in one hand and drew deeply on the cigarette in her other. The draw on the cigarette emphasized the lines around her mouth. She was not yet fifty but she looked ten years older after years of smoking and scowling. Gaudy gems of every kind decorated her fingers. She held herself erect with an almost regal stature, in many ways a younger version of Estella. Except Meredith had clearly just come from bed. Her hair mussed. No make-up to soften the unhealthy pallor of her skin.

Grey looked at the cold, greedy Meredith with distaste but reminded himself that he had no room to judge. Allen and Meredith had been married nearly twenty-five years now and who was he to say they weren't happy? Just because he'd have never been able to stand the woman, didn't mean the marriage didn't work for his cousin. Allen would probably stand in front of an oncoming bus without someone to tell him to get out of the way. If he hadn't had Meredith to order him around, he would have found someone else to do it.

Grey looked at the wreckage of his own pathetic attempts to form a relationship and knew Allen had succeeded where he'd failed, even if he did have to get his backbone removed to accomplish it.

"Let's step away from the door." Grey began walking and the rest of the family could come along or be left behind. A small noise drew his attention to his cousin Clarinda. The middle-aged woman sat silently against the wall, curled up, her arms wrapped around her knees, covered head to toe in a white flannel nightgown.

He heard the slow tread on the stairway that was a footstep he would recognize anywhere.

Sally Bates came into view. She said, "Trevor is coming up the driveway."

Sally, their housekeeper, had been here longer than all of them except Estella. She was fiercely loyal to the family. Her husband had been the gardener throughout his life. The Bates's only child, a daughter ten years older than Grey, had grown up playing side by side with Victor and Clarinda.

Grey asked, "No sign of the police?"

"I saw a boat approaching. Allen and Meredith took two cars down and drove one back so the police can drive up the mountain."

They kept two old Jeeps and one aging sedan for the drive down to the boat dock and back. "It will take them a while to climb that road in this weather." Sally stood in her chenille pink robe with a rolling pin in her hand as if she was ready to fight the world for the Devereaus.

The only way up to The Devil's Nest was on a long, treacherous road to a craggy mountain top. The only way onto the island was by boat unless you flew in on a helicopter. And with all eyes pinned on a hurricane, wondering what path it would take, no helicopters were flying. It was a lonely, wind-swept monstrosity of a place to call home.

Sally set the rolling pin on a table near the top of the side staircase, went to Clarinda and spoke kindly. "How are you, sweetheart? Do you want me to take you to your room?"

"No, let me stay." Clarinda sat on the floor sobbing quietly. She muttered and wept and Grey thought he heard her say, "People die when they're bad."

Grey noticed with some surprise that Clarinda's usually unruly dark curls were pulled back into an intricate braid. His cousin always looked as if no one spent a second paying attention to her. Sally saw that she bathed and brushed her teeth, but who had gotten her to sit still long enough to do her hair? Clarinda usually moved around the edges of the family, never really joining in with anything, disappearing for hours at a time. She reminded Grey of a frightened, wild animal. She was nearing forty. One of those sweet, special souls who remained childlike all her life. Grey was younger than her and she'd been so shy that he'd barely known her. He knew in his distaste for the rest of his family, he'd neglected Clarinda.

With a grunt of effort, Sally lowered her round form to the floor beside Clarinda. Sally held her close, the two of them shutting out the rest of the world. Clarinda was the only one who seemed genuinely saddened by Victor's death. Only someone this innocent could live near Victor without hating him.

The exception to that of course was Aunt Estella. She adored Victor.

Trevor came bounding up the stairs, taking them two at a time. He was haphazardly dressed. His hair in disarray as if he'd just climbed out of some woman's bed. Grey suspected that was the case. Trevor and Victor had tastes in common. Too much hard liquor, too many easy women. Trevor Curtis, a distant cousin with a tenuous claim to the Devereau name, had wormed his way into the house by finding a champion in Meredith and, by default, Allen.

Trevor and Victor caroused together. The few times Grey had met him, Grey hadn't even tried to disguise his contempt.

"What's going on?" Trevor gave them his usual vapid grin.

"Victor's dead." Grey was deliberately abrupt, interested in Trevor's unguarded first reaction. There was definite shock, then Grey saw a flash of keen intelligence in Trevor's eyes. In the past, Grey had judged Trevor to be none too bright. Had Trevor created that impression deliberately?

"Dead? Victor?"

Grey nodded.

Trevor looked from face to face, finally settling on the sobbing Clarinda. Trevor's expression seemed to believe the harsh news at that moment. Grey wondered if Trevor was faking his surprise.

Trevor asked in a level voice, "What happened?"

Grey wanted to gauge Trevor's reaction so, tipping his head toward Victor's room, he said bluntly. "Someone slit his throat."

Trevor's eyes narrowed and he turned toward Victor's room. Without comment he strode to the door. Grey had swung it shut without latching it so he wouldn't have to touch the doorknob. Trevor swung it open the same way. A man mindful of fingerprints. But a guilty man might deliberately touch the door so there would be an excuse for his fingerprints to be on the knob.

Trevor hesitated over the sight of Victor's blood-soaked remains but he went into the room. Grey never took his eyes off of him. Trevor didn't touch anything. He leaned close and seemed to study the body with a kind of detachment Grey envied, then he straightened away and came back out of the room.

Silently, Trevor squared his shoulders, then he looked up at Grey with that familiar careless expression Grey had until now mistaken for stupidity.

Trevor shuddered in a way that struck Grey as false and asked, "What happened?"

Grey didn't answer. He just watched and wondered what Trevor's game was. He decided to confront Trevor on the spot and he opened his mouth to ask some pointed questions, about Victor's murder and Trevor's nebulous claim to the Devereau name.

Hammering on the front door interrupted Grey's interrogation before it could start. "Let them in, Allen," Estella commanded.

Allen trotted, obedient as a trained dog, down the steps.

Two youthful policemen followed Allen back up. "The detective is helping the coroner unload the car. He told us we need to seal off the crime scene."

A detective arrived next and, looking around at the gathering, reached a hand out to Grey. "I didn't know you'd gotten here."

"Yeah, I got a nice welcome home, Case." With a tip of his head, Grey gestured to the closed door. "Victor is in there. Dead."

Case Garrison nodded and, his expression grim, said, "I'm going to need to talk to every one of you, so no one leaves this house without my permission."

Estella sniffed indignantly. Meredith drew deeply on her cigarette. Allen wrung his hands.

"Let me look at the victim first, then I'll talk to each of you, one at a time." Case pulled out a notepad just as the coroner came upstairs trailed by two EMTs. The hall milled with activity. The prominence of the murder victim had gotten a lot of people out of bed.

Case Garrison, former FBI agent, new at the job of chief of police in Gull Cove and a long time friend of Grey's, was pulled away from asking questions and closed himself and the coroner, doubling as a crime scene investigator, in the room with Victor.

Grey hoped he wouldn't have to produce Lanny for a while yet.

Dawn lit the sky before anyone found time to begin questioning the family.

Lanny slept through it all.

Grey made it clear Lanny had an iron clad alibi.

He was subjected to cutting disapproval from family. He didn't say what had passed between them, letting the family jump to their own conclusions.

Rather than strike back, he listened to each member of his family make their snide remarks. From their comments he learned quite a few details of what Lanny was doing. She would need to know all of this if she didn't quickly regain her memory.

Meredith hated her – but then Meredith hated everyone.

Allen avoided her – but then Allen avoided everyone.

Sally mothered her – but then Sally mothered everyone.

Trevor lusted after her – Grey didn't know Trevor well, but he seemed to be a Victor clone so that fit.

Estella used her – but then Estella used everyone.

And Clarinda adored her. Clarinda was scared of her own shadow, hated strangers, and seemed to have no attachment to anyone. That alone was unusual.

Case listened to it all, talking with them first in a group, letting the sniping fade, his sharp eyes taking it all in.

Finally, he said, "I'm going to need to question each of you individually. I need a little more time before I can start, though. Can each of you go to your private quarters until I'm ready for you?"

Trevor, who had long ago slumped to the floor beside Clarinda, asked, "Can we sleep while we wait?"

Case very politely, and perhaps with a bit of envy, said, "Yes."

Grey felt he should remain and observe the proceedings, but Victor's body was gone and Grey had been awake since early the previous morning. He'd pushed hard yesterday to clear his desk before he came up here to have things out with Victor for the last time. He was struggling to keep his eyes open.

And Lanny was asleep in his bed.

He entered his room and saw that she had tossed in her sleep, no doubt haunted by nightmares. She'd kicked her covers off and rolled onto her back.

Laying there in her rumpled blouse and trim slacks, her hair wild across Grey's pillow, he tried to believe she was a murderer. Common sense told him she was. But it was shocking how badly he wanted her to be innocent.

She drew him in a way no woman ever had before. And why would she? He thought she might be a killer. Despite his insinuations to the police, Grey didn't take advantage of vulnerable women. Truth be told, he didn't take advantage of any women. He could have carried her to her own bed, or taken that bed himself. But he wasn't letting her out of sight in a house where a murderer roamed.

He pulled a chair up, sat down and put his feet on the bed. Then he settled in to wreck his spine until it was his turn to face questioning.

Power coursed through the killer like the blood that ran from Victor's throat. His death was so long coming and now, finally!

A smile curved the killer's lips.

It wasn't over.

In truth—it had just begun.

CHAPTER FOUR

Lanny came awake slowly. She had never been so comfortable in her life. It was a perfect moment, she thought drowsily. The perfect night's sleep. The perfect gentle awakening. The perfect comfortable pillow. A firm, warm pillow. Her hand caressed the pillow and realized it was covered with coarse hair. Odd that it would feel so good.

"You're finally awake," a deep, masculine voice murmured into her ear. She jumped and would have screamed but a hand clapped over her mouth. She fought against his hold. She clawed at his face and he caught both of her hands in one of his as easily as if she were a child.

Immobilized, she quit fighting and looked into his eyes. They were gray, the color of thunder. It all came back in flashing pieces. The thunder overpowering her just as it was doing now. Covering her mouth, pinioning her arms. Lifting her and carrying her away from a dead body. The blood.

Lanny began to moan deep in her throat. The hand stayed over her mouth. She looked up at the man with a name like thunderclouds. Grey.

She shuddered deeply as more memory returned. Victor. His eyes open and fixed, staring at nothing. The slack jaw. The blood. The blood! Endless, flowing, sticky blood!

Lanny. Her name was Lanny. At that thought, her mind slammed up against a blank wall. She knew nothing else. She only knew Lanny because

Grey had told her. It was only a word to her and nothing more. That made her shiver until her body was wracked with tremors.

Grey said softly, "The police could come any time to question us. Has your memory returned?"

Lanny shook her head no and whimpered behind his hand.

That whimper settled her down by slapping her with a deep sense of shame. She sounded so weak and she *wasn't* weak! Somehow, she knew that about herself.

She took a deep breath and tried to regain control. She couldn't quite stop the trembling but forced herself to make direct eye contact with him and let him see she was calm. He uncovered her mouth.

"I won't scream. Thank you for stopping me. Now, the answer to your question is; no, I haven't regained my memory. Have you learned anything since last night I should know about?"

A smile quirked Grey's lips. "That sounds more like the woman Estella described. I rather miss my docile, mindlessly obedient little Lanny."

"Mindless is right. I have amnesia, and I'd been scared witless. If that isn't mindless, I don't know what is."

"Well, you appear to have your mind back now."

"Some of it. Enough to tell you to let go of me." She tugged against the grip on her arms.

With a shrug so tiny it amounted to arching an eyebrow, Grey said, "I should, but you look stronger this morning. Something tells me I need every advantage I can get while we talk." Lanny didn't bother fighting him. She'd lose.

"The police are going to come in here and question you...us...at any time. I'm surprised they haven't been here already. I should have woken you earlier and told you what to expect but I fell asleep myself. Then when

I finally woke up, you were sleeping so peacefully I couldn't bear to disturb you."

"Last night when we...met..." Lanny faltered.

"You mean when I dragged you, covered in blood, away from a dead body?"

"Yes, then." The irony of such a sedate recitation to describe the horror surrounding their first encounter wasn't lost on her.

"I've cleaned up after Victor all my life and been faced with a long parade of hurt and angry women. I imagined you'd killed him while fighting him off or in revenge for whatever abuse he'd dealt you."

Lanny quirked an eyebrow at him. "Go on."

"My first intention was to wash the blood off of you. That took us to the shower."

Lanny was determined to deal calmly with this madness but the memory of the blood set off another round of those alarming, deep shudders. She tugged against his hold. "Please, let me up. I'm listening. I'm not going to run."

Grey withdrew a fraction of an inch. "Are you going to be quiet?"

She looked at him as coolly as possible under the circumstances. "Yes, I'll be quiet."

It struck her that she had a logical mind to be able to stay in control. Logical. She knew something about herself.

Grey pulled her into a sitting position. "I'm sorry, but you have to hear the details of what happened. You can't react like this to the police."

Lanny nodded. "Thank you."

Grey's warm touch helped ease the shivering.

"Though honesty forces me to say there is little in this to be thankful for," Lanny added.

He smiled and set off tremors of another kind. It was a nine point eight on the Richter Scale of smiles. There hadn't been any smiling up until now, but it had been worth the wait.

Grey said, "Okay, let's get a few things cleared up."

"Fine. Get started clearing. I welcome it."

"I'm assuming you don't remember anything. So, I'll hit the high points then we'll go into as much detail as we have time to cover. You're here researching my family history."

"Your family?"

"The Devereaus. The proud descendants of famed pirate Pierre Devereau."

"Pirates aren't really much to be proud of as a rule."

"So true." Grey smiled again. "For the last month, you've been sorting through five generations of old junk stored in the attic, everything from love letters to moldy portraits to bills of sale for carrots and potatoes. You've been working in an empty bedroom in the far end of the west wing on this floor. It's been turned into an office for you. Right now, we're in the east wing of this old fire trap. I don't know how far you've gotten but I do know, from asking the family last night, that you stay mostly to yourself. You go to the kitchen and make your own meals, mostly sandwiches, eat alone in your office and only emerge to go into town to the library to search old newspaper files. So, I don't think the rest of the brood knows a lot about your research, except you report to Estella every day."

"So blank spots in my memory about my work won't be readily noticeable," Lanny said in relief.

Grey nodded. "The west wing on the second floor is mainly a suite Allen and Meredith occupy."

"I remember Allen from last night." A voice and the wrist of a bathrobe. That was the extent of the remembering. Lanny's muscles clenched when she thought of the man who had so brazenly entered the bathroom last night. Then backed down so quickly when he found Grey. What would he have done if she'd been in the shower alone? Or if she'd been standing, screaming, in Victor's room.

"Allen is my cousin. Meredith is his wife."

Lanny heard the coldness in Grey's voice when he mentioned Meredith and stored that bit of information away.

"Their part of the house is nearly a private residence," Grey continued. "It's got its own kitchen and they eat alone most of the time. The ground floor on the west side is Estella's living quarters."

None of the names rang a bell, not even the faintest echo of recognition and yet she'd lived with this family for weeks. Tears bit at her eyes. She ruthlessly suppressed them and stared fixedly at the weathered rug beside the bed. "Estella hired me."

Grey didn't answer right away, and she looked at him. There was that compassion again. She remembered it from last night when she'd been reeling from her terror of the thunder and the blow to her head and the sight of Victor. She'd thought he'd come, the thunder in human form, to ravish her and instead she'd found kindness. It threw her off balance by its drastic difference from the swirling assault of the night's violence. His glance fell to her lips and back to her eyes.

She poked him in the shoulder and prompted him to continue. "Right? Estella hired me?"

Grey nodded silently for a moment, then shook his head as if to clear it. "Yes, it was all Estella's idea. Her search really began years ago when she became obsessed with finding descendants of Pierre Devereau. The family has split apart over the years. We descended from the two sons of Pierre and the family has either died off or they've washed their hands of this ugly relic of a mansion. The only children known were Estella and my mother.

They're distant cousins. My parents were away from here, too, but when they died, I was put into Estella's care."

"You called her Aunt Estella earlier, didn't you?" Lanny interrupted.

"Just an old habit. That's what she asked me to call her. As it became obvious none of her children were likely to give her grandchildren, Estella became increasingly desperate to find someone to pass on what, to her, is the great legacy of the Devereau family. Estella is the last of the line to carry the name. But of course, she married. Her married name was Kozinski."

Lanny winced, "Not exactly a name fitting for a suave, swashbuckling pirate."

"No and her husband wasn't a nice man either, but what nice man is going to marry Estella?"

Lanny swallowed hard, dreading her first meeting with the woman.

"He managed to go through what little money was left in the family coffers and then, when he'd made as big a mess as possible, he died. Estella changed her name back to Devereau but her children were all named Kozinski. Her children were grown by then and she pressured Allen into changing his name to Devereau. But the name isn't going to survive through them because Allen and Meredith have never had children. Victor has never married but he has several children, five at last count."

"Five illegitimate children? I don't have to remember your cousin to know I'd loathe him."

Grey gave her a skeptical look. "He's got two sons he's probably never met. Those boys are named Kozinski. Estella wants more Devereaus. Victor delighted in tormenting her. Giving her hope that he'd change his name—and somehow his children's names—if she was indulgent enough. Estella and my mother were the only children we know of in their generation, though there are probably cousins who've shaken the dirt of the Devereau name off their shoes.

"Estella didn't want the name to die out." Grey paused and shrugged. "To my way of thinking it would be a blessing. Estella is getting on in years and she has always romanticized the Devereaus..."

"Devereau. That's your first name. You said so last night."

"That's right. It's a family name. My mother was a Devereau. This house is the Devereau family home." Grey's eyes turned cold. "It's built on the bones of the people Pierre killed to enrich himself. My father's people, the Greys, were wealthy Texas oilmen. The Devereaus, despite their money and their deep roots, weren't...respectable. It's a family whose legacy was steeped in death and ghosts and tales of lost treasure. Estella took great pride in returning to her Devereau name and convinced Allen to go along but not Victor. For all her research, the only lost family member she's found is Trevor."

"Trevor?"

Grey was silent for a moment. "When you see him, you'll believe it. He has the same build, the same dark hair and gray eyes as I do. And I've seen the family tree Meredith concocted to trace down branches of the family that had gotten away from the ugliness of the Devereau legacy. I'm not sure what I think about Trevor. Estella has accepted him completely and it doesn't matter to me one way or the other. I feel sorry for the guy, though."

"Why is that?"

Grey studied her face, none of the compassion was there now. And he certainly wasn't smiling anymore. "Because being a Devereau gives you permission to live down to the family name by being dishonest, self-centered and cruel. Estella is doing her best to bring that out in Trevor and he seems well suited to it."

"Does it suit you?"

Grey shook his head. "It doesn't. But I have it. Some of us revel in it. Some of us consider it a curse."

"And Estella revels," Lanny said flatly.

"Estella," Grey paused for a moment then added, "and Victor."

"And I believe you mentioned ghosts and treasure?" Lanny prompted.

"Allen and Victor were born and grew up in this house. They spent most of their childhood poking around in the attic and the cellar and climbing around in the caves that honeycomb the cliffs, looking for Pierre Devereau's buried treasure. They were adult men when I was old enough to remember them, and they were still treasure hunting. When I'd come to visit, I'd go along with them and explore, so I've heard their ghost stories and the tales of pillage and murder and pirate's booty. Estella believes it's here. I think her obsession with the old records has something to do with finding that dead man's chest.

"The way things stand right now the money is all mine because I have taken over the Grey holdings. But my mother saw to it that upkeep and at least minimal support for her family worked its way into the trust. I keep a tight hold on the purse strings and I never give Estella enough, since I refuse to fund Victor's depravity. Allen works hard for me, doing accounting for the Grey Trust. I pay him an honest wage. But he is bound to this place for some reason and won't leave. Victor has made half-hearted attempts to work for the Trust. But I've learned I can't let him near my money. It drives Estella crazy to believe somewhere around here is a hidden treasure. A fortune in gold and jewels—that would be Devereau money and Estella would have a much stronger claim on it."

"And the ghost?"

Grey didn't smile as she thought he would. "I've heard of several, but I've only seen one and then she appeared only once…maybe."

"She?"

"Her legend is nearly as old as the house. Pierre had a streamlined method of divorce. He tossed his wives off the Widow's Walk."

Lanny gasped.

"The wife who remains most famous is Giselle. Her picture is in the library. A woman in a dark dress with a wide gold collar and cuffs."

"And she's supposed to be a ghost?"

"Well, things are a little murky, but it's said that after a son or two, Pierre came home to his wife and sons bringing a new wife. Pierre grabbed Giselle and took her to the roof. Pierre dragged her to the east side of the house so she'd fall over the cliff and the sea would swallow her up and he didn't have to deal with the dead body. It's said he summoned his sons to watch.

"Giselle told Pierre she'd hidden all the family gold and jewels. When he began to beat the jewels' location out of her, she ran from him along the Widow's Walk. Before he could catch her, she flung herself off the west side of the roof. She took the secret of Pierre's treasure to her grave."

"And she haunts this place?"

There was silence for too long and Lanny watched Grey, wondering what he so clearly didn't want to say.

"I've seen her." Grey's firm hand rubbed her shoulder.

"I don't believe in ghosts." Lanny had enough to worry about without adding fairy tales.

"Neither do I, but it's hard to deny because she saved my life once."

"You're sure?"

With a shrug, Grey went on. "The family calls her Silver Girl because she glows silverwhite. Victor and I were on the roof once, he played into my interest in the treasure. He acted like it was fun for him, too. But while we were up there, he shoved me off the roof."

Lanny sat up straight. "How tall is the house?"

"Tall enough."

"He tried to kill you?"

"When I accused him of that, face to face, he said it was an accident."

"So why didn't he try and save you?"

"Then I told Estella what he'd done and he acted like he didn't know what I was talking about. Of course Estella believed him over me. He was a grown man and I was a child."

"But you saved yourself."

Grey shrugged, hesitated, then said, "I caught at the eaves but my hands were slipping and something…someone boosted me up." Grey's touch on her shoulder turned hard as he looked through her into the past. "Or maybe I just saved myself, who knows? At the time I knew it was her, now I'm not so sure. After I got back on the roof – Victor had run off – I turned and there was Silver Girl beside me. She…"

Lanny's tugged and Grey let her go before he left bruises.

Grey rubbed his hand over his face. "I know this sounds crazy."

"You really saw her, right beside you?" Lanny tried to keep the skepticism out of her voice.

She must not have succeeded because Grey smiled. "I…I was really upset. It was foggy. She was mist, but she glowed brighter than the mist all around us. The dress she wore looked like the one in the portrait, a dark dress on a gray day…I'm sure I filled in the blanks with my own imagination. I was upset from almost falling…" Grey shrugged. "It sure seemed real. She smiled at me, as if glad she saved me. Then still looking at me, she hurled herself off the roof, screaming all the way down."

"Those are some really specific details for a boy's imagination."

There was a long silence between them.

Grey shook his head and continued. "Estella says she wants to find relatives through your genealogical research, but I believe you were hired because Estella hoped you'd lead her to Pierre's treasure. Since Trevor's come, Estella's been able to wield more influence over Victor because his position isn't so secure. I'd heard from Allen that Victor had finally agreed to change his name to Devereau and begin trying to gain custody of his children, particularly his sons."

Lanny had to ask, "Why did you assume I killed him?"

Grey said sardonically, "Victor has that effect on people."

"And...and do you really think...was I in that bed with him because...?" Lanny hesitated, unable to meet Grey's eyes. The thought of casually falling into bed with someone was repugnant. Even with amnesia clouding the issue, she didn't believe she'd done it. But she didn't really know anything.

Her stomach roiled in disgust if she had slept with Victor, especially considering the things Grey had said about him. She'd been in the house less than a month. Were her morals that loose? She tried to pierce the veil of her memory and her head began to ache with the effort.

Grey rested his open palm on her cheek and, with his thumb, lifted her chin until her eyes met his. "Your head wound bled a lot, I could tell by the blood in your hair, yet there was no blood on your pillow. I'm convinced someone knocked you out somewhere else and carried you to that room. The only blood on your robe I could see looked like it'd come from Victor, it was mainly on the back where Victor's blood had pooled. And the blood on your robe was still wet, unlike the blood on your hair. I think someone tucked you into bed with Victor after he'd already bled out."

Lanny flinched at the picture Grey drew with his theory. Then she looked away from him as she felt her face heat up at the thought of someone handling her unconscious body.

Grey's thumb caressed her chin gently until she looked back at him.

She raised her chin defiantly. "So, someone set me up. They put me in that bed, hoping I'd stay unconscious until someone found me with Victor and blamed his murder on me. Did they frame me for murder because I was convenient or does someone have it in for me, too?"

Grey's face settled into a grim mask. "Good question. My feeling is you were just convenient. Everyone would assume Victor would talk you into bed."

"Not if I got to vote," Lanny said sharply.

"I've known Victor a long time. He'd tell you anything, lead you along with lies and promises he didn't intend to keep. He has an abundance of charm. I swear the boy could seduce a rock. If you did resist him, he would relish the challenge and only want you more. And ultimately there are ways, drugs he could use. You might not get to vote."

CHAPTER FIVE

Lanny shuddered at what Grey's words meant about what could have happened to her at Victor's hands. Wouldn't she know? Wouldn't she feel a violation like that?

Grey massaged her shoulder. "I've been privy to Victor's conquests because Estella had to go through me to pay them off."

She recoiled from his touch. "You mean Victor has...forced himself on women and you protect him by...by paying off his victims?"

Grey shook his head, "No, I'd never do that. As far as I know Victor has never raped anyone. I believe he's capable of it, but no one's accused him of that. He prefers to make a woman willing, then break her heart. Before he was out of high school he'd lied and seduced his way through most of the female population near Devereau Island."

"Devereau Island?" Lanny interrupted.

"It's our home. We live in Texas on a little island off the coast. We own it and we're the only ones living on it. It's only accessible by boat or helicopter. We mighty Devereaus believe the island is our own nation and this old heap is our castle. We lord it over everyone from the little coastal town of Gull Cove."

"Castle?"

"You really don't remember a thing, do you?" Grey asked softly.

Lanny shook her head.

"You couldn't because otherwise you could never forget The Devil's Nest, no matter how badly you wanted to."

"The Devil's Nest?"

"It's this house. It's where we are now." Grey looked over his head at the vaulted ceiling and expansive room, murky even in daylight with the inadequate electric lighting that had been added long after the place was built.

"Who would name a home something so dreadful?"

"Pierre Devereau. He came ashore from his years of piracy and built himself a fortress high above the sea. It still clings to this God forsaken mountaintop complete with its buried treasure and its wandering ghosts. He called it The Devil's Nest because he'd certainly sold his soul."

Lanny shook her head, horrified. "Piracy? How long ago was this?"

"Before America was a country. It's said he made a fortune smuggling for the French, then later for both sides during the Revolution. The Devereau name is old. Pierre came to this remote place to put himself beyond the reach of the law."

"You speak so easily of Pierre and evil." Lanny said with a shudder. "You must not believe in anything to be so flippant."

Grey looked thoughtful as he stroked her hair. "No, that's not true. I am a strong believer in God. I think the difference is; few people believe in Satan anymore. I know he exists. His handiwork is too much a part of my family history for me to ever believe he isn't alive and well and roaming the earth. Very often in the form of my cousin Victor."

Lanny gasped. "Then how can you come back here?"

"I seldom do. I had planned for this visit to be my last. I was going to have it out with Victor and have him arrested."

"Arrested?" Lanny's head ached from all the revelations.

Grey continued as if she hadn't spoken. "Then I planned to walk away from the ghosts that haunt these halls and the siren song of buried treasure and never look back."

"Ghosts and treasure? It's too far-fetched to believe."

"You've probably heard all this but with your memory gone, who knows? If you haven't uncovered it yourself, it would be like Estella to keep you in the dark."

And she'd come here willingly and lived here for weeks. She rubbed her head against the pillow and grimaced at the tenderness.

Grey's eyes went to where she'd taken the blow to her head. "I should take you to the doctor. You must have a concussion. I shouldn't have let you go to sleep. I should never have given you that medication. Last night, I thought it was right, but I could be risking..."

Lanny rested one finger on his lips to stop him. "When you said I saved you the trouble of killing him yourself, you were talking about all of this?"

"No, as if 'this' weren't enough. I was talking about the fact that I've just discovered Victor has been dealing with smugglers and using my family's trust fund to launder the money. It was an account I didn't even know existed. He'd covered his tracks well. Victor is smart, but I was surprised by the sophistication of his deceit. I underestimated him and now he's involved the Grey Trust in such a way it could be tainted if Victor's crimes are found out. I had no choice but to have him arrested, it's the only way to clearly underline the integrity of the Trust. The detective who's going to question you is an old friend and his wife is a data analyst. She helped me make sense of the crimes hidden in the Grey Trust accounts. I came home to tell him I was turning everything over to the police. Tomorrow morning..." Grey stopped as if he'd surprised himself. "I mean this morning, I was going to see to it personally that Victor was arrested and spent a healthy chunk of the next two decades in jail."

A loud rap sounded at the door.

"Our time is up." Grey looked over his shoulder then back at Lanny. "They think we met last night and we've been…together…ever since."

"Together? But…"

Grey covered her mouth with his own.

Lanny shoved at Grey's shoulders. He deftly caught her hands and slid them around his neck and deepened the kiss. She gasped in shock at the suddenness of Grey's movements. Grey pulled away from her and she shamed herself by lifting her head, pursuing his lips.

The knocking sounded at the door, more insistent this time. "Grey, it's Case. Your turn."

Lanny saw a dark satisfaction flare in Grey's eyes. He murmured for only Lanny to hear, "Trust me."

He didn't give her a chance to answer, he slanted his mouth over hers.

A short, sharp rap at the door was followed by, "I'm coming in." The door opened and a police detective walked into the room. Lanny tore her mouth away from Grey's and, after a single humiliated look at the intruder she buried her face in Grey's chest.

Grey said gruffly, "Can't you give us another minute?"

Lanny knew her face must be turning fire engine red because of the waves of heat climbing her neck. "Grey!"

Grey laughed at her and tweaked her on the nose as if she had just said something unbearably cute.

Lanny looked from Grey to the detective, wishing she could turn to dust and blow away. On second thought, she wished that *they* would.

Grey turned to the policeman. "Detective Case Garrison, this is Lanny Cole. Can we go into the library and give Lanny a few minutes?"

"That would be fine, Grey. I'd prefer to speak to you alone first anyway."

Grey nodded then said to Lanny, "Take your time. Use my shower if you want."

Grey walked out of the room then Lanny heard him say to Detective Garrison, "The library is at the foot of the staircase, I'll be right down."

The detective said impatiently, "C'mon, Grey. You've had all night to get ready. I've been at this for hours."

"Just a second, I promise." He came back in the room.

He sat beside her on the bed and leaned down as if he was nuzzling her ear. "He may be listening but we didn't finish. I'm going to say I got home around midnight. I found you reading in the library downstairs, it's the room we're being questioned in. Turn right outside my door to find the staircase. The library's at the bottom of the stairs, to the left. We stayed there, talking for a while, then moved up here. We didn't hear anything unusual, although we may have made some noise ourselves. We've been together ever since. You just tell the same story and act like you spent all your time working and can't contribute much to the relationships between the people in the house."

Lanny nodded uncertainly. What else could she say since she remembered nothing?

Grey traced her ear with his lips and continued, "I didn't mention Clarinda. She's a fey, childlike woman, a sister to Allen and Victor. She rarely speaks. Or our housekeeper Sally, she's the only sane one in this place."

Lanny tried to repeat the names and Grey's bare bones description of the rest of the household so she wouldn't forget.

"Come downstairs as soon as you're ready. I think we should be together as much as possible while we talk to the police." He walked toward the door.

"Grey, wait!" Lanny knew she'd spoken too loud, so she whispered her question, "Where's the library again?"

Grey's eyes warmed. He came closer to the bed and repeated the directions. Then he added, "Your office is in the other wing on this floor." Then he nodded his head at a door he'd gone through to get her clothes. "And your bedroom is next door to mine through there."

She stammered, "W...we have c...connecting rooms?"

Grey arched his eyebrows slightly. "That's convenient since we're about to embark on a red hot love affair for all the world to see."

"You mean *pretend* to embark on one," Lanny said repressively.

Grey chuckled softly. "Is that what I mean?" He left the room without a single backward glance.

She's still here! How can she find herself in bed with a dead man, his blood covering her, and not be arrested?

Grey saved her, just as Grey has always thwarted me. If I could have found a way to make him the one they'd suspect, I'd have done it gladly. His iron fist rules this house.

So I picked Lanny, before she uncovered another syllable of Pierre's legacy. Even now maybe she'll go away. That would be as good as having the police take her. The only question is; did she see me?

If she did, she'll have to die.

CHAPTER SIX

L anny waited until the door clicked shut then threw the blanket off and leapt out of bed. The room yawed. Her head gave a sickening throb. She braced her hand on the table beside the bed until things quit spinning. When she was steady, she went to the door Grey had indicated was hers and opened it, careful to check that she was alone.

She saw stacks in precise order on the floor around a wingback chair and on a side table. A heavy sweater hung over the back of the chair and Lanny could well imagine wearing it to cut the chill in this dank room.

There was a lamp on the table along with a dozen notebooks. There were two more lamps on either side of the bed on end tables. Lanny hurried to turn on all three lamps, they each contained a single bulb and barely pushed back the dark in the dreary room. There were tables and chairs, bits of statuary, figurines and random stools and shelves lining the wall. There was so much of it she was overwhelmed. Was this all valuable? Or was it just the flotsam of generations of packrats?

She saw an ornate chandelier overhead. It was centered in a high ceiling and looked suited to candles. The spaces for candles were empty and if it did have wiring for electricity it didn't matter because there was no sign of a light bulb.

The room was huge with two east windows that dripped with a gray rain. A bed on the far side of the room had a massive, heavily carved head-board. All the furniture appeared to be old.

Maybe valuable antiques, but it was such an ugly style that Lanny wanted to throw it all out into the hall.

She saw an open door beside the bed that revealed a bathroom. She considered bathing, hoping to wash some of the cobwebs from her mind. But it would have to wait. Getting herself downstairs seemed like a matter of life or death. The clothes she wore were wrinkled beyond wearing. She went to a dresser in the same wood as the headboard, its varnish blackened with age. Opening a drawer, she found light woolen two-piece sweater sets in one drawer. Five of them in a pattern so similar and in colors so bland it was like looking into a drawer full of oatmeal, with the lively added touch of black and white. She couldn't figure out why she'd bothered to purchase more than one.

She opened another drawer and found bras and panties, all white cotton, all neatly folded. She wondered what kind of woman she was to surround herself with such drab clothes but she didn't take the time to ponder that now. She dressed quickly , then her eye was drawn to a long, white nightgown draped over a chair. She went to it and touched it, to find it damp. It was what she'd been wearing last night and was obviously very old.

The forbidding blankness of her mind was pushed back slightly and she had a glimpse of an elderly woman wearing this nightgown and bend-ing over as if she was reaching for something, or someone. Lanny knew the old lady was reaching for her. It was Grandma Millie. She closed her eyes and focused on her grandmother. Lanny tried to expand the image, make the room take shape behind her grandma. Her head wound sent little darts of lightning pain deep into her brain. She ignored the growing agony as she tried to remember the house her grandma had lived in, even the room she'd been standing in when this memory had formed.

Lanny met only emptiness. But Grandma Millie was real, the nightgown was her gift to Lanny, and the look in Grandma's eyes was pure love. As Lanny closed her eyes tightly and dug for memories, the ache in her head grew, pressure built behind her eyes. She had to give up.

Frustrated, she turned back to her clothes drawers and reached for underwear. Her fingers touched a paper.

Lanny pulled out a sheet of paper so yellowed she immediately dropped it on the dresser top. Horrified to have even touched something so fragile, she looked at the scrolled handwriting and read:

> *Giselle*
> *September—1762*

Lanny gasped. The ghost Grey claimed to have seen was Giselle Devereau. Lanny must have found her diary. Then, knowing just how delicate and valuable it was, Lanny had abused it by sticking it under her bras? No historian of any merit would do such a thing, which led Lanny to wonder if she'd been lacking in merit and goaded to hide this for some reason. Or had someone else put this here?

The words were hard to read and Lanny looked around the room to find a pair of glasses resting on the table top by her papers. She donned the spectacles. The words came into focus.

Reading glasses.

> *Poltron returned to SeaCliff today and is furious to find*
> *I'm not with child.*

Lanny looked up from her reading. Poltron? The French word for coward? Giselle thought of her husband as Poltron? And SeaCliff? But this place was called The Devil's Nest. She went back to reading the ornate handwriting.

I dreaded the beatings. Even more I dreaded the further attempts to father a child with me. That is his dearest wish. When he isn't pursuing that, he'll be boasting of thieving and murder. I will endure until he leaves, for what choice have I?

Lanny realized this was written in French and she read it without hesitation. She wondered what else she was capable of. Lanny read on.

On this trip, Poltron brought another woman home and declared himself to have two wives. She is a vile creature. Vulgar and flaunting. Her laughter is reminiscent of a braying donkey we had when I was a child. Hair a vicious shade of red only a slattern can contrive and her bosom covered with indecent brevity. She laughed at me when Poltron presented her, and mocks me as if I somehow am inferior. I can feel only scorn for her. It's all too clear that no one can replace me with Poltron. Considering what I alone know.

I stay to my room and hope and pray his attentions are fixed elsewhere. There is no doubt that I will be allowed to survive because...

Lanny turned the paper over and there was nothing else.

Because what? Where did I find this paper?

Lanny looked again at the fragile foolscap and the beautiful script.

Pierre. But she calls him Poltron. Coward. Giselle, *1762*, SeaCliff. These were firm facts and Lanny knew any good historian would have tracked them down.

Why was this hidden in a drawer? Would Grey be able to explain this letter? Had he ever seen it before or had Lanny unearthed lost documents? Was this the only one or was there an entire journal hidden somewhere. More importantly, did that journal, if it existed, contain something that led to murder?

Her thoughts circled each other with no answers until the wound on her temple throbbed in time with her racing heart.

Carefully concealing the sheet of paper, she knew she had to get downstairs. Rushing now, she went to the closet and found tidy slacks in various neutral shades hanging neatly side by side with several white blouses like the one she'd slept in. She grabbed the first pair of slacks she touched and put it on. Dark gray pants, light gray sweater set.

"Perfect," she muttered in disgust. She was dressed for a funeral. Apt.

On the floor of the closet stood five pairs of shoes, all in the same low-heeled pump style, all the exact color of a pair of pants hanging above them. She slipped on the dark gray pair, knowing it was what she would normally do. That told her something at least. If she was almost obsessively organized it shouldn't be hard to imitate her natural actions if she just followed an organized line of thought. She hoped she could because Grey was right. It was essential that no one know she'd been hurt. She needed an alibi and no woman with a bleeding head wound had spent the night in bed with a man.

It was distasteful to uphold this pretense. Did that mean she was a moral woman? How could she know? As if it was the most natural thing in the world, Lanny prayed as she dressed. Whatever kind of woman she'd been before, as of today, she would hold herself to a high moral standard. Except now she was preparing to lie to the police. She prayed harder for guidance. Would her lies allow her time to regain her memory and find the real killer? Or were her lies only sin and she made excuses to protect herself?

She dressed in seconds—convenient to be boring. She glanced around the room and found a hairbrush laying on a vanity. She got it and smoothed the tangles from her hair as she studied herself in the mirror. She'd slept on her wet hair and it still brushed out smooth. No sign of body in her hair. There was a hollow look to her cheeks that made her seem almost dangerously slender and the circles under her eyes were so dark they looked like bruises. Nothing she saw pleased her.

She stopped brushing her hair as soon as she could because it hurt and ran her hand over the bump on her head. It was swollen and tender and she parted her hair to find the cut, then she carefully re-covered the spot.

She brushed her teeth, went back into her bedroom, knowing she needed to hurry. She'd already loitered too long. As she prepared to leave, she noticed a purse sitting on one of the tables. A quick look at the wallet told Lanny it was hers. Lana Cole, age twenty-four. There was an address and a quick glance at her checkbook showed a balance that was just barely staying ahead of the monthly bills.

She'd study it more later and see what information could be found about her life. Then she saw a notebook full of neat, handwritten notes. The page was open and she read the last line. 'Giselle said: I tend little Pierre and never tell him the truth. He's too young to be trusted with such a secret. There is no doubt that I will be allowed to live because...'

The notes ended. Lanny knew she'd written this herself.

What secret? What did Giselle know that would allow her to live? And had Lanny found that secret? Was that part of all she'd forgotten?

The notes were extensive, but she didn't have time to read through them now. What had Grey said? They'd hired her away from some museum?

And now this family had dragged her down in their muck. Some of it as new as last night, some that ran deep into the past.

She tapped the notebook thoughtfully, wondering if in it, she'd find why Giselle was so sure she'd live. And if these notes contained a motive for murder.

She'd return to it soon, but first she had to go downstairs and face a murder charge with an alibi based on lies and a heart determined to possess some degree of honor.

The knife through Victor's neck. The power over life and death was a craving now. The blood had washed away but it was still there, the heat of it, the life flowing out of Victor's body. The power was a discovery that needed to be made again and again.

CHAPTER SEVEN

You really walked into a mess last night, Grey." Nodding, Grey said, "I'll tell you whatever I can."

"Tell me you didn't kill him."

Grey felt his temper spike. "I planned to enjoy every moment of having him arrested. And I knew he had information about smuggling that you really wanted. I didn't kill him."

"Okay, now I want to go over last night with you."

Grey nodded, then calmly endured Case's interrogation.

It was simple for Grey to answer the questions because he had nothing to hide. Even the night with Lanny wasn't a lie because they'd been together and Grey refused to go into details that would have been lies, and Case didn't push for that kind of intimate specifics.

Of course, Grey omitted any unfortunate reference to her being in bed with his dead cousin. Still, it wasn't lying to not tell every single thing he knew.

After answering Case's questions, Grey redirected the focus to Victor's theft from the Grey Trust, which gave them a lot to talk about. Case's wife, Nat had done a lot of work on it and Case knew all the details.

Case knew Grey planned to have it out with Victor. He hadn't known

Grey was coming here quite this soon, but it was hurricane season and there were storms out in the ocean. Grey wanted to get this over with before any more time had passed.

They were interrupted when Estella marched into the room. "I'm going across the cove to see about funeral arrangements, Detective. Sally is riding along to do some shopping. I believe we're supposed to ask you before we leave the house." Estella's voice was arctic.

"That's fine." Case responded with a polite nod. "I'm finished talking with you for now, Mrs. Kozinski."

Estella's spine stiffened until Grey wondered if it would snap.

"The name is Mrs. Devereau, and I expect you to use it."

"Sorry," Case said, "But don't leave town." Case had guts. Grey had to give him that.

Estella responded with an indignant, "Hmmph," and left the room.

Just as the interrogation would have continued the last of the policemen came to the door.

"We're done, Chief Garrison. You asked for a preliminary report."

"Excuse me, Grey. This will only take a minute." The detective stepped out of the room.

Grey looked around the library. It was a monument to Pierre Devereau, a man Grey had learned to loathe. Pierre, Grey's pirate ancestor, was captured in a painting that stood above the fireplace. Grey realized for the first time how much Pierre resembled Allen. Pierre's hair was thinning and he had jowls—just like Allen. Pierre's eyes seemed sly and Grey wondered if the artist had put that in deliberately or was there just no way to paint Pierre without including it. As a child, when Grey had seen the picture, he'd seen no resemblance between himself and his forbearer, and Grey had liked that.

As he'd learned the stories of Pierre and his life dedicated to evil, Grey had come to hate that he carried even a bit of Pierre in his veins. Next to Pierre was a much smaller picture. Giselle, the woman said to haunt this house. She was beautiful. Dark haired, gray eyes. Fine boned and regal. She wore a silken gray dress with a wide gold collar and cuffs. After all these years, he still was drawn to Giselle. He'd never been able to figure out why.

Probably because in his wild imagination he credited her with saving his life during that roof top incident. Grey often wondered if she joined Pierre in his decadence or was she his victim?

Once she'd been brought to this remote, stormy coast there'd have been no way to leave.

And the story that she'd died here, throwing herself off the roof, made Grey wonder at the history of his family. Was Giselle driven mad by suffering? He saw no sign of suffering in that portrait. Though there was no joy there either.

Grey had said many a prayer in his life that he could bring honor to the Devereau name. He regretted terribly that his parents had attached it to him.

Garrison came back and Grey heard the outer door shut behind the departing policemen. The house almost echoed with emptiness. He knew where Lanny was. Trevor was probably still around somewhere. Sleeping off last night's excesses. Meredith and Allen kept to themselves, so that left only Clarinda.

Grey needed to find her and spend time with her. Heaven knew how all this was affecting her. But there was no burrowing through all the nooks and crannies of the old house now to find whatever hole Clarinda had crawled into. Grey had to get Lanny through her questioning first.

The rest of the family had been predictably closed mouthed with Case, judging by the questions Grey got. Devereau business was private even if that meant one of their own was killed and the killer escaped justice. Everyone else accused Lanny, and why not? She was the outsider.

If Grey knew Estella, and he did, very well, she would plan to exact her own vengeance against anyone who wronged a Devereau. Grey understood her instinctive desire for retribution. And he too possessed an impulse against airing dirty linen in public. But an impulse could be controlled. He had a gut level distaste for the way Victor had lived, and he wasn't about to cover for the bum. Grey had come back to settle things with Victor. Dying wasn't going to protect Victor's reputation. Everything Grey knew was going to come out.

"Did Victor have any enemies, Grey?" Case smirked. "Besides you."

"I don't know where to begin." Grey gave a sketchy outline of Victor's dealings with women and his heavy drinking. Case hadn't heard that part of it, but it helped identify a bunch of enemies.

"You know the evidence against Victor for financial crimes. You'd have received a call from me this morning except for the events of last night. We have solid proof of what Victor was up to. I also have several leads as to who exactly he was involved with."

Case's eyes sharpened. "You've got names?"

"Yes, a few. I'd hoped Victor would give us more trying to make a deal to avoid prison. Or at least cut his years there. Victor never found a boundary he didn't love to cross. The more forbidden the better as far as Victor was concerned and, if he could bring shame to our family while he was at it, he seemed to consider that a bonus."

With shrewd eyes Case looked up from his notes. "It's no secret you hated him, Grey."

"Anyone with an ounce of integrity got around to hating Victor sooner or later. You'd have hated him yourself if you'd known him well. Hate is too strong a word, though. I didn't feel anything that strong. I had no respect for him. I held him in contempt."

"People have killed for less," Case observed.

"I suppose. I've learned to turn a blind eye to his malicious treatment of women because he was right, they were always willing. Victor was no rapist to my knowledge, and his reputation was no secret. In a sense most of them had no business being surprised when Victor turned out to be a snake who bit them. I'd given up warning him about his drinking. I've assumed eventually he'd run into a policeman somewhere who wouldn't look the other way because of our family name and he'd be dealt with."

Grey hesitated then added quietly, "The ruin of the Trust...I couldn't look the other way on that."

"You're saying it was okay when he was destroying lives but when it comes to your money, watch out, huh?" Case asked.

"I'm *not* saying that." Grey replied, fighting not to let his anger show. "I'm saying I finally have proof of a *crime*. As far as Victor's debauched lifestyle, I talked to him until I couldn't stand to hear myself talk anymore. I've talked to Estella about the way she bailed him out of every jam he ever got into. I've warned women he was interested in what they could expect. I think you'll find a record of me calling the police on several occasions when he boated over to the mainland drunk and I knew he planned to get in the car he kept over there and drive. I was afraid he'd kill somebody. I've tried. Even though I'm a lot younger than Victor I was always trying to protect people from him. My parents died when I was fifteen. They were good people, except my mom really hated Estella. Mom had no use for The Devil's Nest but Estella was obsessed with it and Mom liked having what Estella wanted. She saw to it that the Grey trust made it mandatory that The Devil's Nest be supported, with a pittance going to Estella and her brood. She never wanted Estella to forget who had power over her."

"I never knew your folks, Grey. But your mom sounds a little...um..." Case fell silent.

"Bonkers? Ridiculous? Spiteful?"

Case shrugged and didn't agree or disagree.

"But my parents didn't plan to die so young and when Estella seemed eager to take me in, the Grey side of my family, which is all distant, let it happen. And for three years, that gave Estella control of the trust."

"You may have been her ward, but you went to a boarding school and spent almost every holiday and the whole summer with us."

"The Garrisons were a Godsend. Having you open your home to me..." Grey shook his head. "It made life bearable. I can't imagine being stuck here, even if it was for only three years. Once I was eighteen she had to go through me to get money just like Mom planned it, and she hated that. But I had no choice but to pay the bills.

"When I found proof of Victor's criminal activities, I was talking to you about it. I did everything I could to see you working in Gull Cove."

"Yeah, thanks for the help finding a job," Case said dryly.

They both knew, with his years of experience with the FBI he could have his pick of jobs.

"If you really have to ask me if I hated him enough to kill him, the answer is no."

"I think I'd be wasting my time to look for suspects farther than the people who live in this house." Case's intelligent eyes watched for every flicker on Grey's face. Case Garrison came here because he was a Texas native and wanted a quieter life for him and his wife. Grey had known that finally there was a lawman in Gull Cove who wouldn't bow down to Estella and the law would finally catch up to Victor.

Grey's jaw clenched. The same thought had occurred to him. He said tersely, "An intruder is possible."

"Possible, but not probable. Access to the house is very limited. No one had a friend staying over. A tryst is unlikely considering the people in this house are an elderly lady, a handicapped girl, a married couple, you and Miss Cole who *claim* to have been together."

"We were together, Case."

Without responding to that, Case went on, "Trevor, who was out all evening and has a dozen eye witnesses in a bar in town to prove it, and two men who drove him to the dock to drive his boat over here, after the time of death, and an elderly housekeeper who met me at the door with a rolling pin."

"What about Victor? If anyone had a tryst it would be him."

"Your family said there was no one else here. A visitor would have had to come in late, after everyone retired to their rooms. Your housekeeper says she responds when someone comes to the door and there was no one."

"She didn't meet me. I just walked in. Someone else could have done the same thing."

"True. I doubt it, but it's possible. I plan to ask questions in town as well as with your family."

Grey had probably said too much already. He wondered how his good friend was going to treat Lanny.

The door opened across the room, and Lanny hesitantly stepped in.

He was about to find out.

I move through walls like a ghost.

I hear everything, see everyone. No one escapes me for even a second.

Look at her, so quiet, so innocent, ready to smile her sweet smile and spew her lies. She thinks if she stays beside Grey and their stories match, this will be over. I mustn't laugh.

CHAPTER EIGHT

G rey rose from his chair. "Come sit close to the fire. It cuts the chill in the room."

He indicated a seat next to him for Lanny. She looked at the policeman for permission.

Detective Garrison said, "Anywhere is fine, Miss Cole."

Lanny walked around the couch and would have slipped between Grey and a low coffee table to sit on the couch, but he grabbed her hand. She remembered the part she was to play and found it simple to hold on to him tightly. She let Grey guide her onto the arm of his chair, which put her close to the welcoming fire. Garrison took the wing-backed chair across from them. She looked at Garrison's observant eyes and knew she was going to be very lucky to get out of this room without telling everything.

She let the hearth's crackling flames, their warmth and smell, soothe her ragged nerves to the extent anything could. The library was huge and jammed with furniture, just as her bedroom was. A couch facing the fire-place and chairs on either side formed a sitting area. It would have been nice if not for a coffee table and end tables loaded with dusty bric-a-brac. The stone mantle above the fire was jammed with objects.

Lining the room, there were small tables topped with vases and statu-ettes, as if Devereaus gathered but never discarded. The walls were covered with bookcases, filled with musty tomes. A massive desk stood in front of huge windows that must look to the east, over the sea.

SeaCliff.

Lanny needed to talk to Grey but it would have to wait.

"Now, Miss Cole, I need to ask your whereabouts last night between the hours of midnight and three a.m." The detective's somber voice was a perfect match for the dismal setting.

"I...I..." Lanny felt her face heat up. How many times since she'd met Grey had she found reason to be embarrassed. She couldn't stop herself from glaring at him for a second even as her hand flexed in his and she tightened her grip.

When she looked back at Garrison he was watching her intently. "Go on."

In a rush she said, "I'm sure Grey has told you we were together."

"What time did you first begin...spending time with Mr. Grey?"

"I—oh, it was late." Lanny couldn't force a flat out lie through her lips.

"Grey came home and found me and shortly after that we..." Lanny flushed until she must resemble the rounded top of an overheated thermometer. "...we went to his room."

"I understand you met Mr. Grey only last night."

Garrison didn't say she was a slattern but she knew he thought it.

"That's right." No lies there.

"And you were never separated from him, not even for a short time."

"No," Lanny's voice dropped to a whisper as she thought about Grey caressing her in the shower. "From the moment we met we...we were...I was always...with him."

Grey, sitting on her left, switched so he held her left hand in his left, and slid his right hand around her waist and settled on her hip. It could have been an act of support and comfort but it felt like he was underlining their physical closeness for effect. Lanny didn't shrug his hand away but she wanted to. Even if it did feel nice.

"And what was your relationship with Victor?" Garrison continued.

"I didn't really have one." Lanny tipped her head with a slightly helpless feeling. She certainly couldn't *remember* having one. "I worked long hours, isolated from the family, so I can't tell you much more."

"Can you tell me if Victor had any visitors last night, or if anyone in the family did?"

"I don't know of any." That was the plain truth.

"Can you tell me of anyone who might want Victor Kozinski dead?"

Lanny shook her head silently for a few seconds, then she said, "I'm sorry I can't be of more help."

Garrison looked at her with a probing gaze for a long minute. "Are you sure you're not closer to Victor than you're admitting, Miss Cole? Perhaps we should have Grey leave the room. There might be things you'd rather not talk about in front of him."

"No," Lanny said harshly. "There was nothing like that."

"I think you're keeping something from me, Miss Cole. You look pale, nervous. Something has upset you."

Lanny stared at her hands folded in her lap. "Naturally I'm upset. A man died last night, violently. A few steps from where I was. That's very frightening. In addition, I spend most of my time alone in this large, rather oppressive house where now I know a killer can get in. That's enough to upset anyone."

"Get in, Miss Cole? It's my theory that the killer is already in."

Lanny's head jerked up and she looked at the detective. A chill crawl up her spine. "What do you mean?"

"I mean access to this house is very limited. All clues seem to indicate that Victor was murdered by a member of his own family." Garrison watched her with shrewd eyes as he added,

"Or someone who resides here."

Lanny's stomach twisted with fear. "You think I did it?"

"Mrs. Devereau was sure she heard you scream, Miss Cole. She is willing to swear the sound came from Victor's room. It was the reason she came upstairs, only to discover Victor's body."

"Estella is over eighty years old, Case," Grey said brusquely. "And her rooms are downstairs and in the wing on the opposite side of this very large house. She couldn't hear anything from Victor's room."

"She said there are air vents. She can hear the goings on in Victor's room. She demonstrated it to me. Trust me, you can hear."

Grey's lips tensed. "Estella spends her evenings eavesdropping on Victor, huh? Well, his room is most likely entertaining. Although imagining an eighty-year-old voyeur is nauseating."

Lanny shuddered. She didn't even know Estella except for the regal voice she'd heard outside her door last night, but the thought sickened her.

"As I mentioned earlier, Miss Cole and I made some...noise." Grey's voice was heavy with intentions. "It might never have occurred to Estella that the sounds could be coming from *my* room. She didn't know I'd come home and..uh, retired to my bedroom...with Lanny."

Her cheeks heating up, she said, "Grey, please, do we have to discuss... details in front of the detective?" She tried to ease his hand away from her hip but he curled his fingers over her thigh. She shot him a look of pure embarrassment. She supposed her reaction to his intimacy was exactly right for lovers who were essentially strangers. He the aggressor, she smitten but horrified at how public their dalliance had suddenly become. She pushed at his hand and he laid his other hand over hers.

She subsided before it became ridiculous.

Grey continued talking to Garrison. "Even with the air ducts, it's quite a distance to Estella's room. Add to that the violence of the thunderstorm. Maybe she heard Lanny with me and identified her, then assumed the sound came from Victor's room. You never came into my room, Detective. Did you find out if sound carries from my room to Estella's? We all share the same ventilation system."

Lanny noticed that Garrison, for the first time didn't seem so sure of himself. "No, I didn't check."

"Did Victor cry out for help?" Grey asked. "Was there a struggle? Why didn't we hear that? Even though Lanny and I were...occupied, we'd have heard something."

"The coroner saw no signs of a struggle, we believe someone killed him while he slept."

Lanny shuddered at the analytic detachment in Garrison's voice. That drew his attention back to her. "You're sure there's nothing you're holding back about your relationship with Victor?"

Grey said indignantly, "Detective, I told you..."

"And I told you," Garrison interrupted, "you could stay while I talked to Miss Cole if you didn't interfere."

Grey clenched his jaw but quit talking.

"There's nothing to talk about," Lanny said. "No relationship to discuss."

"Then why do you look like you want to cut and run? I can tell when someone's lying to me."

"I can't believe you *ever* question anyone about a murder and they're not nervous. And I may be uncomfortable discussing last night because of what occurred between Grey and me, but that doesn't mean I can shed more light on Victor's murder."

"It seems like more than that, Miss Cole," Garrison said coldly.

"Grey and I did spend most of the night...awake. I'm exhausted."

"So, after you discovered Victor was dead, you and Grey coolly went back to your lovemaking, is that it?"

Lanny gasped at the cruel tone. "We didn't."

Grey leaned close to her. "You're forgetting this morning."

"Must you keep saying things like that, Grey?" Lanny turned on him in horror that he'd disgrace her like this.

He only smiled.

"I don't think exhaustion, combined with shock over dear old Victor, explains it." Case's eyes slid between them. "You look, well forgive me for being blunt, but you look awful."

Lanny knew he was trying to shock her into saying something unguarded. She was too tired and battered to fall into his trap. She looked up at him and conjured a bit of indignation. "You don't know me, Detective. For all you know I'm positively radiant this morning compared to how dreadful I usually look."

Grey ran his fingertips across her spine and said softly, "Don't get upset. I think you're beautiful."

The detective unbent enough to give them a weary smile.

Lanny realized he'd been up all night. Garrison was probably more exhausted than she was.

"It's my job to dig for answers." Garrison looked down at the small notebook he held in his hand.

"Have you found any?" Lanny really wished he'd settle this, arrest someone—other than her—and leave.

Garrison shook his head, "But I've found a lot more questions. Some very interesting questions."

With that he flipped his notepad shut and stood. "I'll want that information on Victor before I leave, Grey. And I'd like you to help me check the air registers in your room to see if sound carries to Mrs. Devereau's room. I'll have more questions in the near future for both of you, so don't plan on leaving town."

"Can I have just a moment with Lanny before we do that, Case?"

Garrison's eyes shifted between them. "Keep it short." On that threatening note he left the room.

Grey stood and pulled her to her feet. He swept her into his arms and whispered against her ear, "You were wonderful." His lips descended in a ruthless kiss.

Lanny's head was spinning by the time he let go. She forced herself to control her breathing so she could inform him acidly, "And you were an absolute jerk."

"Now wait a minute, if you're referring to the little, flirtatious things I said—,"

"Little? Flirtatious?" Lanny shoved his shoulders but she didn't budge him so much as an inch. In fact, Grey stepped closer.

She whispered, "Don't kiss me again."

"Then be quiet," Grey said simply.

"All right I will." With a sing song mockery of a man's voice, she said, "You're forgetting this morning."

"I might have laid it on a bit thick but two people who end up in bed together after a few minutes acquaintance are—well—it stands to reason we'd wake up and—"

"Don't say it." Lanny tried to keep her voice low but she was practically growling. "Two people who end up in bed together after a few minutes acquaintance are inevitably *fools*. There's no reason we can't call this 'affair' off right now. We'll simply let it be known that you turned out to be a huge disappointment on every level, and we've agreed to never spend another second in each other's company."

"Where's my submissive little angel this morning?"

"And quit hanging all over me. And don't you pull a stunt like the one in the bedroom, grabbing me and...and..." Lanny sputtered to a halt, too angry to speak.

"And kissing you for the nice policeman to discover?" Grey suggested.

Lanny snarled each word under her breath, "Especially! Don't! Do! That!"

"Easy to say. But if my memory serves me correctly, I gave you the first kiss, but you're the one who came back for seconds."

With a strangled scream of frustration, she hissed, "I've got a lot of work to do figuring out where I am in cataloguing your family papers. Hopefully doing that will help jostle my memory and the more I know, the sooner I'll get my memory back, and the sooner I can get out of here. I fact, I found a paper I want you to—"

"That might not be true," Grey interrupted. "I've heard in these situations its better not to push too hard."

"Produce a medical license right now or leave me alone."

"No medical license," Grey said. "Just common sense."

Lanny gave him a last indignant 'humph' and stalked past. He grabbed her arm and wheeled her around to face him. He pulled her close until they were nose to nose and said in a furious undertone, "The affair is on, Angel, and you're going to keep up the front. You may be feeling feisty this morning but the first sign that we were faking our interest in each other is going to be all the police and my family need to start suspecting you again."

"And you, Grey. Don't forget I'm *your* alibi."

"The difference is, I'm covering for you. I didn't get here until after Victor was killed and if I have to, I can prove I'd only arrived. That leaves me in the clear and you twisting in the wind."

"I say you're as big a womanizer as your cousin and you're looking for an excuse to use the only convenient woman in the house. The affair is off!"

The sound of footsteps over Lanny's shoulder alerted them that someone was coming toward the library. Grey gave her a narrow-eyed, challenging look, then hauled her into his arms.

Although she was firm in her decision to call off the pretend affair, for some reason that didn't stop her from throwing her arms around Grey's neck and kissing him back.

Grey broke off the kiss sometime in the far, far distant future. Lanny's heart was pounding so frantically she could barely speak. "Did they go away?"

Grey was watching her lips move as if they had hypnotized him. His only response was, "Did who go away?"

Lanny said, "I don't know."

His mouth, hot and hungry, slanted over hers again. When, after an eternity, he set her roughly away from him, he growled through clenched teeth, "The affair is on."

He swept past her and out of the library, leaving her swaying on legs barely steady enough to hold her upright. She couldn't remember who she was, but she was *not* the weak, lustful woman who had just let Devereau Grey ravish her.

Long after he was out of earshot she said to the empty room, "You mean the pretend affair."

Her words echoed in the room almost like laughter.

More passages.

Why haven't I been told about these before? I could have moved to claim everything much earlier if I'd known. It's a maze, the dead ends, the hidden latches, as dark as a The Devil's Nest.

Had Pierre roamed these tunnels in the night, hidden his treasure here? Locked his women away? Tortured his prisoners here?

I can almost smell blood on the walls. I draw strength as I walk along, planning – always planning.

CHAPTER NINE

The Devil's Nest. Aptly named.

Far better than SeaCliff.

Had they called it SeaCliff at first and changed it later?

The darkness pressing against Lanny, magnified by her grisly memories of Victor's body, enhanced by lingering terror of last night's storm, heightened by the helplessness of having no memory before that.

The house, which she'd barely noticed earlier for worrying about the coming police interrogation, now smothered her with an aura of evil.

The murky weather hung on. The feeble electric lights did little to dispel the gloom. She took her first step up the vast, curved staircase to the second floor and stopped.

The top of the stairs disappeared into the darkness of the upper hall. Someone, or something, waited to devour her at the top. Above her, hallways reaching to the left and right of the stairs seemed to harbor a menacing presence just out of her sight. Wind blown rain soughed around the house like the shallow breathing of a lingering ghost.

A second, smaller staircase yawned open and ascended to a higher floor. The dark maw of the narrow stairs beckoned her as if to her doom. Lanny assumed it led to the attic she was supposed to be exploring. Although she must have done it countless times, she couldn't imagine where she'd found the courage to walk up those stairs. The blank wall of her memory parted.

Thunder cut into her heart but the sound was a memory as the storm outside silently drizzled on. For some reason the memory of the thunder was terrifying.

She looked up those stairs and saw a hand resting on the rickety railing. A man's hand on hers. A short burst of lights behind her eyes nearly knocked her backward off the steps. She grabbed at the banister to keep from falling. A memory? Or part of some long-ago ghostly nightmare come back to haunt her?

She felt a sharp chill crawl up her leg like icy fingers. She jumped away from the draft. She pressed her back against the wall and nearly knocked an ancient portrait of some grim ancestor to the floor, suddenly the icy fingers were his.

With a shriek of terror, she wheeled away from the wall to face the ghosts of the past head on. She clutched the banister as if it were her only hold on sanity. Her other hand went to her throat. Confronting the portraits, they seemed to glare at her, long dead ancestors glowering at an intruder who must be banished.

She had to bite her lip to keep from crying out for Grey. She only controlled the urge through sheer willpower. She stood there, her feet rooted to the stairs as the upper floor beckoned malignantly. The house terrified her, and if she'd been an animal, she'd have hunted a hole and crawled into the depths of the earth. As the image of her running and hiding materialized Lanny realized she was picturing herself as a rabbit, or a mouse. The bottom of the food chain.

Prey.

Her chin lifted. Lanny Cole was nobody's *prey*. If the house wanted her, she wouldn't make it easy. Thinking of it as a challenge, she squared her shoulders. She even managed a smile at the way she'd granted a personality to a pile of stone and mortar. A house didn't prey on anyone. Not even a house called The Devil's Nest.

She walked briskly up the stairs, noticing creaking risers, muted by carpet the dark rust red color of dried blood. When she got to the second floor, it was just a hallway. No one lurked in it, waiting for her. She looked up the next stairway.

No hand on that railing. Had that been a memory? Or had fear created an imaginary terror?

She wanted that notebook from her room so she hurried down the hall to her left to get it. In her room, she snatched it up. Grey swung the door between the rooms open. "I'm helping Garrison for now. Stay with me. I don't like you wandering around the house alone."

Lanny thought of the vent that carried sound and shook her head.

"I'll be in my office. I'm going over notes and old papers." She hoped he'd get the hint that she was trying to jar her memory.

"Everyone's gone but Trevor and Clarinda." Grey studied her for a long moment and she knew he wanted to overrule her decision and continue to keep her close at hand. "I suppose Trevor has his usual hangover. He should be harmless."

Lanny nodded and reached for the doorknob to pull it shut. Grey's hand rested over hers. He jerked his head at the vent barely visible on the far side of the bed, then stole a quick kiss. "Get to work then, Angel."

She narrowed her eyes and tugged on the door. He grinned at her and let her close it.

She didn't take the hidden note, written in Giselle's hand, but grabbed her notebook and left the slim bit of familiarity of her room and went into the wing Grey said contained her office. Right now, it seemed like the best place to try and discover herself.

She opened the first door down the hall and was shocked to face a woman she'd never seen before. The woman was inches away, reaching for the door to come out. Cool, brittle, lines of displeasure cut into her face. Not Clarinda. It had to be Meredith.

"What do you think you're doing coming in here?" Meredith had a cigarette nearly burned away and she drew deeply on it with a hand that trembled noticeably.

"I—I'm sorry." A very good question. If Lanny had her memory she'd have known where her office was. Fumbling for an answer, she stammered, "I—I've been so upset by what's gone on. I wasn't paying attention to which door I opened."

Lanny noticed Meredith lean against the door a bit too heavily as she stood glaring. Wobbly. A whiff of the room told Lanny Meredith was drunk. She didn't bother trying to explain further.

"Hmmph." Meredith blew a long column of smoke upward without taking her eyes off Lanny.

Lanny's eyes followed the line of smoke and that caused her to look past Meredith into the room. To see a bottle of liquor sitting on a table next to a pitcher and a martini glass.

Claws sunk into Lanny's wrist, and she looked into bloodshot eyes. "You killed Victor."

Meredith's voice broke and her knees sagged. Lanny jumped forward and slid an arm around her before she fell.

"Get—get your hands off of me." But Meredith's protest was weak.

Lanny assisted her to the chair. It was old, with upholstery so threadbare it was colorless. Lanny had noticed all the old objects crammed into the house but for the first time she didn't think about how cluttered it was, instead she realized how worn and tired it all was. This was a house with no money. Or at least, none to spare. Lanny thought of all the little tables, mostly solid oak and very old. Valuable. Yes, Grey said he held the purse strings and no doubt he held them tightly, but there was money to be found in this house and clearing it out would only make it better, there was no beauty in their hoarded goods.

The Devereau family preferred to cling to their possessions at the cost of their survival.

Then Lanny looked at Meredith's drink. If the woman could afford that, then Lanny would spare her no sympathy.

"You're not well." Lanny looked at the stemmed cocktail glass and the mostly empty pitcher. "Let me get you something to eat. Some coffee."

"I can't believe he's dead." Meredith didn't respond to Lanny's offer.

"Victor's death has been a shock. Maybe you should rest."

"No. I just need a drink." Tears rolled down from one eye, cutting a path through the heavy make-up on Meredith's face. Her vivid red lipstick had worn away until it was settled into the wrinkles at the corners of her lips.

Lanny wasn't about to pour yet more poison into this woman.

Meredith reached toward the pitcher and Lanny knelt on the floor and caught Meredith's shaky hands. "Another drink is the last thing you need."

Meredith turned to Lanny, the tears flowing faster. "Allen could never give me any children."

The tears and the extremely personal confidence seemed completely out of character for the hostile woman, but Lanny couldn't know for sure. Perhaps they'd become confidantes since Lanny had arrived. "Would you really want to raise a child here?"

"It's what Mother Devereau wants."

"You still hope for a child?" Lanny wasn't sure of her age, but surely it was too late for a child.

"But Victor fathers children without effort."

"What?"

"And Mother Devereau wants a new generation, she said it would be fine. Victor said it would be fine. Allen would never find out."

Lanny could only imagine one thing Meredith might mean.

"I wasn't supposed to fall in love with him." Meredith wrenched free and buried her face in her hands, the sobs wracking her whole body as she curled down.

Horrified, Lanny stood and backed away.

Meredith erupted from the chair and swung her hand hard. She slapped Lanny so hard Lanny staggered back. She braced herself for another attack. Instead, Meredith crumpled back into the chair.

"Victor laughed when I told him. He said you'd agreed to marry him."

"No!" Shock rattled that single word out of Lanny as she rested her hand on her burning cheek.

"All he wanted was you. But that was always the way. He wanted a woman until he got her." Meredith covered her tear stained face with one hand and rested her other low on her stomach.

The gesture made Lanny think of a woman expecting a child.

Or one who wished she was.

What started as the devil's bargain to secure an heir to the Devereau name, had deepened further into a nightmare when Meredith fell in love. With Victor, her husband's brother.

Had Allen found out and turned on Victor?

Had Meredith confessed her love and been sneered at and cast aside, then killed Victor in a frenzy of rage?

Either one of them…or both of them together, might have done it, then dragged Lanny in as a scapegoat.

Had Estella affirmed that a child was on the way, thanks to her Machiavellian scheme and decided she no longer needed to put up with Victor?

Lanny had just found three people with a motive for murder.

Bile rose in Lanny's throat as she backed away from the weeping woman and stumbled out of the room, leaving Meredith behind, crying her heart out as if…as if…the man she loved had died.

The question was, by whose hand?

Every time Lanny learned more about Victor, she could see why someone would want to kill him, maybe including her.

Lanny wanted to run to Grey. She wanted to tell him what she'd learned. But he was with the police. Would this bring up more questions from the detective about how Meredith had acted around Victor and Allen? Lanny certainly couldn't answer them.

Her cheek throbbed and she knew that if Grey saw a red, swollen mark on her, he'd storm down to Meredith's room and exact vengeance, which would draw the police's attention to his temper.

No, she had to talk to Grey alone first.

With her hand still resting on her stinging cheek, she tore her eyes away from the direction she knew would lead her to Grey, and rushed down the hall to the last door and pulled it open.

Another ridiculously cluttered room. But in this one, she found signs of occupation. The desk was clean except for neat stacks of paper. Lanny recognized the tidiness of the desk as her own work. She apparently spent her time here or in the attic or her room.

Thinking of Meredith, drunk and so grief stricken she was barely sane, Lanny closed the door firmly behind her, to shut out the gloom of this family.

And maybe she was now isolated, but the room was so overrun with junk she felt buried alive. The brooding sense of evil she'd felt on the stairway returned and she battled it back.

Her office was huge and dimly lit with only north windows coated by relentless wind-driven sheets of rain.

Facing the window, the room was dominated on her left by a fireplace big enough for her to stand in upright, but no sign a fire had been lit in ages. On the right was an oak desk blackened with hundreds of years of varnish.

The desk, six feet long, five feet wide, ornately carved, immense and scarred with age, had a brutal kind of beauty. The piece reminded Lanny of a mountain. It looked harsh and noble at the same time. Only the top was smooth. Whoever had carved the fleur-de-lis and twisting vines that covered the drawer fronts and legs, as well as all the sides, had been obsessed with decorating every inch of space. In their arrogance they had believed it would be more beautiful than smooth, natural wood. Now it stood, apparently forgotten for years until Lanny had intruded into this room. It could claim a gruesome, baroque monstrosity, it's only value simple survival over the years.

The oak desk chair was tucked so neatly into the knee hole of the desk Lanny knew she had done it herself. With padded red leather back and seat cushions and arm rests, the same excessive carving was repeated on the chair.

There were books and papers everywhere on and around the desk. Ancient and crumbling, they lay neatly stacked in some order Lanny needed to discern, on every inch of the desk and in orderly piles on the floor and several other surfaces. There were two straight-backed arm chairs with the same elaborate carving sitting in front of the desk. They too were stacked with papers.

She glanced around the rest of the room to file away knowledge she might be expected to possess. It didn't look like she'd touched any other part of the room. A couch with wooden trim and red leather padding with dozens of large buttons tufting it, was lined up to face the fireplace. A matching overstuffed chair sat at a right angle to the couch.

The walls were covered with red wallpaper, heavily flocked with red flowers. The curtains were red velvet with black tassels dangling along the edge. They looked fragile with age and seemed to serve no purpose except to heighten the garishness of the room and block out what meager bit of light might find its way in the window. Lanny thought the furnishings were more appropriate for a bordello than a home.

The room was lined with an endless succession of decorative tables in a mishmash of styles. They held the results of some long ago obsession with brightly painted porcelain figurines, overly embellished vases, and flamboyant, ornamental boxes. Bric-a-brac covered every horizontal surface and heavy dust covered the bric-a-brac. Only Lanny's work area was dusted and clean.

A life-size statue of Pan complete with satanic horns, a goat's hind end and a fife, stood in one corner next to the fireplace. The only connection between all the pieces was gaudiness, as if generations of collectors had been unshakably burdened with hereditary bad taste.

Any uncovered space on the walls held more old portraits, no doubt all Devereaus, but lesser family members who weren't worthy enough to make the main staircase or the library. Lanny wondered if she'd been assigned this room or if she'd picked it hoping to use the portraits to get a feel for whose documents she was reading. That might have been her thinking at the time but now they just made the room sinister. She felt them watching her as if they knew she was vulnerable and they only waited until the right time to strike.

She shook off the foreboding thought and made her way to the desk. She saw a pile of spiral notebooks filled with her orderly handwriting. With a sigh of relief, she switched on a lamp that sat on the desk and settled into her chair. Eager to think of something beside ominous evil and a family with too many secrets.

The center drawer in the desk was open an inch and, considering the neatness Lanny was beginning to recognize about herself, she doubted she'd left it open.

Tugging on the brass drawer pull, Lanny opened the stubborn drawer enough to see a sheet of paper laying inside. A sheet of paper that matched exactly the one she'd found in her room, also tucked inside a drawer.

Lanny carefully pulled the paper out and saw there were two sheets this time, both covered with the elegant, flowing handwriting of Giselle Devereau. French again of course.

Lanny lifted the paper to lay it on her desk so she could touch it the least amount possible.

February—1779

Poltron's fourth wife has given him a son.

Lanny gasped. Fourth wife?

He came home from the sea and spent days intolerable with pride at the chubby little boy. Then he caught Magda with the stableman. From the first she's been in league with the devil, even more so than Poltron, if such a thing is possible.

She had earned pin money on her back, welcoming every man with a coin who came near.

Poltron is enraged that he'd been cuckolded and of course must wonder if the boy is his. As do I.

My little Pierre is nearing ten and there have been no other children to any woman that I know of. Poltron dragged Magda to the roof of The Devil's Nest to cast her into the sea.

Grey said Pierre divorced his wives by pitching them off the roof? But Giselle survived. Maybe all four of the wives lived in the same house.

But as in all things, this wife was different. She didn't go meekly. Instead she attacked.

I watched in secret as she slapped and screamed threats.

Poltron was a coward as always and cringed away. Magda drew a knife and stabbed him, escaped past him and left The Devil's Nest. Just stormed out of the house and down the road to the dock. She rowed herself to town. No man stopped her as I know they would have me. Perhaps she earned their favor as well as pin money. If Poltron were dead, would they let me go? But he is not dead. I couldn't defy my Father in Heaven far enough to sneak in and finish what Magda had started. His men reached him while I hated myself for hesitating.

They took him to his bed and tended him.

I'm caring for the newest child, whom they have called Bayard.

I have no motherly affection for the child and regret that. The child is not responsible for his parents. I tend him gently and pray for him always, but I fear he can tell his mother has abandoned him to his fate and his caretaker is too full of despair to give him love. I keep little Pierre at my side when possible. We are a strange sort of family.

I hate the waiting. His routine is to come to me daily and ask if I am ready to talk. Odd to think something so horrendous could become routine. This time his wounds kept him away.

I wonder if I can kill a man?

Is it wrong to pray to God for such courage? I pray such dreadful prayers with nearly every breath.

What is the right of it, Dear God? Of course, it is wrong

to kill, but to stand by while a man is so evil, harms so many,
harms me over and over, isn't that the greater sin?

That was all. Lanny looked at the pages. Nothing she read there was familiar. Had she seen them before? Why would she bring two sheets of paper here and one to her room? She needed to talk to Grey. But the drawer being slightly opened made her wonder if she had brought them. Was someone else leaving them for her to find.

Why?

Lanny reached for the notebook she'd brought with her and flipped to the first page.

Reading it would teach her what she'd forgotten. It might even restore her memory.

Within moments she was lost in the sadistic mind of a pirate.

Case and Grey could hear each other clearly through the vents. Grey tried to think what he and Lanny had discussed that morning and the night before. They'd been quiet, but it was possible Estella knew everything.

The two men experimented with other bedrooms and hallways and talked back and forth easily. The cold air ducts carried the sound and Grey found he could muffle the noise from his room by laying a blanket over the vent. He didn't leave the blankets over it though. He hoped Estella wouldn't realize they had discovered her secret. And he might be able to use it against her.

They found several spots that didn't seem to be audible from any of the other rooms and, even though the house was virtually empty, they picked one of these, a small alcove at the far end of the hallway outside Grey's room, to confer.

"I now know Estella has been privy to every private conversation anyone's ever had in this house. It's a pretty unpleasant thought. When I was a kid, I thought that old bat could read my mind. Then later I just thought she was an insufferable snoop."

Case, a newlywed and very happily married, said wryly, "I wouldn't want anyone to eavesdrop on my bedroom that's for sure."

"I've always had a sense that there was no true privacy in this house, but it never occurred to me that there could be such an obvious reason for it."

"You brought Miss Cole up here," Case pointed out. Case knew him very well and knew how out of character that had been.

Grey's jaw tensed. True, he and Lanny hadn't really done anything but somehow that seemed like a small detail. He felt a bond more intimate than if it were physical with Lanny. The thought of someone intruding on that made him furious.

"It makes me sick to think she might have heard us. I'm having a plumber start work tomorrow to make changes to assure this doesn't happen again."

"No, you're not."

Grey's eyes narrowed as he studied Case. Then he nodded, "We don't want Estella to know we've found her little secret."

"Well, she told me. She had to. It was the only way I'd buy her hearing what went on in Victor's room. But she's out of the house and doesn't know we've been checking the loudspeaker system that your air ducts seem to be. And she doesn't have to know I told you. Not yet."

Grey studied the deserted hall that stretched out in front of them and rubbed the tense muscles on the back of his neck. "If this whole place caved off these cliffs into the sea I wouldn't spend two minutes regretting it."

"Does that include your family going over the cliff, Grey?"

Grey shook his head then, incongruous as it was, he grinned. "Don't try and pin this on me, Case. It's a waste of your time. I know you can't take my word for it. I know you have to keep asking questions, and I won't sleep peacefully in this house until you find who did this. But you could save yourself some time if you erased me from your list of suspects. I was really looking forward to watching a jail cell door slam shut on my cousin."

"If you were that angry, you have a powerful motive for murder."

"I might agree if Victor had been beaten to death as slowly as possible, but I'd have never let him die in his sleep. He deserved worse than that."

"That's the worst excuse for why a guy should be removed from a list of suspects I've ever heard."

"It's always nice to excel."

"You know I don't suspect you of this, Grey. I know you too well. And even if I didn't, I'd be inclined to believe you. I mean if you're going to kill the guy, why bother gathering all the evidence you have? But someone did it."

Grey looked around the empty alcove with sudden awareness.

"Did you remember something?"

Grey shook his head and looked at Case, for a second he'd forgotten the man was there. "No, every once in a while it just hits me that I might have a murderer in the family."

"You'd better not forget it. An intruder is possible but there's no evidence of one."

"No one is safe here," Grey said.

"No," Case admitted. He spoke to Grey in a way he probably wouldn't if they weren't old friends. "No one is. I need the information you have on Victor's activities right away, it will no doubt open up some solid lines of inquiry. It sounds like he was dealing with some bad apples with his smuggling. People who don't hesitate to kill and who might have the wherewith-al to breach your security."

"I've got everything in town. I didn't bring it here with me."

"Can you bring what you've got to the station? I'd like to go over it with you."

"I'll follow you. I won't give you any political hassle and I'll block the rest of the family to the best of my ability and overrule them when I can't block them. The governor is a personal friend, I was vice-chairman of the committee to reelect the county judge and I go to Bible study every week with the Attorney General."

"I'd appreciate you keeping your aunt out of my hair."

Grey started walking toward the stairway. "Have you talked to every-one?"

"Everyone but Clarinda." Case fell into step beside him. "I tried but she was so grief stricken we asked your aunt to call a doctor in early this morning to give her a sedative."

Grey's eyes sharpened, "So you knocked her out?" He didn't like the idea of anyone in this house being so helpless.

"We would have but she slipped away from us and we haven't seen her since."

Grey nodded. "That sounds like Clarinda. I doubt she can tell you any-thing." Grey mused silently for a moment then he said, "She's the only one of us who feels any true grief for Victor. And the only reason she's crying is because her childlike nature makes her forgiving of Victor's cruelty."

"Victor was cruel to her?"

"Victor was cruel to everyone. The list is so long you can't hope to wade through it in a lifetime." Grey thought of Victor shoving him off the roof as a child. That went far beyond cruel.

"I'm willing to bet that whoever killed him had been hurt badly by him and won't be dangerous to anyone else. If I didn't fear for the rest of the family, I'd urge you to just close the book on this, Case. Not that you would, of course. But my cousin did so much damage in this life it's a blessing he didn't live longer."

"That may be as sad an epitaph as a man ever had. Do you want to go into town with me? We could cover a lot of ground working together. I can have a patrolman run you home later."

"No, I'll follow you. I want my own vehicle and my own boat." Grey should get Lanny. He hated to leave her but he didn't want her exposed to questioning again. She was too shaky to keep up the pretense of their alibi.

Grey heard a door open below and moved to the top of the stairs to see Trevor leaving. That meant the house was empty except for Clarinda. Lanny would be safe and Grey wouldn't be gone long.

He escorted the detective out into the dismal Texas morning.

CHAPTER TEN

Like a monster clearing its throat, the thunder made itself known.

It pulled Lanny up from the depths that had swallowed her. Like a salmon fighting its way upstream, she forced herself to break the grip of murder and depravity. With a final act of will, she surfaced, feeling soiled by the saga of Pierre Devereau.

Looking up at the room, she saw the statue in the corner move. Lanny screamed. Her notebook went flying and she leapt to her feet. Her chair slammed against the bookshelves behind her.

The devilishly horned head turned to look at Lanny. Lanny opened her mouth to scream again just as a shape separated itself and emerged from the dark corner on the opposite side of the room.

It was a woman. Lanny clasped one hand to her chest, trying to calm her hammering heart.

She sank back into her chair, gasping for breath. Only her fear had brought the satyr statue to life.

Blank for a moment, Lanny came up with Clarinda. This had to be the cousin Grey had spoken of.

Clarinda standing, half concealed behind the statue of Pan.

As that flash of panic eased, she blamed Pierre Devereau for her fear. He'd climbed into her mind and wrapped his malice around her like tentacles. There was no sin in which the man didn't indulge fully. No cruelty he didn't savor. He was a pirate with none of the current romanticized view of what a pirate was. He was a thief who took human life without a qualm, who tortured captives for pure sadistic pleasure, who brutalized women with relish. In her notes, Lanny had drawn a picture of pure evil.

Pierre's depravity had her nerves on edge and now a simple thing like Clarinda creeping in had scared the living daylights out of her. Daylights? She glanced at the gloomy window and heard the distant thunder and wondered if she'd ever see a clear sky again.

As Clarinda separated herself slowly from the statue, Lanny had a sudden flash of memory. Clarinda had done this before. This was familiar. Clarinda the Lurker. She couldn't remember much else except the image of herself jumping half out of her skin on another dreary afternoon.

Because it seemed like the natural thing to do, Lanny said, "Come out and sit with me for a while." Then Lanny got up and met her far more than halfway. Lanny walked the length of the room and sat on the bordello-red couch.

Lanny couldn't lock onto a specific memory, but she was sure Clarinda came in here and sat regularly. She was sure, from the wary look on Clarinda's face that the poor, shy woman-child wouldn't have come even this close if it was the first time. Lanny had the impression of a half-wild animal, slowly gentled over time, who would come out from cover, ready in an instant to dash away if the human became dangerous.

As Clarinda crept closer, Lanny could see her fully for the first time. She looked like a faded, distorted, female version of Allen. But where Allen looked weak and soft, Clarinda was beautiful. Her face was wide-eyed with fear, barely repressed by curiosity. Her skin was an ashen white against her dark brown hair, as if she'd never seen the sun. Her hair was long and unruly. It was straggling down her face to be pushed aside constantly with nervous motions from Clarinda's shaking fingers. She was so painfully thin Lanny wondered if she ate. A drab housedress hung on her skeletal frame. Her feet were bare and filthy. Lanny wondered if anyone ever took the time to see that she had a bath. Clarinda edged out from behind the statue and came slowly the five feet to sit on the couch as far from Lanny as possible.

When she was close enough, Lanny noticed Clarinda's hair and teeth were clean, so someone took time with the girl. Dirt under her fingernails and splattered on her damp dress, looked as if she'd just come in from walking in the mud in this inclement weather. Clarinda clasped and unclasped her shaking hands in her lap and stared at the motions of her fingers. She rocked herself slightly and, except for occasional furtive glances, didn't make eye contact with Lanny.

Lanny said, "Hello, Clarinda."

Clarinda looked up at her then glanced back down quickly. With jerky, uncoordinated movements, she reached into a pocket in the housedress, so faded Lanny could only suspect it had once been light blue. Clarinda produced a comb and a rubber band and offered them to Lanny. Lanny hesitated wondering if this was a daily ritual. "I'll be glad to comb your hair. Turn around so I can reach."

Clarinda obediently turned her back to Lanny and Lanny looked with dismay at the tangled mess of Clarinda's hair. It occurred to Lanny that her quiet visitor might know something of what went on in this house and, if she crept around silently, she might have answers to a lot of questions.

Could the woman even talk?

Lanny combed, careful not to cause Clarinda even a moment's pain. Then started with a simple question. "Have you been outside?"

Clarinda nodded her head up and down.

Lanny tried to think of a question that didn't have a yes or no answer. "Why?"

Clarinda whispered hesitantly, "Walking." Her voice had a childlike quality to it, so soft and fearful it was almost unearthly. Thunder rumbled overhead and tension wound in Lanny that was at least partly the fault of the storm.

"Are you cold, Clarinda? You're all wet."

Clarinda shook her head back and forth.

Lanny tried to suppress her frustrated sigh. Clarinda could talk, she just didn't. She asked gently, "Why did you go out in the cold for a walk, honey?"

Clarinda said softly, "Victor's dead."

Lanny's hands froze against Clarinda's hair. What did Victor being dead have to do with Clarinda taking a walk? Lanny said carefully, "Did you see what happened to Victor?"

Clarinda shook her head frantically.

Her fear was palpable. Not the same shy fear she'd shown when she first came in. Lanny was suddenly certain Clarinda knew more about Victor's death. Something that terrified her.

Lanny worked silently on Clarinda's hair for a long time, willing the girl to calm down. A couple of times, Lanny accidently caught a snarl too roughly but Clarinda never flinched or complained. At last Clarinda's shoulders relaxed and Lanny thought she could chance talking again. She turned the topic away from Victor hoping Clarinda wouldn't bolt from the room. Speaking very calmly, she said, "We're good friends aren't we, Clarinda? I'm combing your hair for you. That means we're friends doesn't it?"

Clarinda sat painfully still for so long Lanny thought fear had frozen her in place. At last she nodded her head once quickly. "You always comb it good."

Which Lanny took to mean they'd done this before many times. "You have pretty hair. So thick and curly. I wish mine was dark and thick like yours instead of so boring and colorless."

Lanny spoke of neutral things as she smoothed away the last knots in Clarinda's hair and pulled the brunette mass back. It surprised Lanny that her hands nimbly formed a braid. She wasn't conscious of remembering how to braid hair but apparently her hands knew how without direction. She continued talking quietly, getting an occasional one syllable answer from Clarinda.

They'd been sitting together for a long time, maybe more than an hour, Lanny thought, when Clarinda's hair finally lay neatly braided. When Lanny was done she laid her hands on Clarinda's shoulders and turned the girl to face her. As soon as Clarinda turned around she slid as far from Lanny as the couch would allow.

Lanny said, "Should we go to your room and get some dry clothes?"

Clarinda shook her head and said with a modicum of pride, "Dress myself."

"Good. I'm glad you can take good care of yourself. That's good."

Clarinda shook her head, all pride gone from her expression, "I'm not good. I'm bad."

Lanny was shocked by Clarinda's comment. "What do you mean? How could you ever be bad?"

"I'm bad. I'm bad." Her voice rising from its whisper for the first time, Clarinda stood shakily from the couch and backed toward the door watching Lanny closely as if Lanny was going to attack her.

Lanny started to rise but Clarinda backed away more quickly and Lanny immediately sat again. "Don't go, Clarinda. You're not bad. You've been really good while you were here."

"I'm bad." Clarinda's voice rose to a screech as if Lanny was doing something terrible by saying Clarinda was good. "Victor says he's bad, and I'm bad."

"Don't go, Clarinda." Suddenly, knowing why Victor thought Clarinda was bad seemed vitally important, though Lanny couldn't imagine why. It was probably just the sadistic teasing of a cruel older brother.

"I'm bad." Clarinda glanced behind her as if searching for a way out and started moving more quickly toward the door.

"Tell me why you're bad, Clarinda." Lanny was afraid that each word might be the one that sent her running. "Maybe I can help you be good again."

"I'm bad. You and Grey were bad last night." Clarinda wheeled and dashed silently to the door. She swung it open then stopped and looked back at Lanny, her eyes wild with fear.

"People die when they're bad." She disappeared around the corner to the hallway.

Lanny jumped to her feet and raced to the door. The hallway was nearly pitch black. Tables loaded with artifacts cast shadows and Clarinda could have ducked into a darkened recess, but if she had, Lanny couldn't tell it. There was a window behind Lanny's back to the east and a bolt of lightning gave some illumination, but there were no lights or windows along the entire length of the hall to the west.

No door opened or closed, no running steps, even barefoot ones, sounded on the creaky old floors. Clarinda had vanished as quickly and silently as she had appeared. Icy fingers caught Lanny's ankles and climbed up her legs and ran the length of her spine. A deep rumble of thunder broke Lanny's concentration. A wail of wind whistled around the outside of the old house in a high -pitched moan that almost sounded like sobbing.

Lanny could imagine voices in that wind saying, "People die when they're bad."

Those cold fingers of wind closed on Lanny's neck. She jumped back into the office and slammed the door. She stood there trembling for long minutes, shaken by a soul deep fear of Clarinda's words. Her fear seemed to wed itself to the increased ferocity of the storm. Closing her eyes to hunt around for control, she forced herself to scoff at her imagination. Clarinda was childlike. To her simplistic way of thinking maybe everyone was bad. Did Clarinda believe Lanny and Grey had lied about last night? Maybe, with her quiet ways, Clarinda saw more than anyone and knew Lanny was in Victor's room. Or maybe, Lanny rubbed her aching head, Clarinda heard the family say Lanny and Grey were lying.

Clarinda might not know anything first hand. A child would think a lie was bad. If she thought she was bad, then did that mean that Clarinda had told a lie? The real bad thing, murder, Lanny couldn't imagine Clarinda doing that, so when she said she'd been bad—Lanny stopped the questions that circled around in her head. She would find Clarinda and simply ask the girl what she meant. Clarinda couldn't have been too afraid or she wouldn't have come to have her hair combed.

Lanny looked around the horrid office and wondered again why she had stayed here in this house of darkness. This Devil's Nest. She wasn't ready to cut and run yet but she couldn't go back to her reading. She couldn't spend another minute studying the vile Pierre Devereau.

Lanny had looked through her purse, including her checkbook containing deposits. She was being well paid to unearth Pierre's history. But it was unfortunate his life story had survived. Not just the tales themselves but his life survived in the hearts of Estella Devereau and Victor Kozinski.

Without her memory, Lanny really knew nothing of either of them. She might be judging unfairly, based strictly on what Grey had said. But as she went to her desk to tidy her notes, she scanned the last words she'd written. She'd read through several notebooks and, because of her amnesia, she had the objectivity of an uninvolved observer. She could see the change in her work. Fear had crept slowly into her records. She could see how she'd been increasingly affected by the house and its inhabitants.

She hadn't specifically written of interaction between her or the family, since the notes weren't a personal account of her stay here. But the notes had taken on a defensive almost cryptic tone that was sometimes in a sort of shorthand that Lanny couldn't decipher even though it was obviously her own system. From the encoded work Lanny could see she'd censored herself. The most logical reason for that was because someone was reading her work. But then why not? Estella was paying her salary, of course she'd expect to read what Lanny wrote.

Why had she holed herself up in this tomb? Why hadn't she quit if she was afraid? It was all a puzzle and the more she knew, the more confused she was.

The thunder cracked again and Victor's lifeless eyes stared at her out of the night.

The little slut has been so distant, avoiding Victor's charm like no woman I've ever seen before.

Then lately, as Victor has gone into his 'I respect you for saying no, I've been waiting for you all my life' mode, the little iceberg started to thaw. It always worked. I could see love shining in her eyes. He'd've had her in a few more days. Ah...I love the sport. It's what I'll miss most about Victor.

No one can believe that someone with Victor's charm had such a hard time with her, and stubborn, cold-blooded Grey swept her off her feet.

The police are fools! I thought they'd at least take her away. She's already back to her research. She sits, defenseless as a child. I itch to march in there and watch her terror.

When Victor's blood poured onto my hands, the bright red was like life.

I'd taken life. The power was incredible. I'm hungry for it again. And there she sits reading, the little fool.

She would be so easy to kill. But not quite yet. Another should go first.

CHAPTER ELEVEN

Grey pushed his foot firmly on the accelerator even though the road to The Devil's Nest was little more than a rain-soaked goat trail.

The road was cut into the side of a mountain. A sheer rock wall stretched up on one side with a straight drop on the other that fell a hundred feet to the pounding surf of the stormy gulf.

He hadn't meant to be gone so long. But pushing to leave the police too quickly was a bad way to get them on his side. Especially when he and Lanny lined up to be the prime suspects.

Placing himself completely at Case's disposal allayed the suspicions and hopefully sped up solving this.

Somehow the day had been swallowed up and Grey had grimly hung on to self-control as the knowledge of Lanny alone in that house gnawed at him. Estella would be back by now, along with Allen and Meredith. He should have cut the interrogation short.

Just because someone killed Victor didn't mean anyone else was in danger. Lots of people had a motive to kill Victor. But knowing that didn't quell his sense of urgency. He was furious at himself for staying away so long. Lanny should be in a hospital for heaven's sake. Or at least under a doctor's care. Doctors were sworn to confidentiality. Grey decided he'd take her in the morning and have her checked. He should have done it today.

Worry made him step harder on the gas and the rear end of his Jeep fishtailed toward the cliff.

It was just too much of a miserable shame that she hadn't forgotten Victor's vacant, staring eyes along with the rest of her memory.

She distracted herself from reliving the horror of Victor by thinking about her amnesia. She didn't know people or her personal history, but what did she know? She couldn't remember current events or what was happening in the world. Then she thought, 'I don't know who the president is' and it registered that she knew there *was* a president. Of the United States of America. She remembered her country. A flashing vision of four heads carved in stone came into her mind and she knew it was Mount Rushmore. She knew who each president was. Then, after a second, she remembered who the current president was but not whether she'd voted for him.

She knew where Texas was on a map and for that matter that Austin was its capital. She could spell any word that popped into her head, but she'd had to check the notebook for the spelling of her own name.

She could braid hair. As her hands moved mechanically tidying the desk, she realized that orderliness was part of her nature. She could go a long way by just letting her subconscious take over and have her hands do the work they'd done many times before, allowing her mind to lead her in whatever direction it was her habit to go. Lanny sank into her chair and played with the few memories she'd had. She thought about Grandma Millie. She tried to build something beyond that.

The storm outside grew more violent and a bolt of yellow lightning flickered across the window. Lanny saw a bright yellow kitchen and her grandma pulling cookies out of the oven.

Lanny could smell them. Chocolate chip. She knew she'd been there for grandma's cookies. She leaned forward in her chair, thinking she might finally be remembering.

The thunder cracked. Fear jolted her out of her introspection and the memory was lost. She had been driven to terror by the sound last night, but then she'd been stirred from unconsciousness while the storm was in full fury. Now she could prepare herself. She knew that her fear of the storm went deeper than this current trauma. She carried it around with her. She tried to think when she'd learned to be afraid of thunder.

She saw the lashing rain on the tall, narrow windows. The outside darkness was more profound than could be accounted for by the storm. She'd turned a single desk lamp on early in the day because of the murky room, so the growing darkness hadn't been apparent. She looked at the foot-high stack of notebooks she'd read thoroughly and wondered how long she'd been lost in her reading. She searched for a clock and there wasn't one. She had no watch, which didn't seem in keeping with the orderly Lanny Cole. A phone. Hadn't she had a cell phone? She'd looked in her room and couldn't find one. She had a checkbook, but hadn't studied it closely. Maybe there were bills she was paying that would tell her something.

She stood and a wave of dizziness made her sink back into her chair. Her head throbbed and her stomach rumbled. If the darkened window was from the sun setting rather than the storm worsening then she'd been engrossed in her reading all afternoon. Which meant she hadn't eaten all day. Breakfast had never occurred to her. During lunch she'd been in the middle of an interrogation. Now dinner had come and gone. Forgetting to eat wasn't amnesia. It was stupid.

She propped her elbows on the desk top, rested her head on her open hands and tried to steady herself. It struck her as strange that no one had come and told her she'd missed lunch or dinner. Were there regular mealtimes in The Devil's Nest? Grey had said she ate food she scrounged in the kitchen. Sandwiches mostly. Where was the kitchen? Did she have a car here and drive herself where? This was an island. Were there ferry boats big enough to carry a car? Did the family have cars on the island, boat across the water, then have cars in town? Did she occasionally go into town for meals? Or did she just stay here?

She hadn't given it any thought until now, but it seemed, considering the blow she'd received, Grey might have made sure she was aware of mealtimes or at least checked to see if she'd eaten. For all he knew she might have collapsed in a heap somewhere. Him paying her that little bit of attention would be expected considering his Academy Award caliber pretense that the two of them were involved. She squelched her indignation. For all she knew the man might have a job to go to. He might have left the house with no plans to return, maybe not for months. Didn't he say he stayed away from the house whenever possible?

The stab of fear was understandable but the unhappiness made no sense at all. She braced her arms firmly on the desk and rose slowly to her feet. The dizziness came again but Lanny held herself upright until it receded. She stepped away from the desk and precisely tucked in her chair without making a decision to do such a thing.

She turned off her desk lamp and plunged the room into darkness. Picking her way carefully, she left the room and headed down the unlit hallway for the stairs. Why didn't someone turn some lights on? She ran her hand along the wall but never touched a light switch. She moved slowly, wary of a misstep.

The kitchen would most likely be to the back of the house, downstairs. She hoped no one noticed her wandering about lost. She heard a stair step creak under slowly moving feet just as she reached the top of the stairway. She looked down and could see the stairs were empty. The steps creaked again and she looked toward the room where she'd left Meredith, then toward Grey's room. No one. Turning, she faced the stairwell that led to the attic. The wind moaned outside the house and again Lanny thought the wind had an almost human cry. The sound got louder and suddenly Lanny was sure someone was crying in the attic.

Clarinda.

Lanny had upset the poor woman. She should have gone after her and cared for her. The sobbing grew louder, and Lanny looked up into the unlit gloom of the stairway. There was definitely someone up there. It sounded like a woman. She'd heard Meredith's harsh sobs and this was nothing like that.

Lanny hesitated for just a second before she got a handle on her fear. She had been living in the house, obviously in perfect safety, for weeks. There was no reason to think that whoever attacked Victor had anything in mind except framing her because she was handy. That had failed and she was most likely safe because, if whoever killed Victor had wanted to kill her…she'd be dead.

She was very interested in questioning Clarinda more thoroughly. And even if she didn't get more answers, simple human decency demanded that she check on sweet Clarinda. Besides, Lanny had a feeling the answers to many of her questions might be found in the papers Grey told her were stored in the attic. Lanny needed to protect those papers.

Clarinda, or whoever was up there now, might be messing up her chance at reconstructing the Devereau family history accurately. Even with no memory, that offended her sense of professionalism. She needed to tell Clarinda to be mindful of what she did in the attic.

Lanny shook off her childish fear and headed for the stairs.

My fondest wish is to have them all dead.

I'll have to move carefully with Grey. It would have been much better if he'd never come home. He's too strong to face, but no man is strong when he's sleeping.

Hadn't Victor proved that?

I had her earlier but thought it better to wait. But she's coming right into my lair. How can I resist?

Grey fought for control of the car, twisting the wheel into the slide and pulling it back from the precipice. Heart slamming from the close call, he slowed down, knowing he risked his life by driving too fast. More importantly, if he really thought Lanny needed help, he'd better survive to give her some. But urgency rode him hard. He stayed at his slower pace through pure rigid self control as he approached the worst stretch.

The Overhang. A stretch of road nearly a quarter of a mile long that wasn't meant to exist. It defied nature.

When Pierre had built his fortress, he had chosen this impregnable spot. Alone, among the low, sandy barrier island, and out farther than any of them, stood this rock. Pierre had found it, claimed it and made it his kingdom. He and his men had personally dug away at this sheer rock wall. Pierre's men chiseled until it was wide enough for a horse and precious little else—which made it simple to defend—something Pierre was called upon to do with some frequency.

Later generations had widened it to accommodate buggies, then freight wagons, then automobiles. But there was no way to go out so they had to dig into the mountain. Each time carving deeper into the rock.

It would accommodate a good-sized car, just barely. Carved into solid rock, it malignantly lurked over the heads of drivers.

That looming mountain seemed always to be waiting to pounce down from above. There had never been a rock slide so Grey's uneasiness was as much fear left over from his childhood as anything. Still, he always gripped the wheel firmly driving this stretch. Half of him wanted to speed to get past the quarter mile overhang quickly for fear it would cave in. The other half, the reasonable half, knew he had to drive slowly so he wouldn't go careening off the narrow ledge and drop hundreds of feet to the merciless rocks and battering waves.

Grey crept along strangling his steering wheel, at fifteen miles per hour. While he inched along, he kept up an internal rant for leaving Lanny alone all day.

Maybe with a murderer.

Lanny slowly made her way up the attic stairway. Cold wrapped around her ankles. The impression of deathly cold fingers clinging to her sent a savage shudder of fear through her.

"Old houses are drafty," she muttered to herself to bolster her courage as she took another step. "Stop being ridiculous."

She groped for a light switch but found nothing. It would be useless to go up there in the pitch dark, but someone else had. She looked above just as the room was illuminated by the flickering lightning. The thunder was louder up here and the rain hammered on the eaves until it was a drumbeat in her ears.

All pretense of beauty and comfort were forgotten on this upper floor. The stairs were worn wood. On both sides of her, unpainted plaster walls rose above her head until they disappeared in the dark. The stairs were so narrow she could touch both sides easily. The splintered wooden railing she rested her left hand on wobbled. A wave of dizziness assailed her and reminded her of her battered head and her empty stomach. She stopped and gripped the railing until the dizziness passed. She looked down and saw her hand, clinging to the rail with another, larger hand covering it.

He'd almost convinced himself today at the police station that an intruder, some confederate of Victor's, was responsible. But this road changed his mind.

Grey got through The Overhang. His foot pressed harder on the gas and the car slewed in the deteriorating road. Grey had wanted to fix it, widen and even pave it. But Estella had fought him. She liked her mountaintop aerie. She liked her Devil's Nest to be a fortress. When he was finally old enough, with his power solidified enough to fight her, he no longer cared about The Devil's Nest enough to sink a fortune into a better road—and for years there was no fortune, not until the Grey Trust assumed responsibility for the Devereau holdings.

There were sharp switchbacks all along the narrow road. It had been raining for days and there was talk of the hurricane season. Grey thought about what someone would be up against if they tried to gain entrance. The only other way up the craggy peak would require a long walk that included climbing this massive rock. The hike would be almost impossible in the foul weather. It would be a Herculean task to fight the rugged, mud slickened incline. Someone could have driven up, but the last stretch was a long, straight slope. Sally had a sitting room that had a view of the road. A car could have avoided her notice if it was driven with its lights off, but that would be death defying.

Grey eased off on the accelerator as the back end of his Jeep began to fishtail. He wrestled it under control and, as soon as his heart quit trying to pound its way out of his chest, he increased his speed. Yes, an intruder could have made it in, definitely. And Victor played with a dangerous crowd, something Grey was just finding out.

Maybe those confederates of Victor's did what they came to do and left. Lanny would be safe. She had to be.

Even with that common sense to reassure him, impending doom hung over his head like the Sword of Damocles. He thought about Lanny alone in The Devil's Nest and he pushed the car faster.

If she had walked on, I might have let her live for another day. But she is the same stubborn, interfering Little Girl she was before I tucked her into bed with Victor. I don't think she learned her lesson at all.

Well, tonight I'm not a teacher. Come up, Little Girl. Come to your precious attic and say good-bye to The Devil's Nest. Perhaps I'll be more like Pierre tonight than ever. Perhaps I'll set my knife aside and separate a woman from my life in the way Pierre separated them from his.

Grey passed through the gate and punched the gas firmly on the last mile of the wretched road.

He was away from the cliff now. How long had he been gone? He didn't risk a look at his watch, and the old car left on the island didn't have a clock. A split second's inattention might be the last thing he ever did. He roared on, skidding around corners, fighting to control the steering wheel as mud sucked at his tires. He was driving one of the old Jeeps they'd hauled to the island years ago. It brushed against shrubs and dangling branches, missing the tree trunks by inches.

He caught his first glimpse of the house through the thinning trees as lightning jagged across the sky. Three full stories. Made completely of enormous ghostly white stones sitting high above a pounding surf that exploded violently against the rocks a hundred feet below. Salty mist shrouded the house and distorted Grey's visibility. A tower jutted from the otherwise rectangular mansion, off-center slightly to stand as a sentry beside the front entrance.

The tower guarded this side just as the sea guarded the east. The flat roof was lined with a corroded, cast iron railing along the Widow's Walk, surrounding the entire length of the roof. Pierre Devereau's wife had probably emerged from the doorway in the tower and moved around the house on that walk, most likely hoping the sea had swallowed him at last.

There were no welcoming outside lights. Everything about the forbidding facade of The Devil's Nest said, 'Stay Away!' A single light flickered weakly out of one second floor window, most likely Meredith and Allen's sitting room.

Other than that, the house sat in utter darkness.

Lanny jerked her arm back. The hand vanished. She whirled around to see…nothing. No one. She was alone.

It had been a memory. She squeezed her eyes shut and pictured the larger hand. She could feel its warmth. The hand slid up and down her wrist several times, raising farther each time. It caressed her elbow and upper arm. It molded the curve of her shoulder. Gentle fingers brushed the side of her neck, then tilted her head around to face...

The door to her memory slammed shut.

To face whom?

She went back to that first image of the hand over hers but the floor overhead squeaked and she returned to the here and now with a dull thud. She didn't lose the memory but she couldn't expand it. Who had touched her? She was aware that included in the memory had been a pleasant feeling. The touch wasn't unwelcome. Whom had she let caress her so warmly?

She heard footsteps above her again, focused on Clarinda and began her ascent.

That's right, Little Girl. Listen and follow.

Come to me, Little Girl. Come deeper into The Devil's Nest.

CHAPTER TWELVE

Grey could picture Meredith and Allen sitting, ignoring each other, watching television.

Estella would have gone to her rooms. He approached the house from the west and with the library to the west of her rooms, her lights wouldn't show on this side of the house. If it was like every other night, Trevor wouldn't have come home yet. If the water around the island was choppy enough maybe he wouldn't try and make it home.

Grey caught another peek at the gloomy house and, though he had no use for Trevor, he couldn't blame the boy for going out every chance he got.

Clarinda.

Grey sighed deeply over his isolated, childlike cousin. She should have been sent away years ago, as a child. Instead she'd been locked in here like the family skeleton. Like Clarinda's sweet innocence was a shameful thing, and Victor's corruption was a source of pride.

As he pushed on toward Lanny, he made the decision that Clarinda would get away from here. Estella would fight him but Grey would wrest that power from her like he had every other bit of authority he'd accumulated over the years.

He would start work on Clarinda's escape immediately. As soon as the police let him leave town, he and Lanny would go with Clarinda.

He caught himself as he realized he planned a future that included Lanny Cole, a woman he'd just met last night. A woman that, despite his powerful instincts to the contrary, could very well have murdered his cousin. Yes, Lanny was going with him. She just didn't know it yet. And Lanny, more than any of them, with her blood untainted by the Devereaus, would help handle the wraithlike Clarinda.

To Grey's knowledge, Clarinda had never been off the grounds except for the brief time Grey had virtually stolen her from this place. Hoping to find help for her.

Clarinda had nearly died. It had seemed as if her life was connected to The Devil's Nest. Then Estella had come and rained down her fury on Grey, demanding Clarinda come home.

Because Grey was worried for Clarinda's life, he'd let her go home, but he shouldn't have.

He got another glimpse of The Devil's Nest rising up like a ghost in the eerie fog.

Lanny's head slowly emerged into the vast darkness of the attic.

She looked around the huge room at the top of the stairs. There were niches she could only make out when the lightning flared, but she couldn't appreciate nature providing light in the darkness because thunder rumbled close on the heels of the lightning.

The narrow walls of the stairs fell away as she ascended. She reached the top and stepped toward the right. On the side of the house where the tower grew up to a fourth story.

She didn't know where she was going, but she tried to let her instincts guide her, hoping she'd move toward the place she'd been working last and that there would be some trace of her passing that would guide her.

Lightning flared. A row of dirt encrusted gabled windows gave enough light that Lanny saw the vast cluttered attic. The thunder rioted across her nerves. She breathed deeply, struggling for control. Just noise. It would pass.

"Hang on and let it pass, Lanny, hon. It's the angel's clapping because the farmer's need rain. Let's clap, too. Let's yell, hooray for the rain."

Lanny clapped and the sound startled her. She looked down at her clapping hands.

She murmured, "Grandma Millie knew I was afraid of thunder."

She stared at her hands and clapped again even though the thunder wasn't bursting in the sky right then. She thought of her grandma's gentle, caring voice and felt the strength her grandma had helped her discover in herself. Lanny's jaw firmed and she clapped her hands sharply just to hear the sound. Then she looked around the attic calmly in the flicker of lightning that she knew meant another thunderbolt was coming. She saw an open chest with papers on the floor in meticulous piles. She smiled to herself.

"This looks like the work of Lanny Cole." She moved toward the papers and clapped with the thunder. It helped— a little.

My Little Girl's not right in the head, clapping at nothing, talking to herself, smiling at the floor.

It's just as well Victor didn't get her. I had a vision of her bringing a baby into the family to carry on the Devereau name. She was the type to demand marriage first, but Victor nearly had her worn down.

He might have even married her. Probably not, but he'd have planted a baby in her belly and we'd have kept this one. But Victor's gone. Grey is too stubborn. So, the Little Girl lost her chance at being part of a dynasty. I wonder if she saw me when I tucked her in bed with Victor? It doesn't matter. Her slender neck won't survive a fall from the tower.

Pierre would be so proud.

Lanny heard the floor creak and whirled around. Her heart hammered.

No one there.

She heard the noise again. It came from just in front of her. The lightning lit up the room and she could see a door tightly shut.

Clarinda must be behind that door. Lanny started forward, hoping she could comfort the distraught girl. The thunder rumbled and lodged itself in the pit of Lanny's stomach.

She reached the door and turned the rusty knob. It resisted her grip but she forced it to turn and with a reluctant creak of metal against metal, almost as if the house didn't want her to enter, the door unlatched.

"Clarinda, are you in there?"

There was no answer.

Lanny pulled the door open slowly.

Grey had left his family alone for too many years. It was time to make his final move and change the dark path they had traveled down for too long. With Victor dead and Estella growing old, he might be able to accomplish it at last. He'd get Allen and Meredith moved to town. He'd find a group home…or a private facility…something…for Clarinda that would give her special treatment. Trevor was getting the boot.

He hurled his muddy car up the last steep incline. Lanny's office was on the south east side of the house. Her bedroom was on the northwest. Where was she?

Something on the uppermost level of the house caught his eye. A face appeared in the skyhigh door of the tower. The door opened onto the wrought iron Widow's Walk, but no one had stepped out on the rickety old thing for years.

It was too far away to be seen and yet he *did* see it. The face seemed to glow out of the upper floor despite the lack of lights and the stygian darkness of the night. White, ghostly, though too far away, he was struck by an ineffable sadness.

Lanny? Up in that shrine to the Devereau's infamous past? But no light shone in the tower.

The attic was in total darkness. Whatever light glowed from the face came from within.

Silver Girl. Ready to choose death at her own hand over being murdered by Pierre.

Lightning blazed and the face vanished. The house pitched into utter blackness save that window in Allen's suite. He could not possibly have seen anyone standing in that unlit window. A fluttering curtain maybe? It was too dark to be sure.

Grey slammed on his brakes, skidded to a halt in front of the main entrance, and flung open the door.

Imagined or not, he sprinted for the house with only one goal in mind. The tower.

Lanny pulled the door outward on creaking hinges. She'd definitely heard something out here. Had it just been the sound of an old house being buffeted by the wind?

The door opened to a room that was circular and empty save for curved benches lining the wall, one under each of three windows.

Then she noticed another door straight across from her. That must lead onto the roof. It was open just an inch. The wind must have blown it open. That could explain everything. Even the crying could have been the weeping of the wind.

She stepped into the tower to close the door before the rain soaked the tower floor.

That's it, Little Girl.

One more step.

One more step.

The police will think you committed suicide, steeped in guilt because you killed Victor.

Grey will have no reason to cover for you once you're dead. Oh, you're a good Little Girl to step right into my nest.

The door was warped, which was the only reason it wasn't swinging out into the wind. She tugged on the stubborn thing. A soft click off to her right in the tower caught her attention and she turned to see what had made the noise. A faint movement in the gloom sent an icy river of fear flooding down her spine. Turning she faced the circular room with her back toward the door to the Widow's Walk.

She backed up at the same instant whisper quiet footsteps came toward her. Lanny nearly jumped out of her skin when the footsteps changed and someone charged at her in the dark.

A hard hand grabbed her wrist and she screamed.

"What are you doing up here in the dark?" Grey's fury thundered over her. He hauled her out of the tower.

Stunned by his sudden appearance and his anger, Lanny let herself be drawn along. Fury radiated off of him and Lanny didn't speak. No sense poking a rabid dog.

He dragged her toward the steps then he wrapped his arm like a vise around her waist and pulled her close so the two of them could be side-by-side on the narrow stairs. He practically lifted her off her feet as he force-marched her down one level and veered off to the right. He slammed a door open, yanked her through and closed the door. He moved so fast and Lanny was so shocked by his sudden appearance, she didn't know where he'd taken her. He turned the light on and the glare blinded her.

He grabbed her by both shoulders, turned her to face him, and lifted her onto her toes.

"What were you doing in the tower? Are you crazy?"

Grey shook her shoulders until her head rattled. "That Widow's Walk wouldn't have held your weight. No one has gone out there, to my knowledge, since I was a child. What were you trying to do, kill yourself?"

"I didn't..." she began, patting his chest to soothe him.

"What kind of a stupid idiot wanders around a gloomy attic late at night?"

Before she could catch a breath to reply he raved on. "I thought there was one person in this house who wasn't a complete idiot."

He shook her again and her head whipped back and forth. He had cut off the circulation to her arms and her hands were beginning to go numb.

"That bump on the head must have scrambled what little there ever was of your brain!"

Something snapped inside her when he piled on all those insults at her intelligence. Without planning it at all, suddenly she had his shirt front in her fists and she jerked him forward until they were nose to nose.

"Get your hands off of me." She didn't recognize the voice. She discovered something. Up until now she'd been mostly cringing away from this house and the situation like a fearful rodent. But now she knew why she'd stayed here, why she'd changed her writing style to cryptic, almost encoded notes. Why she'd braved the dark attic. Because Lanny Cole was no coward, and Lanny Cole didn't let people push her around.

Her growling tone caught Grey off guard. He quit shaking her. They glared at each other for a long second.

Lanny twisted the fabric of his white oxford shirt more tightly. "I said let me go!"

Some of the fury left Grey's expression and Lanny saw a spark of amusement. She said, "So, you think my temper is funny, huh?"

"Ummm...no."

"Well, you don't know the half of how funny I can be." She let go of him and knocked his hands off of her.

"This is a new woman. Not the one I so bravely rescued last night."

"If you were hoping for a damsel in distress you're out of luck."

"Has your memory returned?" Grey asked sharply.

"I've had a few flashes, it'll come. But...no...nothing significant. But I don't have to remember my name to know I don't like your insults." She jabbed him in the chest with her index finger. "If you've got something you want me to do, you say so. Don't drag me around. *And don't yell at me anymore!*" It occurred to Lanny that it was high handed of her to demand at the top of her lungs that she didn't want to be shouted at, but she didn't care to deal with logic right now.

Grey's expression switched from fury to guilt as quickly as a light being switched on. "Are you all right? I never should have left you alone all day.

The police needed me to bring some papers I have about Victor, then they had more questions, then..."

"I didn't expect you to hover." Lanny stepped away from him, her arms crossed to hold her temper in. "I'm fine. I have a feeling I'm very self-sufficient. Why else would I take this ridiculous job? You may have wanted an affair with a shrinking violet. But I suspect you'll think better of it once I'm more myself."

"You were so adorable as the weak, clinging maiden." Grey curled one corner of his mouth in a sad smile. "Can she come out and play once in a while?"

Lanny snorted in disgust.

"But I think I like this version better." Grey's head dipped and caught her lips before she knew what he had in mind.

She jumped away from him. "Grey, there's no one here to impress."

"I'm here." His arms wrapped around her waist and reeled her right back in. "Impress me."

She meant to shove him away. She really did. Some perverse moment of weakness mixed her thinking up so she wasn't sure if she was submissive 'Save Me' Lanny, or the tough 'I'm Fine On My Own' Lanny. And by the time she figured it out she was a very warm 'Kiss Me' Lanny, lost in Grey's embrace.

Her brain must be scrambled. But scrambled felt great and it'd been a lousy day.

She was due for a little great.

Lanny moved closer to see just how wonderful she could feel and how warm she could get.

After way too long, she said, "Grey, stop. You can't do this." She turned her head away from his kiss and he let his lips trail along her jaw line and down her throat.

"Yes, I can." His strong hands tilted her head back toward his lips and just as he covered her mouth with his, he said, "I'll show you."

Lanny fought against his gentle allure. No, truthfully, she fought against herself. "Stop, Grey. I mean it."

He ignored her.

She shoved hard on his shoulders. "You don't want to make me mad."

Grey nuzzled her neck. "You're so perfect. So sweet. Such a beautiful, compliant, angel."

She shivered. "Get your hands off of me."

Grey let his head fall back and dropped his arms from around her waist.

"I went up there because I thought I heard someone, and I didn't want..."

Grey blew up. "You went *alone*, into a *pitch dark attic*, in a house were a *murder was committed last night*, because you *heard someone*? Are you completely crazy?"

Lanny reached up and kissed his ranting mouth. "Shut up and listen, Sparky."

He quit yelling. Lanny decided she was onto something.

Grey glared at her but his eyes flickered toward her lips so it ruined the tough guy effect. "You left me alone in this..." Lanny dropped her voice an octave to mock Grey's voice, "House where a murder was committed last night." She went back to her normal, if slightly testy tone. "Don't come in here pretending like I'm in terrible danger. If you'd thought it was danger-ous you would never have left."

"Actually, I did think it was dangerous, and I never should have left. I feel like ten kinds of a fool about it, and I'm sorry I left you hurt and in dan-ger all day. I'll never leave you alone again. Day or night." He grinned at her.

"You think me being in danger is funny?"

"Nope, I was just thinking about the night."

"So why were you acting like a madman?"

"I thought you were going out on the Widow's Walk. Plus, I didn't mean to stay away so long and the whole drive home I was driving myself crazy worrying. I thought I'd find you in a coma or, worse yet, tucked in someone else's bed. You're up to two in one day now and Trevor's quite a stud." Grey's eyes narrowed.

He must be paying her back for 'shut up and listen'. "Who is Trevor again? Have you mentioned him before?"

"You have amnesia." Grey sighed deeply. "I forgot. Which is really ironic when you think about it. Trevor is my long lost, distant cousin who got found and now lives here like a blood sucking leech. He's Victor's shadow. We can't leave here tonight, because the road is too bad. But tomorrow I'm getting you and Clarinda out of this madhouse for good."

Lanny took a second to catch up with the sudden change of subject. "Go on ahead if you want but I've got a job to finish." He really did seem to like kissing her. She didn't see any reason to discourage him. Add to that it was a good chance to annoy him again, she found she liked it.

"Call me sometime. I'd give you my number but I don't remember it."

Grey growled and pulled her hard against him before she knew it was a warning sign.

I had her! I was within an inch of taking her.

Grey can protect her all he wants but there will come a moment when he won't be watching. Or, there will come a moment when they can die together. The hunger burning in my belly won't let me rest.

CHAPTER THIRTEEN

Lanny grunted softly from the impact then she sighed so deeply Grey felt it. The sigh felt like longsuffering patience rather than surrender.

"What now?" She looked at him, then rolled her eyes.

"Go ahead if you want?" Grey heard himself screech and tried to bring it down an octave. Speaking slowly, through clenched teeth he said, "You were on the verge of stepping out on that tottering Widow's Walk. I can't leave here. I can't even let you out of my sight for fear of what you'll do next. You scared ten years off my life with that stunt."

His control was slipping so he stopped and fought for reason.

"I wasn't! Going! Out! On the *Widow's Walk*! Will you quit saying that? What kind of idiot do you take me for? The door was ajar. I was shutting it."

"I saw you leaning out the door when I pulled up." When Grey had seen where she was in the attic, he'd figured out it was Lanny with her white hair and delicate fair skin that he had seen when he drove up.

"I'd only been in the tower a few seconds. You couldn't have seen me from the driveway. And I was not leaning out. That would make me stupid and *I am not stupid*."

"How do you know?" Grey roared back. "You can't remember any-thing. Once your memory comes back you'll probably remember you are a complete moron!" Grey realized he was the complete moron because Estella could hear everything they said.

"Don't you call me...mmmph..."

Grey slapped his hand over her mouth.

She shot daggers at him with her eyes. He actually felt a few of them stab into his skin. He almost checked to see if he was bleeding. Her hand made a move that would have left Grey a very unhappy man if he hadn't blocked her in time. Grey remembered she'd objected to him doing this gagging thing before but honestly the woman was always needing to hush up.

He leaned down until his forehead touched hers and hissed, "Estella can hear every word we say. Shut up."

He pulled his hand away from her mouth and held her gaze, daring her to say anything.

She narrowed her eyes at him then she mouthed, "Estella?"

Grey nodded.

Using hand gestures she mouthed, "She hears..." Lanny pointed to her ear. "...your..." Lanny pointed to Grey. "...bedroom?" She made a little circle with her index finger to hopefully encompass the room.

Grey nodded.

Lanny said softly, "Ick!"

Grey nodded.

Then he whispered, "I know a place we can talk."

Grey pulled and prodded her out into the hall using the finesse reserved for a tug boat trying to get a lumbering cargo ship into an undersized seaport.

He dragged her into a bay window at the end of the hall. The earlier storm had passed while he and Lanny were so thoroughly occupied. Now another storm flashed in the west.

Looking out the floor to ceiling window of the alcove, Lanny muttered, "I'm sick of this weather."

"You and me both, Angel."

Heavy drapes hung alongside the windows and Lanny was tempted to close them just so she could pretend there wasn't another thunderstorm in her near future. She turned and her eyes met Grey's. "Why do you call me that?"

"Angel?" He rested his hands on her shoulders.

"Yeah."

"Because that's how I think of you." He slid his hands to her hair and gathered it behind her shoulders, smoothing it down her back. "The first time I saw you I thought you looked like an angel come down from heaven. Like a perfect vision of feminine beauty."

Lanny narrowed her eyes at him. "The first time you saw me I was covered with blood, screaming my head off and you thought I was just another in a long line of tramps who'd had sex with your low life cousin. After which I lost my mind and slit his throat."

"Good point." Grey quit playing with her hair. "My very, *very* first impression of you was of a hysterical, murderous, psycho slut. But right away my impression changed."

Grey thought for a moment. Honesty forced him to add, "Except for the slut part."

He rubbed his chin, "And the murderous part."

He shrugged and smiled a little weakly, "And really you were still pretty hysterical and the whole thing did seem psychotic. But even with all that, I'd already started liking you real well."

"Lucky me," Lanny said dryly. "Now what's this about Estella hearing everything we say? Are you telling me an old lady eavesdrops on your bedroom? That is so sick I can't stand to think about it."

Grey shrugged one shoulder. "If you knew how boring my bedroom was, you probably wouldn't feel that way."

"I don't think it's boring." Lanny said. She clamped her mouth shut and opened her eyes wide with shock.

Grey held her gaze for a long moment and almost caught fire from the heat that raged through him.

At last he shook his head, cleared his throat and said, "We might as well assume that Estella knows everything. She hasn't ratted us out to the police for reasons of her own. Anyway, even if she talked it would be our word against the word of an eavesdropping pervert so if we stick to our story we should be okay."

"So, should we talk to her about it? You said she was..." Grey watched Lanny's pretty blue eyes lose focus as she thought about all he'd told her about Estella. Finally, she said weakly, "...bad."

Grey snorted. "Headstrong two-year-olds who are denied candy are 'bad'. Puppies who chew on your good shoes are 'bad'. Saying Estella is 'bad' is like saying the Great Fire of London was 'toasty'. It's like saying the Johnstown Flood was damp. It's like saying the atomic bomb they dropped on Japan was—"

"All right." Lanny cut him off. "I get it."

"We should *not* talk to her about it. We go on as planned. She would have said something already if she was going to, so she's playing some deep game of her own."

"No one would play a game with their son's death," Lanny protested.

Grey's mouth quirked. "Hmmph."

Grey heard the first distant rumble of thunder, and Lanny took the tiniest possible step closer to him.

"Now," Grey said, "you said you remembered something. Tell me. Maybe I can make some sense out of it."

"Well, mostly it was my grandma. I remember her name and what she looked like, so I'm sure I'm right about her."

"Anything else?" he asked gently.

"I remember her making cookies in a yellow kitchen. Chocolate chip. I remember how they smelled and how good they were. I've tried to back away from the image of her taking cookies out of the oven, you know, see the whole house, see myself watching her, but I can't do it."

"Your grandma made chocolate chip cookies?" Grey asked wistfully.

Lanny nodded.

"I never had a grandparent," Grey said. "My parents were almost too old to have children when I was born, so my grandparents were all gone."

"But you lived here and learned about your ancestors."

"I didn't when I was young. My mother had a fixation on this place. There was always a battle between her and Estella over who would own it in the end. My mother's father was older than Estella's so she had a strong claim."

"They were brothers?"

"No, cousins. I'm not sure how close the relationship was. Ownership descended through the male Devereaus, and there weren't any. My parents didn't come here often but my mother was determined that in the end, she'd take it away from Estella somehow."

"But they died before they could gain control of The Devil's Nest?" Lanny sounded unconvinced that the house was any prize.

"I was at boarding school when my parents died. Estella gained custody, but I stayed at school, and I spent most of my time with the Garrisons. Their son was in my class, but they weren't boarding there."

"I got that Case was an old friend."

"Yes, his parents practically adopted me when my folks died. But sometimes I couldn't avoid being brought home. Estella got to raise Allen and Victor in her image. Allen was always too mild mannered to be truly deviant, but she did a bang up job with Victor."

Lanny said, "I'm sorry."

"For what?" Grey asked.

"I can tell you feel responsible for Victor's messed up life."

"I'm *not* responsible for it." Grey snapped. Then he heard his own tone and forced his shoulders to relax. "I'm just mentioning it because of what you said about your grandmother baking cookies and how different that is from my family."

"Okay, not responsible. Guilty. You feel guilty because you escaped and Estella's children didn't."

To Grey that was just a statement of the obvious. "I did escape. They didn't. And I lived here just long enough to know how bad it really was."

Lanny lay one hand on Grey's arm. "And now Victor's dead."

Grey stared over her shoulder into the storm for a while. Finally, he exhaled slowly and looked at her squarely. "I wish I had one drop of grief in me for Victor. I won't be a hypocrite and pretend I had any use for him, but I wish things could have been different."

"What about Allen?" Lanny prompted. "Is he your older or younger cousin?"

Grey shook his head. He often found Allen forgettable. "All of Estella's children are older than me, but like an old English aristocracy, the estate is passed down through the oldest child. That's my mother and she had me very late in life. Even so, my mother gets to own everything and now I do. But she's also charged with caring for the family. The Devil's Nest passed down through her, and she always knew she owned it, but because my father had a business away from here and a beautiful home of his own, mother left this place in Estella's hands."

"Doesn't Allen resent being passed over when he's the oldest grand-child?"

"Hard to tell with Allen. He does as Meredith tells him and that's the end of it." Grey looked back at her. "What else did you remember?"

Grey tipped her chin up from where she looked at her arm. Holding her gaze, he asked, "Are you remembering making love to Victor? Is that what came back to you?"

Lanny shook her head and dropped her eyes, even though Grey held her chin tilted upward.

"Tell me."

"Someone touched me. That's all. Someone ran their hand up my arm and onto my shoulder like this." She stroked two fingers up the back of her hand and down to her fingertips. Then in gentle back and forth strokes, worked her way up to her elbow and back down, going a little farther each time before Grey caught her hand.

"I remembered the touch was loving. I remember I...I welcomed it."

Grey said in disgust. "The Mother of My Children."

"The what?"

"Actually, it's a good sign. I've been a reluctant witness to that gen-tle stroking thing he does a few times. He's trotted out the speech for the family and laughed about it. Women have quoted him verbatim, at least a dozen of them over the years. It's not one he uses very often, only when a woman is proving intractable. Good for you, Angel. You were giving him a run for his money. Victor gets all squishy and tears fill his eyes and he says, 'Up until now, I'll admit I wanted you because you are so beautiful. But that was just physical attraction. I'm so thankful to you for demanding more from me. I have so much respect for you. A woman who holds herself to a high standard...'"

Like a bolt of electricity, underscored by the lightning that flickered through the alcove, Lanny raised her hand and Grey quit speaking. She said, "...to a high standard is someone I want to commit my life to. Your honor and decency have given my emotions time..."

Together they said, "...to catch up to my desire. I want you to be the mother of..."

They both broke off at the same time.

Grey said, "keep going."

"I remember." Lanny said breathlessly. "The Mother of My Children. He said I was the woman he wanted to make a home with."

Lanny's rubbed the goose egg on her head. "It was so beautiful, so moving."

She stared sightlessly into the hall past Grey's shoulder. Grey wondered what she was remembering. Victor usually led them straight to bed after that speech.

Lanny went on. "Come with me this weekend. It's the first of June. Summer has come to Devereau Island. We'll take the boat out, cruise down the coast. We'll find a justice of the peace and be married."

She murmured the loving words. "I...I agreed to go. I believed every word of it." She looked up and Grey fought with every ounce of self-control not to hate her for giving in to Victor.

She added, "Then I went to bed. Alone."

A satisfaction so fierce he couldn't control his expression, flooded through him. "Tomorrow is Thursday. Victor didn't make it to the weekend."

Tears burned at her eyes. "I remember I intended to insist we get married first and I knew he'd say yes. He was so adoring. He said my virginity was a treasure he valued greatly."

Driven by an urge he didn't even try to control, Grey pulled her into his arms so she couldn't see the thoughts that he knew had to be written on his face.

He tightened his hold, enraged at Victor when he thought of how eager his cousin would have been to devour such rare fruit and inflict the pain that went with being her first. And how Victor would have relished - immediately after the physical pain - assaulting her with terrible emotional pain. They would have never found that justice of the peace. There would have been engine trouble or fear of a possible storm. Victor would have thought of something. There would have been time for lovemaking but Victor would never have married her.

Lanny wound her arms around his waist and buried her face against his chest. "You're saying he had a whole routine down? You even knew it well enough to have the words memorized?"

"I'm sorry." Grey pulled her close. "You have no idea how many times I've said 'I'm sorry' for something my cousin did. But I've never meant them more than I do right now."

"So, that means I was one of the...the..."

"You didn't fall for his line."

"I played hard to get."

"You didn't play hard to get, Angel. You *are* hard to get. Big difference."

"I suppose when his usual approach didn't work, he told me how desperately he loved me. And I went for it. I was falling in love with him. "I...I..." She let go of Grey to press her hands to her head. "I can't remember anything else. I believed him."

"Victor couldn't bear to let a woman go once he set his sights on her. It became a matter of pride with him and there was no lie he wouldn't tell, no promise he wouldn't make." Grey fell silent. Everything he said only made it worse.

He could see the pain written across her face and the tears pooled in her luminous eyes. On a purely masculine level he knew she was so vulnerable she might turn to him to salve her wounded womanhood. But at this moment he cared too much about her to do anything but take care of her.

A single tear slipped from the corner of her eye and he brushed it away with one caressing thumb. "Just because you didn't make love doesn't mean he didn't hurt you. I'm so sorry."

She made a sudden movement and laid her fingers gently on his lips. "Don't. Don't ever say those words to me again. It was him, not you. You have nothing to apologize for."

"I know." Grey said simply. "But I'm not apologizing for him. I'm just so genuinely sorry you were hurt."

The kindness in his eyes was the last straw. The sharp, salty tears spilled onto her cheeks and Grey pulled her into his arms and held her while she cried.

Grey carefully controlled his bitter anger over Victor's cruelty.

He held her and murmured sweet sounds of comfort. He touched her hair repeatedly, greedy for the feel of its silky weight. He caressed her and let her weeping run its course.

When her tears ebbed, Grey decided to replace Victor's cruelty with new memories. He sank both hands into Lanny's luxurious hair, tilted her head back and kissed her.

The thunder was coming. A murderer still roamed the halls of The Devil's Nest. He didn't know Lanny the way a man needed to know a woman before he felt for her all the things Grey felt, but none of that mattered.

He pulled away to tell her.

CHAPTER FOURTEEN

Her eyes flickered open and something moved in the hall. With a short, sharp cry of fear she jumped away from Grey.

Estella.

Grey whirled around.

"I see last night wasn't a one time thing," Estella said sarcastically.

Except Estella knew last night was a pack of lies because she'd been listening to Grey's bedroom as well as Victor's through her air duct. Grey had said so. Lanny wondered if Grey would call her on it.

"Lanny and I don't want to discuss last night, Aunt Estella. It's private."

Estella strode forward.

This was the first time Lanny had seen Estella since her amnesia and she didn't recognize her. Despite the late hour and the hard rigors of the day, her hair twisted elegantly into a French chignon that looked as if it never dared to waver in a stiff breeze. Her hair glowed a bluish white that so many older women tried for and just ended up blue. Estella wasn't particularly short, maybe five foot four, but so slender and finely boned she seemed to barely take up space. Her personality however commanded the entire hallway.

Her back ramrod straight, eyes the kind of cold blue that burned anything it touched, lips locked in a disapproving line that looked so natural on Estella's face, Lanny didn't take it personally. Estella stepped to within arm's reach of Grey and Lanny refused to cower behind him. She stepped out to stand by his side.

Estella gaze slid back and forth over them. "Well, it's all public knowledge now."

"True enough." Grey responded. "Did you come to wish us good-night? It's not like you to come to the second floor but under the circumstances I can understand you wanting to feel connected to the family tonight."

Grey's sarcasm nearly slashed the air.

"What I'm here for is to tell Miss Cole I don't believe she is innocent in last night's treachery. I don't believe she went so easily from Victor's bed to yours, Grey. I know what I heard in that room."

Estella turned her gaze from Grey to Lanny, glaring until her eyes sliced like a razor. "I know you were in there."

Lanny opened her mouth to defend herself.

Grey spoke before she could. "We're not impugning your word, Estella. I'm sure you just misunderstood what you heard. It's quite a distance. I've already attested to Lanny's whereabouts and, as you can see, the police didn't arrest her." Grey slipped his arm around Lanny's waist.

Estella's jaw became rigid. "And I'm just as certain that you must have fallen asleep, Grey. It was very late and you'd been traveling. Obviously, you'd exhausted yourself with Lanny's easily won favors. You would only have had to doze off for a second for Lanny to slip out, kill Victor, and return."

"I can assure you that I didn't sleep for an instant. We were intensely involved every moment from the time I got home. The police trusted my version of the night's...activities."

Lanny watched them spar. Neither of them coming straight out and calling the other a liar but both, in their own way, insulting the other. It was fascinating, like two powerful predators facing each other. Both strong. Both used to domination.

Then it got old.

Lanny found her backbone. "I didn't kill him, Estella."

Estella gasped sharply and Lanny knew she'd made some mistake.

Estella said, "I believe I've informed you that the *help* is required to call me Mrs. Devereau."

Which Lanny had no doubt been doing for the past month. She wondered how many other landmines awaited her. 'The Help' indeed!

Grey stepped in. "I consider Lanny much more than an employee now, Estella. What happened between us was very special. It may be that she'll end up a member of the family." He turned to Lanny and stroked her cheek softly.

She nearly got lost in the warmth of his eyes even though she knew this performance was for Estella.

He leaned close and added, "Wasn't it special, Angel?"

Lanny smiled, throwing herself into the role so easily because she was dying for an excuse to say loving words to Grey. "Incredibly special. And I was never with Victor. Not that night. Not ever."

"I know you weren't. You were too wise for his nonsense. Victor always did look for the dumb ones. But you were so beautiful and so convenient. He wouldn't have been able to resist trying his trite seduction. He was in over his head with you from the first."

Lanny saw the edge in Grey's eyes and knew his barb at Victor was launched for Estella's benefit. She thought if she hung around the two of them for long she'd have to take to wearing body armor to protect herself from the slings and arrows.

Turning to Estella, Lanny said gently, "I can see why you thought there was something between us, though. He was quite a flirt, and I'll admit I enjoyed his attention from the standpoint of having an attractive man pursuing me. But it never developed. And yet with Grey it was love at first sight." Lanny looked sideways at Grey and said meekly, which took quite an effort on her part because she wasn't feeling real meek, "Victor's gone now, Grey. Let's don't speak ill of the dead."

Grey seemed to get lost in her eyes. As a performance it was masterful. Academy Award stuff. Lanny tried not to enjoy it too much.

Finally, never looking away from Lanny, Grey asked, "Was there something else, Estella?"

Estella stepped closer to them and, when Lanny glanced away from Grey, she saw the burning hatred in Estella's eyes. Lanny saw a thirst for revenge so consuming that, if Grey hadn't been with her, Lanny believed Estella would have physically attacked her right there.

Estella's scorching eyes flashed. Lanny saw that rage at another time. Aimed just as surely at her then as now. Estella sitting in...Lanny let her eyes drift closed as she tried to picture the room behind Estella—it was the library, where she'd been questioned by Detective Garrison. Estella holding a spiral notebook open on her lap and lifting her eyes from it, furious. Lanny recognized the notebook as being just like the ones she had filled with her work. Estella hated her for more than supposedly murdering Victor. Lanny had read all the notebooks. Something in them made Estella mad enough to kill.

Lanny moved closer to Grey. He pulled her tight to his side. Grey turned to face Estella. Estella diverted her murderous gaze from Lanny and turned it on Grey, as if the two of them were locked in mortal combat. The silence stretched until tension arched like lightning bolts between them.

Finally, when Lanny decided neither of them would ever back down, a loud rumbling in her stomach gave her an idea of how to break the stalemate. Lanny tugged on Grey's arm. "Can we go find some dinner? Please? I haven't eaten all day. I'm starved."

A smile quirked Grey's lips as he looked away from Estella. "Of course, Angel. Estella and I are done."

He made it sound like forever.

Without looking at Estella again, he took Lanny's arm and stepped around Estella. As they passed her Lanny saw Estella's hand clench into a tight fist as if only her strong will kept her from striking out at them. Grey escorted Lanny toward the stairs.

At the top of the stairs Lanny looked uneasily down the hall at Estella who stood, silent as a ghost, staring after them. Lanny saw fury, rolling like thunder, in Estella's black heart.

Then a bright jag of lightning illuminated the alcove Lanny and Grey had been talking in and, because the angle was just exactly right, Lanny could see a man hovering behind the floor length curtains. He must have been standing there the whole time!

The lightning died away then flared again and this time Lanny was watching closely. She couldn't remember him but she knew who it had to be. Allen was short. This man was tall. Unless there was an intruder in the house, there was only one possibility. Trevor.

And he'd just eavesdropped on a conversation she'd had with Grey that admitted to all their lies and her amnesia. What part did Trevor have in the secrets and mysteries of this house?

Hadn't Grey made it sound like Trevor was mainly interested in whatever money he could get from Estella? So, did that mean anything Trevor knew, he'd passed on to Estellla and probably Allen, who'd tell Meredith? If that was so then Grey's and Lanny's lies were now an open secret in this house. And if Estella accepted Trevor so completely, then why hide from her as well as Lanny and Grey.

Lanny clung to Grey's arm as they walked away. She didn't mention seeing Trevor because she wasn't sure whether they could be overheard. After all Grey hadn't just dragged her into the hallway to talk to her. He'd very deliberately chosen that alcove. She had to assume the hall wasn't safe.

Grey escorted her to the vast kitchen and made himself at home in the dim recesses of the barely modernized room.

The walls were stone. An ancient stove sat at one end of a tiled countertop. A huge stainless steel refrigerator—the only modern thing in the room—anchored the other end of the kitchen. Cast iron pots hung from racks on the ceiling as if they'd been there since pirates strode the halls of The Devil's Nest.

Grey urged her to sit at the well-worn rectangular table then he turned to pull lettuce out of the refrigerator, along with a covered dish and mayonnaise. Lanny refused to let herself be waited on, so she overrode Grey's protest and the two of them worked side by side making roast beef sandwiches. He set them on the kitchen table along with a pitcher of iced tea.

"You're treating me like 'The Help' by making me eat in the kitchen."

He laughed as he pulled a chair from the end of the scarred oak table and slid it next to hers. He leaned close and whispered, "The only 'Help' we have around here most of the time is Sally, and she has her own little apartment. We have a few other people who come in once a week to keep the yard in order and clean the few rooms that get real use. Estella doesn't like outsiders hanging around. Sally doesn't eat with us, but she doesn't eat in here either."

"Sally?"

Grey shook his head and studied her closely for a minute. He spoke barely above a whisper and Lanny tried to match the low tone.

"You seem so good most of the time, I forget about your memory. I'm taking you to the doctor in the morning. You should have gone last night."

"I'm fine, Grey."

Grey shook his head firmly, "No, you're not."

"Well, no. I'm not. But I don't think a doctor can help me. I just need time. Now can Estella..." Lanny pointed to her ear.

Grey sighed and nodded.

Leaning inches from his ear, she said, "I found some papers today, I want to show you." She wanted to tell him about the man in the alcove, too. "And Meredith said some strange things."

"After we eat." Grey bit into the roast beef.

Lanny unhappily stuffed her sandwich in her mouth and started chewing. The two of them ate quickly, without any conversation between them except an occasional comment from Grey along the lines of, "Do you want another sandwich?"

Lanny shook her head. Grey poked her and pointed to his ear to remind her they needed to act natural. She said with cloying sweetness, "No, thank you, sweetheart. This is fine."

Grey grinned impishly at her, and Lanny went back to gulping down her food, dying to get away from Estella's eavesdropping. Only where did they go to accomplish that? She didn't think she could pass the night standing in the alcove. It occurred to her that Estella probably made the trek from her quarters to the second floor because she wasn't able to hear anything going on in Grey's room and she wanted to find out what they were up to.

Lanny sighed as she considered the last twenty-four hours. She felt better when she'd eaten, only realizing how shaky she'd really been when the worst of her hunger abated and her hands steadied. Her head felt a lot better, too. Lanny decided she was inches away from being fully human again. Too bad she couldn't remember *which* human.

As they finished, Lanny finally thought of a topic that should be innocuous enough to discuss regardless of who heard them. She tapped Grey's arm so he'd know she didn't mind being overheard. "I'd like to show you some of what I've found about Pierre Devereau." She'd show him the diary pages she'd found, but there was no reason they couldn't discuss what she'd written in her notebook. Those wouldn't be secret. Not considering her flash of memory of Estella holding one.

Grey smiled wryly, "I'm not a huge Pierre fan. If it was up to me, we'd burn all those old papers and let the memory of Pierre Devereau be wiped from the face of the earth."

From the cutting way he said it, Lanny knew he wanted Estella to hear.

Grey added more equably, "It's quite late. I'd prefer we wait until to-morrow."

Lanny tipped her head, asking him if he meant it or he just disapproved of the topic.

Grey pressed an index finger to his lips. He stood, quickly washed their plates, cups and the silverware he'd gotten dirty making the meal. He wiped off the counter and table and made sure everything was back in the refrig-erator where it belonged.

"You're acting like the help." Lanny didn't bother whispering that.

In an about face from his tidying he said, "Let's go to bed, Angel. I ha-ven't had you for so long I'm desperate."

Lanny raised one eyebrow at him as she stood and planted both hands on her hips.

Grey crooked one finger at her and she couldn't imagine he had what he appeared to have on his mind, especially now that they knew Estella could hear them, both here and in his bedroom, so she went to him. He crooked his finger again so she leaned close enough to hear his whispered instructions. He bit her earlobe, just the tiniest bite. Lanny gasped and jumped away. Grey laughed with pure lechery and dragged her back into his arms.

"Grey, no! We..."

He silenced her very efficiently with his mouth.

He swept her up into his arms. Lanny didn't know what was going on. She hesitated to slug him or loudly demand he let her go because of the eavesdropping. She pulled away from his lips to see him grinning broadly at her. He was two steps up the staircase when Lanny finally wriggled loose from his grasp.

He let her down but kept heading up the stairs, and he held her so firmly by one wrist she could either walk along with him or be dragged.

Halfway up the stairs Grey leaned close to her and whispered, "I think it's safe to talk for a few minutes. There are no air ducts on the stairway. We have to go through the motions of an affair. Estella may know we faked things last night but she has to believe it's the real thing now. She'll think twice before she harms you once she knows you're really involved with me."

"Harms me? She's an old lady. She can't do anything to me. She may be as cranky as all get out, but she's eighty years old."

"Eighty-four actually," Grey interjected.

"Whatever," Lanny hissed in exasperation, "she's old. She didn't knock me cold and toss me over her shoulder and tuck me in bed with Victor. You may hate your aunt but she cannot be the killer."

Grey said with macabre amusement. "I learned long ago never to underestimate Estella. She's small but she's made of pure gristle and spite. The woman is tough. If she wanted to slit Victor's throat then hunt you down, bash you on the head, carry you halfway across the country on her back and frame you for the murder, she'd find a way to do it."

"Then she'll find a way to do it, whether we're faking an affair or not."

"It's about more than Estella. The rest of the household needs to believe it because the police will ask them about it. Your bed needs to quit being slept in."

"I'll make it myself."

"You need to get caught coming out of my bedroom in the morning."

"Grey, this isn't necessary," Lanny began as they neared the top of the stairs.

Grey hissed, "Air duct dead ahead. We've got to make it sound good." He caught her and swept her up into his arms again and kissed her as they made their way to his room.

Lanny didn't notice an air duct and she'd have told him so if she wasn't so breathless from Grey's exuberant passion, resigned to the pretense and not all that averse to Grey kissing her for any reason, Lanny let herself be carried into his bedroom.

CHAPTER FIFTEEN

"Kiss me, Angel," Grey did his best to sound romantic but since he was reading a book in one chair while Lanny read her own, he didn't really sell it.

Lanny whacked him with the book she'd found on her nightstand and brought into this room. It had a bookmark in it, but Lanny couldn't remember a thing so she started over.

Grey grinned at her. He leaned up to her ear and whispered, "Say you have a headache. I've always wanted a woman to try that one on me."

"As if you don't hear it all the time," Lanny muttered, then took another swipe at him with the book, this time aiming for his head. He ducked, then snatched it out of her hand.

She said in an indignant hiss, "That was just getting good."

"All right, Angel." He spoke aloud. "I'll let you rest, for now. You're so beautiful. So passionate."

Lanny snagged the book away from him and started thumbing through it, searching for her page. "Same goes, hon."

Grey grabbed a pillow off his bed and buried his face in it to drown out the noise of his laughter.

Lanny's eyes flickered open. She was lying on her stomach looking to her left with both arms hugging her pillow and the first thing she thought of was Grey.

He'd kissed her good-night, very chastely. Which was a good thing because she didn't believe in having sex without marriage.

Lanny jerked upright in bed. She remembered!

Then she remembered everything. She got up, got dressed in fast, angry bursts of temper and stormed into Grey's bedroom.

His eyes popped opened and he sat up, scanning the room for danger. He saw no threat and turned to Lanny. "What?"

Lanny had been awake long enough to be clear headed. Memories were rioting through her head. Without looking at him she said, "Shhhh."

Grey rubbed his eyes for a few seconds then his head came up and he glanced at the air duct and nodded. He whispered, "Did something scare you?"

"No, I remembered something..." Lanny sat in the chair she'd spent such a pleasant hour in last night and stared sightlessly across the room. Memories washed over her. College. High school. Her childhood home. Her parents' traumatizing death. Grandma Millie...

"Grandma!" Lanny jumped for the land line phone on Grey's beside table. "I need to call my grandmother."

Grey threw back the covers. He was wearing flannel pajama pants and a t-shirt. It was a good thing because she wasn't putting up with any more of his nonsense about an affair.

He got to his feet, watching her quietly. Then she thought again and remembered that she hadn't been calling anymore. Grandma Millie had failed so badly in the last two months that she was nearly comatose.

Grandma's debilitating stroke. The nursing home. That's why she was here in this dreadful house. The money for Grandma's care. That was why she'd written those huge checks, not rent. Lanny lived in Grandma Millie's house. The same house she'd grown up in. The money was for a nursing home. An excellent nursing home that Lanny had chosen for her grandma's special needs. A nursing home that had grown more expensive as Grandma's health had deteriorated. Her grandma had given her life to care for Lanny and now it was Lanny's turn.

Lanny remembered her parents' death. Her parents' death in a car accident. And she'd been in the car. The terrible rainstorm, the exploding thunder. A slick road. She'd been pinned in the car with her parents while the thunder raged at her as if it wanted to get in the car and drag her away.

Then help had come, and Grandma Millie.

And now Grandma's care ate up most of what Lanny made every month and when Lanny'd had to decide between selling her childhood home or changing jobs, the chance to earn more from the Devereaus had been irresistible.

The Devereaus. Victor!

She whirled to face Grey and jabbed her finger at him, coming inches from nailing him right between the eyes. "Your cousin is a pig!"

Grey watched with fascination. "Was a pig."

"Oh, that's right. He's dead. Good riddance!" She plowed her fingers into her hair and looked at the ceiling as she muttered in disgust. "Don't speak ill of the dead!"

She turned to face the direction of Victor's room and snarled, "I can't believe I said that. Whoever killed him deserves a medal."

Grey slowly rounded the bed. "I thought you were in love with him?"

Lanny jammed her fists on her hips. "For about two hours, one evening."

She paused and sorted through the jumble of reawakened memories. "I can't remember..." she mused. "It must have been Monday or Tuesday..." She fell silent and stared at nothing.

Grey stepped in front of her but she was looking into the past, far and recent. He touched her lips to shush her and her eyes focused on him.

She looked at him, chagrined.

Grey plucked the pillows off the couch and dropped them over the air vent. He came back and whispered, "That might help, but keep it down."

"I still can't remember anything after going to sleep Monday night." Whispering, she ignored the headache she was giving herself. "I think it was Monday night. I didn't get hit until..."

Grey said, "I got home late Tuesday night or rather, early Wednesday morning. It couldn't have happened long before that."

Lanny wrapped her arms around her waist tightly as she tried to force her memory to produce what had happened to her. "All day Tuesday is a blank. Early in the day, Monday, Victor had cornered me in the stairway and given me his speech."

"Mother of My Children?" Grey supplied.

Lanny nodded, remembering how touched she'd been. "I bought it." She speared Grey with an angry look. "He was a pro, wasn't he? Boy, he really sold it. He'd changed his tactics in the last week. Less the arrogant, You-Are-So-Lucky-I-Want-You, approach, and more the tender, love sick puppy. I can't believe he had any luck with women. The man was an idiot!"

Grey prompted her gently, "You said it worked for a while."

Lanny finally really looked at Grey and saw how worried he was about what 'it worked for a while' might mean. She smiled at him and stroked one finger down his unshaven face. The bristles of his beard tickled her finger delightfully. Then she thought of Victor again.

She replaced her smile with a scowl. "He spent the whole day Monday worshiping the ground I walked on for refusing to be seduced. I went to bed Monday night in love. I was planning my blasted wedding to that rat! Right up until he came into my bedroom, drunk out of his mind. I thought you said he'd wait till the weekend with his Mother of My Children routine?"

"He probably meant to, but he was too drunk to remember the game plan." Grey shrugged, battling the rage he felt at the idea of Victor attacking Lanny. "So, he came into your room..."

"And when I was done teaching Octopus-Boy a lesson, he crawled back out. Literally. He wasn't up to anything but crawling."

A burst of laughter escaped Grey's lips.

Tempted to do something that would make Grey crawl out of the room, she glared at him.

The laughter, laced heavily with relief, escaped again.

Lanny gave him a disgruntled look and crossed her arms in front of her. "You think this is funny?"

"No, although the image of Victor crawling does have a certain appeal. I've always wondered why someone didn't do him some type of permanent damage. He's certainly had it coming."

"How could I have bought his line for even a minute?" She left one arm hugging her waist and rubbed her mouth with her thumbnail. "His endless, tacky come-ons made work here insufferable. I'd taken to virtually hiding in my office to avoid Victor and your whole nasty family. Not that he left me alone there either."

Then Lanny hesitated. "You know, I take back the 'whole nasty family' crack. Clarinda was a sweetheart. Prone to sneaking up on me but essentially harmless. I braided her hair almost every afternoon. Then she'd sit in the office with me or go up into the attic with me while I worked. I tried to talk to her but if she answered at all it was usually in words of one syllable."

"I need to get her out of here." Grey shook his head. "There's no excuse for neglecting her for as long as I have. I can't believe I haven't done something before now. It's easy to forget such a ghostly, quiet woman is even here."

"I liked her a lot at first but lately she'd started coming in the office constantly and bugging me. I learned Clarinda was afraid of Victor, slinking away like a half-wild kitten whenever he'd come in to make one of his smarmy propositions. Clarinda has a strange habit of appearing unexpectedly and standing in corners until I notice her. That had really started getting on my nerves. She scared me half out of my wits several times until I'd started to find even her tiny effort at friendship intolerable."

"That sounds like Clarinda."

"She came into my office yesterday afternoon again. She had a comb with her and sat down. I could tell I'd brushed her hair before."

"It was you then who had done her hair. I noticed it the only time I've seen her since Victor died. She was crying in the hallway by his room – the only one of us who could manage any tears for dear old Victor."

Lanny thought of Meredith.

"She must trust you." Grey went on before Lanny could tell what she'd learned. "Clarinda is incredibly shy around strangers. Why wouldn't she be? She never leaves the house and we don't have many visitors."

"She said something very weird to me. She said she was bad."

Grey shrugged. "That sounds like her. She was always afraid she'd been bad if she broke something or got in someone's way."

"Does she always say, 'People die when they're bad?'"

Grey started. "What do you suppose she meant by that?"

"She said Victor was bad, too. And Victor's the only dead person around."

Grey tried to sort out Clarinda's cryptic comment.

Lanny added softly, "She said you and I were bad, too. Does that sound like a threat?"

Grey dismissed the idea immediately. "Clarinda wouldn't threaten anybody. She's afraid of her own shadow."

"Maybe she wasn't making a threat. Maybe she was warning me. The whole topic terrified her. She ran out of my office. I'm sure it was her I heard upstairs. That's why I went to the attic. She was so upset, I wanted to make sure she was all right."

"That's why you were up there? Why didn't you say something earlier when I was so worried about you?"

"Worried? Is that what you call screaming at me and jerking me around? How am I supposed to explain myself when you're roaring away?"

"Next time make me listen," Grey said sternly.

"Next time, shut up and listen," Lanny snarled back.

Grey said with chagrin, "This is the real you, isn't it?"

Lanny slammed her fists onto her hips, "What do you mean by that?"

"You said Clarinda was upset. Why?"

Lanny wondered over the 'real you' crack but decided to leave it for now. "I'm sure she knows something about Victor's death."

"Victor was awful to her," Grey muttered in contempt. "Practical jokes, cruel pranks. Constantly making sneering remarks about how stupid she was, right in front of her. Even though she was an adult, she was childlike, just as she is now, and she didn't understand. You know he taught her every filthy cuss word in the book. I heard her say terrible things when I was living here, desperate to grow up and get out of this place. Victor thought it was a huge joke to teach Clarinda some dreadful sexual phrase and tell her to come and ask me if I'd do it to her." Grey ran his hands into his hair as if he was trying to wipe the memory out of his brain. "Some of the obscene things she'd say so innocently. It got so I was afraid to talk to her. And Victor would make sure he was in the room and he'd start laughing his head off when she'd ask me to..." Grey lapsed into silence.

"That's the main reason I tried to get her out of here. Estella couldn't stand to let anyone she exerted power over slip through her fingers. Shortly after I'd turned eighteen and moved out, I virtually ran off with her and took her to a special hospital in Houston. But Clarinda was like a fragile flower who couldn't survive being transplanted. The first few days she constantly tried to run away. I stayed nearby and spent every waking minute with her, but she curled up in a ball on the floor and quit talking. She sat there hugging her knees, rocking and crying. She refused to eat. She wouldn't get herself to the bathroom. At the time I believed she would have stayed there on that floor until she died. Finally, with Clarinda killing herself, Estella caught up with us, bearing a court order from some judge she'd bought, screaming that Clarinda had a family who loved her and wanted to take care of her, and I just wanted her out of the house because I didn't like her because she was disabled. I caved. I let her come back to The Devil's Nest."

"What else could you have done? She would have died."

"And this is living? What she does here in this house?" Grey asked morosely. "I should have let them experiment with medication. I should have stayed right there in that hospital day and night. I should have force fed her myself until she got through the first shock. I was too weak to do what I knew was right. I let her come home, and I've ducked my conscience ever since by looking the other way. Well, I'm done looking the other way. I'm getting her out of here." Grey turned on her fiercely, "And you too, Lanny."

Lanny waved a hand in his face. "Clarinda may need a guardian. I don't. I'm not going anywhere."

"Lanny," Grey said with rising anger.

"I'm not leaving here until I find out what's going on. I'm finally getting my memory back. The rest should return soon if it's going to. I think being here will help jog it."

"What if you don't recover your memory until you're face to face with the knife that killed Victor?"

"Grey," Lanny said frustrated. "If someone wanted me dead, I'd be dead. I was clearly at their mercy when they tucked me in that bed. Now, I want to ask you about..." Lanny thought and a new memory assailed her.

She remembered taking a report to Estella.

"I called your aunt by her first name." Lanny pressed both hands over her mouth and shuddered when she thought of how she'd addressed Estella yesterday. No way would she have made that mistake if she'd had her memory. Mrs. Devereau was adamant that she be treated with near reverence. Lanny whispered from behind her hands, "I'm lucky to be alive."

"You are," Grey agreed.

"Mrs. Devereau." Lanny punched herself lightly in the forehead with the side of her fist. "I know that. The old bat nearly froze me to death with her eyeballs the only time I called her Estella."

Grey added, "And she had her name legally changed back to Devereau after her husband died. But she kept the Missus. She loves that name Devereau to distraction. She forced the name change on Clarinda and bullied Allen into changing his. When it became obvious Allen and Meredith wouldn't have children, she turned to Victor. She wanted grandchildren named Devereau."

"I reported to her every day at precisely five o'clock. It was always an ordeal." Lanny nailed Grey with another dark look. "Your aunt is a nasty old battle-axe."

Grey tilted his head briefly to acknowledge Lanny's accuracy. "I didn't pick my relatives. Can you remember who hit you, or for that matter, why?"

Lanny kept letting her life reel past her. She remembered her parents' deaths again. She got lost in the memory until Grey pried her hand away from his shirt. She was strangling him.

He said, "What? Is it about Victor's murder?"

Lanny shook her head, "I...I was just remembering why I'm afraid of thunder. I've learned to control it over the years but..." She sheered away from the horrible memory and tried to focus on the day after she'd used her knee to nearly separate Victor from his reason for living. There was nothing.

"Tell me about the thunderstorms. Why are you afraid?" Grey asked.

"I don't want to deal with that now. I need to remember Tuesday night." Although she was feeling pretty good this morning, her head ached when she pushed. She wasn't aware of rubbing her battered skull until Grey caught her hand.

"Enough for now. You're close. It will either come or it won't."

Grey led her toward the door of her adjoining room and opened it. He went in ahead of her without letting her go. He searched the room carefully, even looking in the closet and double checking that the door to the hallway was locked.

"Get ready for the day, but quick. I'm not letting you out of my reach until we can get out of here. I'll be right through that door." He pointed to the door to his bedroom.

He left the room and Lanny was right on his heels. He swung the door shut but she caught it before it closed, slammed it open and faced him, her arms firmly crossed. "Grey, I told you I'm not going anywhere."

"Lanny, listen to me. I'm getting you and Clarinda out of here." It was an order.

"Grey, listen to me. I'm not going." It was a fact.

"I am finding a facility, maybe a group home." Grey ignored her. "One Clarinda can board at so she doesn't have to spend the rest of her life imprisoned in this place. I'll pay whatever tuition they require. I'm giving Trevor one chance to go with us. If he goes, I'll give him enough money to live on for a couple of months while he finds a job, beyond that I'm cutting him off. There's a murderer in this house. I don't know who it is and I'm not going to have you endangered. I still get half crazy thinking about you in that attic yesterday."

It occurred to Lanny that now that she remembered everything, she wasn't quite so adoring of Grey. The man was unbelievably bossy. "Now that I have my memory back, I remember why I was here. I need the money to keep my grandma in the nursing home. I know enough to be on the look out now. I still don't believe that whoever hit me had any goal other than framing me for Victor's murder. I'll be fine. Take Clarinda away. That's a good idea. She needs to get out of here. But I'm staying."

"I'll give you the money for your grandma's nursing home bills. You're going." Grey loomed over her like a cranky vulture.

Lanny stepped closer to him. "I take care of my grandma myself. And I'm not a child to be told what to do and where to go. I said I'm staying and I am."

"Your grandmother's care isn't worth your life. Your grandma would never accept money you made like that. She'd want you to be safe. You're going if I have to throw you over my shoulder and drag you out of here."

Lanny poked him smartly in the chest with her index finger. "You know what? I'm starting to remember a lot of things about myself. One of them is that I don't take orders. You put your hands on me and you'll find that out, just like Victor did."

Grey said smugly, "What am I worrying about anyway? Estella's going to fire you. She thinks you killed her golden boy."

Lanny smirked and nodded her head. "I remember that, too. Victor the golden boy. What a lousy piece of judgment that was."

"Yeah, well that's Estella all over."

"If Estella was going to fire me she would have already. Victor was my main problem and he's gone." She waved her hand dismissively at Grey. "Go take care of Clarinda. I'll be fine."

Grey caught her hand and pulled her fully against him. He pressed her hand to his chest and slid his arm around her waist and switched to a soothing, persuasive voice, "I can't bear to have you in danger, Angel. I can't let you stay knowing you could be hurt. How about if we just go down to the nearest town? There's a nice little motel in Gull Cove. It's not far away. We'll sleep down there and you can come up here, with me, and we'll do your research during the day."

Lanny bit back the angry retort. Grey was trying to keep their conflict from turning into an all out war. "I can't afford the room."

"I'll pay," Grey snapped, the hold he'd put on his temper was slipping.

"Will you quit saying that?" Lanny exploded and she shook his hands off of her. "Quit tossing your money around. Give Clarinda money. Give Trevor money. Give my grandma money. Give me money. Not everything can be solved with your filthy pirate's treasure."

Grey's eyes darkened. "Every cent that cutthroat made has been long ago spent. Any money this family has, I earned by working myself half to death. And I did it all honestly. The Grey Trust was sucking fumes when Estella got done with it. Nothing here is from a pirate's booty. Even this house was mortgaged to the rafters when I took over."

"So, you saved this mausoleum? You're actually proud of that?"

"I saved it to keep a roof over my family's heads. I'd have had to drag Estella out of here by her fingernails. Even though I can't stand the old bat, I let her stay. If it was up to me, I'd have put a match to this hulk years ago!"

"Grey," Lanny said, deciding it was her turn to be reasonable. "I know you want to take care of me. How old were you when everything landed squarely on your back?"

"I took over the finances when I turned eighteen."

"So, you've been taking care of this family since then."

Grey grabbed her by her shoulders. "Don't start psychoanalyzing me. This isn't about some misplaced sense of responsibility. As long as you're in this house, you're in danger."

Okay, that was it. The man could not hear her. She was done trying to be nice. "Then you'd better stick to me like glue, Grey. Because I'm not going anywhere."

"I respect your desire to make your own decisions but I don't think you're making the correct one here. Be reasonable."

"I have no intention of being reasonable." Lanny stopped. That sounded so wrong. Then she plunged on. "I'm staying."

"I want you to be safe, Lanny. I care about you."

Grey said he cared about her. The words touched her deep inside and Lanny didn't really think it through before she slipped between his clasping hands, wrapped her arms around his neck and kissed him. Kissing a man to get him to do things her way was the oldest trick in the book.

CHAPTER SIXTEEN

G rey used the oldest trick in the book to get his own way.
Then the kiss deepened and he wasn't sure what they'd been talking about. Nothing important, that was for sure.

He was just getting to the point where he didn't remember any of those things a person never forgets. How to ride a bike. How to swim. His name.

Lanny's amnesia might be contagious.

All he could remember is where they were. Alone, together.

He pulled her hard against him.

A loud knock sounded on the door. "Grey, I have to talk to you. It's about that police detective."

Grey lifted his lips away from Lanny's. "Go away, Allen."

"Good grief, Grey. It's the middle of the morning. Aren't you ever done in there?"

Grey muttered, "More like, I never get started."

Lanny giggled.

He slapped her smartly on her neat little backside, helped her peel her arms off his neck, and turned wearily to face the door. "Come in."

Her memory had returned, but she hadn't really thought of Allen yet. Allen wasn't the kind of man who left a strong impression. The rest of the family was memorable. Despicable Victor, fragile Clarinda, dictatorial Estella, and arrogant, cold Meredith.

Allen was different. Lanny remembered her research and all the photos and journals, plus the extensive gossip supplied mainly by Victor. Allen was only a couple of inches taller than Lanny. His thinning hair was light brown liberally salted with gray. He had a middle age spread.

His chin was weak, his nose beak-y, his complexion badly scarred from acne and he didn't make eye contact often and then only glancing up to hope for approval.

Now that she was confronted by him, Lanny remembered Allen. She remembered everything, including the time Allen had shaken off his spineless nature for long enough to corner her in the attic and make a crude pass at her.

Allen had gotten physical enough to frighten her. Despite his short stature, he out-weighed her by fifty pounds and he had a man's strength. Lanny could still taste his artificially mint-y breath when he tried to force a kiss on her. She could remember his almost feminine soft hands, the palms soaked with sweat. The thought of it made her shudder. She'd shoved him, escaped from the attic and gone to her room to pack and abandon this house that was already giving her the creeps. Allen had come to her and apologized contritely through her locked door. He begged her not to tell anyone what he'd done, with enough whimpering that she'd believed he meant it.

Lanny had stayed.

Despite Victor's endless, tacky seduction attempts, he'd been an annoyance but he'd never made her skin crawl the way Allen did.

She was standing behind Grey because he'd had his back to the door when Allen had knocked. She couldn't bring herself to be such a weakling as to hide. Something in her movements must have caught Grey's notice because he turned sharply to look at her and narrowed his eyes. She tried to adopt a bland expression because she didn't want to deal with what Allen had done. It had been a one-time thing and she'd handled it herself. But she hadn't covered her reaction well enough because Grey turned back to his cousin.

"You said Victor was a pig but you didn't mention that Allen was one, too."

Allen paled visibly and opened his mouth but no words came out.

Lanny said, "Why don't you just assume I can't stand anyone in this house unless I tell you different?"

Grey smiled at her. "That include me?"

Lanny sighed and jerked her head sideways in an abbreviated shrug. "So far I like you pretty well."

Grey's expression lightened and he looked back at Allen. Lanny wasn't looking forward to another war of words so she tugged sharply on Grey's arm. Grey arched a brow at her.

"I'd have mentioned Allen being a pig if his pathetic excuse for a seduction had been important enough to discuss."

A flush of anger colored Allen's pasty cheekbones. "I didn't come in here to discuss that. Detective Garrison and some of his cronies are downstairs with a search warrant. I haven't allowed them in. They did enough searching yesterday. I have a call in to our lawyer. Estella is on the phone to the lieutenant governor. Meredith is talking to the police commissioner. You'd better come downstairs, Grey, and send them packing."

"What I'll do is call off our lawyer, tell the lieutenant governor to get off the phone, reassure the police commissioner that we want to cooperate fully, then come downstairs and let the police in so they can tear this place apart."

"Let them in? This is harassment. They've been all over the place already. They're just trying to be as disruptive as possible."

"Don't you want to know who killed Victor?" Grey asked smoothly.

"I believe we know who killed Victor." Allen shot Lanny a malevolent look.

"She was with me, Allen. She didn't do it."

"She's convinced you to cover for her. I don't blame you. I understand her appeal well enough. She's made a try for every man in this house. She thought Victor would marry her and when he laughed in her face she waited until he fell asleep then she slit his throat."

"Watch it, Allen. You're talking about the woman who is going to be my wife."

That was news to Lanny but she didn't react by so much as a twitching eyelid.

Allen continued in his smirking voice, "I don't blame you for thinking with the wrong part of your anatomy where she's concerned, but I'm not going to let Victor's murderer go free just because you can't resist her."

"Allen," Grey said with barely controlled anger. "You are not listening to me. She was with me. While you're focusing on her, you're letting a murderer go free."

"It's obvious you're beyond reason at the present. Have you ever heard of a polygraph test?" Allen didn't give them a chance to respond. "I know a police department in the state that has one and I'm going to insist the police give both of you a test."

"Insist all you want, Allen. Lanny and I were together and Detective Garrison agrees that neither of us is the prime suspect. Quit wasting your time and let the police in here to do their job."

"Grey..." Allen began.

"Get out, Allen," Grey commanded. He strode toward Allen, grabbed the collar of his white dress shirt and lifted his cousin onto his toes. "The only reason I'm letting you walk out of here with all your teeth is because I don't want Lanny to watch me beat you senseless. You came on to her. We both know what Trevor and Victor are like and she turned every one of you down." Grey shook his cousin slightly and said with sardonic amusement. "And yet she can't keep her hands off of me. I think that says good things about her taste in men. This is your first and last warning. I don't want to hear any more malicious talk about Lanny. I don't want to hear another word about something scurrilous going on between her and the men in this house. If I do, after I'm done knocking your teeth in, I'll make sure the police know you're lying."

Grey released Allen with a little shove that sent him stumbling backward. Allen opened his mouth but the only words he could manage were an outraged sputtering. He backpedaled his way out of the room and in a limp wristed attempt to salvage his pride he slammed the door.

Grey whirled to face Lanny. "Why didn't you mention Allen?"

Lanny was a little surprised at Grey's anger. He had defended her so magnificently. "I didn't remember it until he came in."

"What about Trevor? What am I going to hear from him when the time comes?"

Lanny narrowed her eyes. He'd caught her off guard with his suspicious question about Allen. She'd answered his question by reflex, but she didn't plan to stand here and get scolded for Allen's nonsense. "You can't possibly believe I had anything to do with that greasy little worm, Allen. And don't try to pretend you think I let Trevor seduce me either. I remember he tried but he is a Victor wannabe with the single redeeming quality of not having so much practice. I refuse to dignify any accusations you make with a denial."

Grey stared at her for a long time as if he was trying to see inside of her, then finally he said irritably, "I know nothing happened."

"Then why are you upset?"

"Because it made me jealous," Grey erupted.

"Well, that's just..." Lanny paused for a second as what Grey said registered. "What?"

"You heard me. Listening to Allen talk that way about you and other men...I know it's not true." Grey rolled his eyes at the ceiling. "How could Allen think I'd believe..." Grey chuckled, slowly at first, then gaining strength as the idea caught up with him.

"You hitting on Allen?" Grey laughed until he had to sit down. He rubbed his hands over his face while he laughed, then tousled his hair with both hands and looked up at Lanny. "Not in his wildest dreams." Grey started laughing again.

Lanny couldn't help but join in, although she was so lost in all the craziness that had been surrounding her, not just for the days since Victor's death but ever since she'd come to this madhouse. "So, you believe me, then?"

Grey nodded and wiped his eyes, another burst of laughter escape.

"How did one family ever come up with so many slutty men?"

Grey's eyebrows arched in surprise. "Slutty? Men?"

"Give me a better word," Lanny asked dryly.

Shaking his head slowly, Grey was silent a minute. With a tiny shrug of one shoulder he said, with a glint of humor, "But slut is a female word. Men can't be sluts."

"I think your family is living proof that's not true."

Grey, his eyes still bright with amusement, said more seriously, "That polygraph test thing worries me, though. We can fight it. I don't think the police can compel you to take one, but it will look funny if we refuse."

Lanny said quietly, "What are we going to do?"

They stared at each other for a long time.

Lanny saw it in his face, the moment he decided what to do. She saw his eyes light up with a conviction that was burning from deep inside of him. Then determination settled across his face and she knew whatever it was, he had decided irrevocably to do it.

"What?" she asked nervously.

With an intensity that left singe marks on her, Grey said, "A husband can't testify against his wife."

Lanny's stomach churned at the implacable tone in Grey's voice and she knew her life had just slipped completely out of her control. "H...h...his wife? What wife? What does that mean?"

"It means..." Grey said with barbarous satisfaction worthy of a pirate, "...Lana Cole, will you marry me?"

They're leaving! It can't be! Without Lanny there's no one.

Wait! Indeed, there is someone.

I wanted Lanny, but there might be an appetizer in this house.

CHAPTER SEVENTEEN

I think I will ride along with you to town. We need to have an uninterrupted, un-eavesdropped upon talk."

Lanny certainly didn't say anything so stupid as 'Yes, I'll marry you'. Though from the pounding of her heart she knew it held a treacherous appeal and that worried her. Could a woman fall in love with a man—while she had amnesia—then, when she remembered who she was…did the love come along with her return to…sanity? Or was that whole crazy attraction to Grey a product of her vulnerability?

Honesty forced her to admit that whatever had caused it, she was still drawn powerfully to the man.

"Talking sounds good." Grey had a glint in his eye that worried Lanny. "Including talking about whether or not we should come back at all."

Her backbone stiffened at Grey's high-handed zeal for running her life.

"I want to talk about some papers I've found." Lanny couldn't bring herself to take the papers out of the house, expose them to rain. The historian in her rebelled at the terrible abuse of ancient documents. She thought of Meredith's shocking confession. "And—"

"I don't suppose you'd agree to pack your suitcases." Grey interrupted her. He sounded like a man with no hope.

Which was wise of him. "No. I'm coming back."

Lanny rushed into her room, snapping the door shut in Grey's face, changed into another outfit which might well be boring, but it was smart to be able to pick her clothes out in ten seconds flat. Practical. Wise. Efficient. But that impression of boring couldn't quite be shaken.

She jerked her drawer open and immediately saw a second sheet of paper resting on top of her socks. It hadn't been there before. The historian in her balked at taking such an old piece of paper, a piece of surviving history, out in the weather.

"Are you decent?" A sharp rap on her door told her Grey wasn't going to give her any time alone and, considering the spooky house, complete with murder suspects galore, she couldn't blame him.

Her paper couldn't be folded and it couldn't be exposed to rain. Her eyes landed on one of her notebooks and she opened it, lay the paper inside and snapped it shut. "Come in."

Grey swung the door open. "Let's go."

Lanny grabbed her purse, shoved her feet into her very sensible shoes and followed Grey down the stairs and out into another in the endless parade of thunderstorms.

When Grey drove her down that miserable road a few more things came back to her. "This road is awful in good weather. We shouldn't be on it."

A grunt was his only response about the driving conditions. "Tell me about the papers you found."

"I just found a new one." Lanny opened the notebook to show Grey the paper. "It's written by Giselle."

"You just found it now?"

Which reminded Lanny of even more that she'd forgotten. "I've found a lot of old papers in your attic, but *I've* never found anything from the era of Giselle and Pierre Devereau."

"Nothing? How come I know so much about Pierre then?" Grey eased the car down the slick road.

"I think a lot of it has been written down by later generations."

"Which means it might not be that accurate. I've heard only terrible things about my pirate ancestor."

"I'd say you'd better hang on to your low opinion. Giselle writes terrible things about him. She doesn't even call him Pierre, she calls him Poltron, which is French for coward." Looking at the paper in her lap, Lanny said, "Someone has been leaving these for me to find. Estella maybe. I've never known who for sure. Maybe Estella is leading me to certain conclusions about the family by what she shares and what she withholds."

Grey had his eyes riveted on the road and it was a good thing. They approached that ugly stretch with the mountain hanging over the top of the drive.

"I hate this road." Lanny felt herself leaning sideways, as if she could avoid the avalanche when it came. She knew it wouldn't help but her body language was almost uncontrollable. "You and me both," Grey muttered, gripping the wheel tightly and slowing to a crawl, which was about two miles per hour slower than before because he'd been creeping along. Lanny didn't talk while they passed The Overhang. She glanced out into space compulsively. There was only a few feet to spare on this road and any sudden stop or swerve could send them hurling out into certain death.

When they emerged from the shadowed stretch, she realized she was holding her breath.

Grey blew out a long breath in relief. "You want to read that to me?"

Lanny nodded. "It's in French. By the way, I can read French." She lifted the paper, touching it as gingerly as possible.

August—1802

This wife lasted only slightly longer than the earlier ones. The coward pitched her off the roof into the sea when, after two years, no child was forthcoming.

Grey scowled. "That's one story of Pierre we know is true."

"I've read several of these. I now believe every horrible thing I've ever heard of the man." Lanny went back to reading aloud.

I've become someone I hate. Nearly as much as I hate Poltron. How can I watch his depravity with such detachment?

"Poltron? What did you say that means?" Grey asked without taking his eyes from the road, which Lanny appreciated.

"Poltron means coward."

Grey blew a low whistle through his lips. "I've always wondered if she was with him in evil."

"She talks about God. Talks about praying for protection, and for protection for her son."

"Just her son? Not her other children?" The road straightened and widened enough that Grey could pick up a little speed, but they still crept along.

Lanny wondered about going back up. The road was graveled, but water stood in the ruts and the edges of the road were a mire.

"Near as I can tell from reading my notes and these letters I've found from Giselle, she only had one child, and that was a son with Pierre. Any other children he had were with other women."

"Illegitimate children," Grey shook his head in disgust. "Sounds like his blood ran true in Victor. I hate knowing I came from such a man, but blood doesn't really run true in anyone. We each have our own lives."

"There's a Bible verse that says, 'the sins of the father will be visited on his sons to the third and fourth generation.'" Lanny thought Grey was beyond the fourth generation. She wondered if that really mattered.

"I don't believe that." Grey's knuckles turned white as he gripped the steering wheel. "I refuse to. I can't be condemned because of something my great-great, however-many-great grandfather did. God isn't like that. He lets us choose or reject our faith. There are enough Bible verses that say that. There is no hope for redemption without that."

"I agree, actually." Lanny looked at the yellowed paper bearing proof of Grey's dreadful heritage. "I don't think that Bible verse means punishment from God is visited on the third and fourth generation, I think it means evil runs in families because of the way those families live."

"Are you a believer, Lanny?" Grey's hands relaxed a bit. He risked a glance away from the road. "Now that your memory has returned, do you have a personal faith in God?"

Lanny exhaled and realized how tense she was, too. The road, the letter, the murder.

Leaving the house suddenly seemed like a stroke of genius.

She smiled and rested a hand on Grey's arm. "Yes, I am. And I did not…involve myself with Victor. Although I know you've already realized that. But every time he'd make some disgusting proposition to me, I'd try and talk with him. He might have even listened a bit, but more likely he pretended to." A thought suddenly struck Lanny. "After his 'mother of my children' pitch ended with him crawling out of my room in agony, I talked to him the next day. I thought maybe he really heard me. I told him there was no possible way I'd ever get involved with him under any circumstances because I wanted a man of faith. A man to be a spiritual leader in our home and I wasn't going to settle for anything less."

"But Victor would have probably immediately started faking that to try and woo you."

Lanny lifted one shoulder. "I made it clear that there was never going to be anything between us, that I had no interest in him and I'd never trust him. He said some of the right things anyway. You don't suppose…" Lanny tried to think where she was going.

"Suppose what?" Grey prompted her.

"If Victor really did change, he might have said something to his smuggling confederates that made them angry. He might have told them he would no longer be a part of their crimes."

"And the Grey Trust held a lot of their money. I caught on to what Victor was doing and I watched the money in his account go up and down for about two weeks, money flowing in and out. Then once I knew where the money trail led, I waited until a big chunk of it came in, enough to almost cover all they'd siphoned out, and I froze the bank accounts, then transferred all the money out that was there. I did it the day I drove up there. If smugglers suddenly realized their money was gone, they might have blamed Victor."

Lanny heard the worry in Grey's voice, the thread of guilt. "Victor chose to be involved with very dangerous men, Grey. If he'd been honest, no bank transfer could have put him in danger. Don't even think of blaming yourself."

Sighing deeply, Grey nodded and said, "Read the rest."

I creep through the house like a ghost, hoping he won't turn his attentions back to me.

"A ghost." Grey shook his head. "She was a ghost while she was still alive." Lanny went back to reading.

Poltron has finally used up all the wealth—sold off everything of value in the house except that which I have hidden. His last beating left me near death and with my son grown and gone— though not gone enough to be safe from Poltron—I would have welcomed the end.

The quiet voice of God whispers in my ear that it is wrong to turn my hand against myself and I believe that, so I survive. But there is nothing the coward can do that will make me reveal the treasure.

As always, I listen to him without him knowing. He's never discovered the secrets of The Devil's Nest and he never will. He is too stupid to grasp all that is hidden. He said to his men that he was returning to the sea tomorrow.

Another reprieve. My life is mostly lived without him and that has to be enough.

I write this account so someone may one day know the truth. I keep it hidden even from the servants so the truth and the wealth are safe, perhaps for all time. Someday it will all be found out. When I know I am alone, I slide the hidden stones aside and the secret room becomes my haven.

"What hidden room?" Grey turned off the hair-raising road onto a much better maintained gravel road.

"I've never found a hidden room," Lanny shrugged. "You lived in that house a lot longer than I have. You've never heard of stones sliding aside to reveal a room?"

"Nope." Grey nodded at the paper. "Is that all there is?"

Lanny flipped the paper over. "Yes."

Now Lanny had to ask the question that was far too much on her mind. "A little while ago you said a wife—"

"Hang on."

Lanny looked up to see a car round a curve just below them.

Grey battled his car to the very edge of the road. It wasn't along a cliff, but if they got too far to the side, they'd be stuck.

By the time the car passed them and they'd gotten away from the soft shoulder, the dock was in view. They climbed into one of several speed boats and in the buffeting, summer rain, they zipped across the sea that flowed between the coast and the island that held The Devil's Nest.

After they docked, Grey led the way to his car, left parked in a lot along the ocean. The town was small but it was a tourist spot and there was plenty of traffic and commerce. He drove along, very familiar with the place.

"I want you to see a doctor." Grey pulled up to a small building along a quiet main street.

He swung his door open and got out before she could insist he stay here and finish their talk.

He was clearly a man on a mission now, so she set aside all she needed to tell him until later and together they entered the small waiting room. There was no one present except a nurse sitting behind a counter.

After a few quick questions, the nurse said, "Come on back, the doctor should be here shortly."

The nurse took Lanny's pulse while Grey leaned against the wall, watching every move the nurse made, as if she somehow threatened Lanny.

"Sir, if you would go to the waiting room, I think—"

The phone rang in the outer office. With an impatient huff, the nurse said, "I'll be right back."

She stepped out and Grey swung the door shut.

"What's the matter?" Lanny watched him approach.

"We never finished talking about—"

The nurse bustled back in. "The doctor is going to be a bit longer. He was delayed with an emergency. Do you mind waiting?"

Grey said, "Would it be all right for us to have some privacy for a bit? We have some things we need to discuss."

"That's fine, take your time, he might be another half hour." She stepped out and pulled the door shut. Grey came to Lanny's side and before she could ask him what he wanted to discuss, he lowered his mouth and kissed her.

The kiss set her trembling deep inside.

When Grey lifted his head, Lanny wondered how much of the half hour was left. She'd lost track of time.

"I'd take you to Las Vegas and marry you today, Angel. But the police won't let us leave town."

A sentence that helped Lanny shake off the thunderstorm in her brain and start thinking again.

"That," she said dryly, "is about the most unromantic thing any man ever said."

"I expect that's right." Grey patted her on the shoulder.

"What exactly did you mean 'a man can't testify against his wife'? Since we're each other's alibi and we can't be compelled to take a polygraph test, we don't need to get married. If the police want to push the point until we look guilty as sin, they will, married or not. There really is no point to the wedding."

"Yes, there's a point. It's the only sure way to keep us both safe."

"Grey, they can't find evidence because we didn't leave any because we didn't do it."

"You being stuck in that bed is planted evidence if ever there was any. So, there may be more planted evidence. With our alibi and a marriage, we've protected ourselves."

"It's not necessary."

"Don't you want to marry me?" There was an extended silence as Grey stared into her eyes.

"Grey, we haven't—"

He leaned over and kissed her until she didn't have a single sensible thought in her head. When he pulled away she sat bemused on the examining table.

"Let's just get the license. We don't have to decide right now. I want the doctor to take a look at the wound on your head. We can ask him if Texas requires a blood test."

"There's really no point having my head examined." Lanny paused, shocked to realize she was going to go along with the blood test and license, and very probably the wedding, too. She honestly *did* need her head examined.

"I've always thought when I got married it would be a sensible decision. I've—"

"What's more sensible," Grey cut her off, "than marrying a wealthy man who's very attracted to you, shares your faith and can keep you out of prison?"

Those were really sensible reasons. And she hated every one of them. But she was the one who'd brought up sensible. "But we don't know each other, Grey. We just met. And nothing we've been through comes even close to normal."

"We know each other better than two people have any right to after so short an acquaintance. I've seen you terrified, hurt, furious. I know you're brave and funny and smart. I've realized you're very organized, well educated and honorable. I've seen that you befriended Clarinda. That reveals the kindness of your character more than anything else."

"I befriended Clarinda, but I'm really tired of her popping out at me. I'm not all that kind."

"Good, that would get old real fast."

A smile quirked Lanny's lips. "It's still been just two days."

"If these had been normal days, I'd agree with you, but we've been through so much I think our characters have been revealed."

With no way to evade Grey she was forced to really think about what he'd said. "You jumped in to rescue me."

"Not for great reasons, mostly just because I detest Victor."

"My white knight reveals rust on his armor." Lanny's smile grew.

"You're not afraid of Estella."

"That *is* a sterling quality, I'll grant you that one. I'm wildly brave to not be afraid of that old harridan."

"You're honest."

"Except for the part where I lied to the police."

"Yes, except for that part. And you're really good looking." Grey frowned over that.

"It was a compliment. Why are you frowning?"

"Because it's a shallow reason to marry someone."

"You included being attracted to me in your list."

"Yes, I did, and I think you're the most beautiful woman I've ever seen."

"Okay, there's a strike against you, you're blind."

Grey leaned down and kissed her again, more deeply than last time. When he was done, she had her arms wrapped around his neck.

He pulled back enough to whisper. "I think you're the most beautiful woman I've ever seen, and mine is the only opinion that counts. So that's settled."

The melting in Lanny's already vulnerable heart was unstoppable in the face of Grey's heated kisses and gentle flattery. "You make me feel beautiful."

"Will you marry me, Lanny? I think we will do very well together."

She wanted to tell him she loved him but it was too much, too outrageous. Too soon. Being a woman of extraordinary common sense, she said, "I'll agree to get the blood test and apply for the license. That gives me a little more time to decide, right?"

The look on Grey's face was more frustration than triumph and for some reason that made Lanny happy. She thought frustrating the very take-charge man she was most likely going to marry was a very good decision. She wanted to see how he'd act. "Right."

"And we need to go back to The Devil's Nest. I want my papers out of that house."

"And we need to find Clarinda and get her out of there." Grey hesitated. "But I can do that alone. I'd prefer we find a place for you to stay in town."

"No. I'm staying with you."

Grey looked into her eyes so hard she thought he might be reading her mind. "I want you to stay with me, too. But I can't protect you all night, Lanny. I can't make sure you're safe. No one is safe there."

"Are you sure I'd be safe in town?"

More silence before Grey finally said, "All right, for just as long as it takes for us to find Clarinda."

It gave Lanny hope for the future that Grey was letting himself be swayed. He didn't seem like a man who was easily turned from his course.

"Let's skip the head examination, too." Lanny thought she might as well get her way in as many things as possible while he was still trying to convince her to marry him.

"You really should be checked over. Any blow that renders you unconscious—"

"I feel fine, Grey." Fine was stretching it a little, but she was much improved. "I hate the idea of anyone else knowing I've been injured. I think that might put our alibi at risk."

Grey nodded just as there came a sharp rap on the door. The nurse came in, saw them in each other's arms and her eyes narrowed as if she'd caught them in some compromising position.

"We'd like a blood test please. We're applying for a marriage license." Grey smiled as he stepped out of Lanny's arms.

The nurse relaxed and gave them a huge smile. "Oh, in Texas there's no blood test requirement, but there is a three day waiting period. If that's what you came for, there's no need."

They stopped in the courthouse, applied for the license and returned to the car.

"Let's eat before we go back," Lanny said. "I don't seem to have much of an appetite in The Devil's Nest."

Nodding, Grey drove to a diner and they went in. Lanny smelled the aromas and her stomach rumbled. She was suddenly starving.

It was early for lunch and there were only a few tables and booths occupied. Grey led Lanny to a booth with red vinyl seats and white Formica table tops, streaked with red, to look like marble.

Once they'd placed their order, Lanny waited until the waitress had stepped behind the long counter and handed over the order. Once the woman was out of ear shot, Lanny said, "Now I need to tell you what Meredith said to me."

"When did you talk to her?" Grey was busy lining the silverware up. He stopped and studied her.

"Yesterday afternoon." Lanny left her silverware in its rolled-up paper napkin for now.

"I thought she went to town with Estella and Allen."

"No, she stayed behind. I walked into her room by accident looking for my office."

Grey's hand snaked across the table and caught Lanny's wrist. "I left you there with her? I thought everyone was out of the house but Clarinda."

"She was drinking heavily. She probably stayed behind to mourn."

"She didn't mourn Victor. He was a terrible bully to Allen and her both. He treated them with the same contempt he showed everyone else."

"Not all the time, apparently." It must have been her tone, but Grey's eyes sharpened and his grip tightened.

"What does that mean?"

"It means—"

The waitress, chewing her gum hard, interrupted them to pour coffee. The soft hiss of the savory hot liquid made Lanny's stomach growl. "Thank you. This smells great."

The waitress smiled. "Rotten weather. A hot drink hits the spot."

The waitress, in her white uniform dress and sensible shoes, gave Grey an equally friendly smile and served him. "Your food will be up quick."

"Thank you." Grey picked up his white stoneware coffee cup and curled both hands around it. The waitress left and Grey said, "What was that about Meredith?"

"She was having an affair with Victor."

Grey flinched so hard the coffee splashed on his fingers. "No."

Nodding, Lanny said, "Yes."

He set the cup down and wiped his hands with his napkin.

Lanny told Grey all Meredith had said.

"Estella encouraged it?"

"And Meredith always obeyed Estella. Except Meredith—"

The food came to the table and they had to break off their conversation. She served them hot beef sandwiches and a salad, the noon special.

The diner was getting busier and Lanny chafed to get the story out before anyone sat close enough to them to overhear.

When the waitress left, she said, "Meredith fell in love with Victor."

Grey shook his head silently, eating, his eyes looking somewhere in the past. "When I think it through, it makes some sense. Why would Victor leave Meredith alone? There seemed to be no boundary he didn't cross. And if she fell for him, then he'd have enjoyed hurting her."

"Which gives her a very good motive for murder," Lanny concluded.

"Meredith and Allen both."

They ate as Lanny considered all the possibilities.

"It's against all my common sense, going back to The Devil's Nest for the night. But there's so much evil there. I have to get Clarinda."

Nodding, Lanny said, "We have no choice."

She told him about Trevor spying on them. Another person in that house with secrets.

After the bill was settled, Grey drove to the dock in the picturesque little town, crossed the bay and they drove up the hill toward that dreadful house. She *did* want to marry him. It was stupid to marry a man she didn't know who came with a family of eccentric lunatics, one of whom was a killer who had framed her for murder. Even with all that, she wanted to marry him so bad she'd decided to do it, even though she wasn't going to tell him that right away.

Lanny looked at the ominous drizzling day, the world looked as if it had been draped with white gauze as they crept up the narrow drive toward the nuthouse.

"I'll keep you safe, Angel. I promise."

And she knew he'd keep that promise, as long as it was within his power. The realization that it might not be made her tense. She ducked when they went through The Overhang.

The car slewed as the tires dragged them up the hill.

Grey said, "It gets worse with every new rainstorm. It's as slippery as if someone came out and poured oil on it."

"Do you think God's trying to keep us out?" Lanny looked overhead at the looming rock. She'd been on the ocean side of the road going downhill, now she looked out her window at a stone wall so close she could have reached out and touched it.

"I wish He'd have made it impossible, because I obviously don't have enough sense to listen to Him if this is His only sign." Grey inched along the nasty stretch of road.

Lanny had planned to go back anyway, but she had to admit she was glad Grey hadn't taken her at her word when she'd told him to leave her behind. Anyway, she'd mostly said that to torture him when he was being such a tyrant. She knew he'd never abandon her.

"I'm going to have it out with Estella. I'm going to tell her Clarinda is leaving with me and neither of us will be back. I'll tell Allen things are going to change with the Trust, too."

"Will you tell him about Meredith and Victor?"

"No. I won't go into that. I don't want you with me while I talk to them. I'm going to leave you with Sally. And even then, it won't be for long."

Lanny remembered Sally. She'd liked the elderly woman, though she'd often wondered why she stayed. The housekeeping was clearly beyond her, judging by the heavy dust in every room.

Why didn't the woman go find a job somewhere less oppressive?"

They got to The Devil's Nest in the late afternoon and Grey towed Lanny along behind him into the kitchen.

Sally, a short, gray-haired woman, nearly as round as she was tall, was up to her elbows in flour, rolling out a pie crust. Lanny smelled apples and cinnamon as she came in. The whole room was old but somehow Sally had made it habitable. In Lanny's opinion it was the only room in the house that was.

Grey made a rather elaborate ceremony out of shushing Sally then hunted up a stack of linens and covered the cold air duct in the kitchen. Sally quit rolling and looked on so calmly that Lanny knew Sally was aware of Estella's eavesdropping. Grey didn't seem to notice, but Lanny sure did.

Lanny thought Sally had sad, tired eyes, and she had the sudden desire to help the aging woman get the evening meal.

Sally set the rolling pin down as if it was heavy. Her eyes slid between Grey and Lanny with a knowing look. Lanny felt herself begin to blush. Considering how many times she and Grey had been caught in a compromising position since they'd met, she would have bet embarrassment was beyond her. But the minute they stepped into the kitchen she'd remembered Sally warning her about Victor and Trevor.

Sally had even sought her out on Monday, after Lanny had decided Victor's intentions toward her were honorable. Lanny was wearing her feelings on her sleeve. Sally had told her sternly that Victor had hurt a lot of other women with empty promises.

Lanny had assured Sally blithely that she knew what she was doing, and Sally had gone away grumbling. And now, here Lanny stood, latched on to Grey only days after being in love with Victor. Lanny again faced the fact that she was behaving rashly by going along with this wedding insanity, but she couldn't make herself regret it.

Grey tipped his head at Lanny. "We're getting married as soon as we can arrange it. I'd like you to be there. You, and maybe Clarinda, are the only ones from the family I'm inviting."

Sally stared at Grey for a long moment. "Clarinda won't come. But I'm proud that you asked me. I wouldn't miss it for the world."

"Thanks, Sal." Then Grey grew more serious. "I'm taking Lanny and getting out of here as soon as I can find Clarinda. She's going with me, too. I know she won't leave without a protest but that's not going to stop me. I'm going to settle her in a residence home or a special facility somewhere and take legal steps to ensure she never comes back to this dungeon. I want you out of here, too."

"Clarinda can't be away from here, you know that, Grey," Sally said sadly. "She won't survive apart from The Devil's Nest. And she needs me. Taking care of her is the only reason I stay. She's like my own child."

Grey walked over to Sally and put his arms around her. "Sally, you've cared for Clarinda faithfully all these years and protected her in every way humanly possible. But it's time for you to put down your sword and shield and let me take over. Clarinda is leaving. They've made advances in the care of the disabled since we tried before. We can find some medication that helps her cope with the change. Anyway, if we can't, I don't care. She has to get away. Being kept a prisoner here isn't living. She's going and she *will* learn to live away from this nightmare of a home, or I'm prepared to stand by while she dies trying. And you're leaving, too.

"You've served this family long and well. You know I've set up a respectable retirement account for you and I..." Grey looked around the dreary kitchen and its antiquated appliances. "...I don't think anyone is safe in this house anymore. The evil has taken over. What happened to Victor...I suspect it was personal and the only danger was to him. But I don't want you here. I'm going to get Trevor out too, if I can."

Sally returned Grey's hug fiercely then she released him, dusting floury hand prints off his back and turned back to her baking. "Trevor won't go. He's found the goose that lays the golden eggs, and he's too enamored of his newfound wealth to see he's had to sell his soul to get it."

"I know," Grey conceded, "but that will be Trevor's choice. He's a grown man. His only handicap is his lack of a moral code. I'm giving him one chance—and part of that chance is telling him I'm going to strangle that egg-laying goose to death, so the money stops now. I'll tell him, then I'm washing my hands of him."

Sally nodded, paused, then nodded with more assurance. "I'll go. I'll find an apartment near Clarinda and do what needs doing for her. Yes, you're right, Grey. My time in this house is over."

Grey leaned down and kissed her wrinkled jowl. "If you want to stay near Clarinda that would be wonderful, and I'll keep you on full salary while you do it but, if you want to retire, I'll understand. You've got your own daughter. You could move closer to Marcia if you wanted."

Sally picked her rolling pin back up and went to work on her crust. "No, I'll stay with Clarinda. Marcia isn't one to stay in one place for long. There's no sense me trying to live near a tumbleweed."

"I'm going into the lion's den now. I need to tell Estella and Allen what Victor was doing with the Grey Trust. I've told the police everything and it will all be made public in the next few days. We'll have a scandal on our hands. I'll tell them I'm getting married, then I'll find a way to talk to Trevor alone. I don't see any point in warning them about Clarinda until the time comes to leave. I don't want Lanny with me when I confront Estella." He looked over his shoulder at Lanny.

Lanny crossed her arms firmly. "I can take whatever they dish out, Grey."

Grey looked hard at her, then said confidently, "I know you can, Angel."

Lanny fell a little more in love with him for saying that.

"But I don't see any reason you should have to. I have no desire to have a further relationship with anyone in my family. So, it doesn't matter what they think and I don't want you to have the memory of all the dreadful accusations they will hurl at you. This little meeting will be bad enough. Besides I may have to punch Allen in the nose and if you're there I might pull my punches a little to avoid a bloodletting out of deference to your feminine sensibilities."

"We wouldn't want that," Sally said dryly.

"Don't punch your Aunt Estella." Lanny patted him on the arm.

Grey seemed taken aback by her comment. "I'd never punch a woman."

"That's good, 'cuz I think she can take you," Lanny said.

Sally nodded. After thinking about it, Grey nodded, too.

He said to Sally, "Don't let Lanny out of your sight. I mean it, not for a minute."

Sally flipped her pastry onto her arm then adeptly slid it onto a pie pan. "I'll sit on her if I have to."

"You won't have to," Lanny said indignantly.

"Good girl." Grey kissed her until she didn't know if her knees would still hold her up, then left the room.

Lanny stared after him for a full minute, sighing.

"Switched sides pretty quick, didn't'cha, girl?"

Lanny turned back to face the housekeeper. Her whole head heated up as a blush climbed her neck. "Grey knows all about Victor."

Sally watched her for a minute then she seemed satisfied with whatever she saw in Lanny's expression and she relaxed and smiled. "The truth is, except for that last day, I've never seen anyone give Victor such a run for his money. Well, maybe I've seen it once before. Grab yourself a cup of coffee if you want. I've already got the first pie out of the oven. Have a slice."

Lanny realized she had just enough space after her lunch to accommodate Sally. She scooped out a wedge of the apple pie and poured some coffee. "Have a piece with me, Sally."

"In a minute. You settle in while I finish my baking." Sally lined the pie pan with the first crust and poured in a bowl full of sliced apples, heavy with sugar and cinnamon.

Lanny ate her pie with enthusiasm but it was soon gone and an awkward silence stretched as Sally rolled out the top crust. Lanny really hadn't spent much time with the woman while she'd been working here. Feeling desperate for a topic of conversation, Lanny finally said, "So who was it besides me that gave Victor a run for his money?"

"My Marcia."

Something about the way Sally said it, with a lifetime of sadness lacing her words, caught Lanny's attention. "Your Marcia, the tumbleweed?"

Sally nodded as she covered the pie with a second crust and crimped the edges with nimble fingers.

"Was she Victor's age?"

Sally balanced the pie on one hand and turned it as she used a razor sharp paring knife to trim the excess crust away. "About five years younger. She and Clarinda were the same age and they got on well together, even with Clarinda's shy ways."

Lanny imagined how awkward that would have made things for Sally. "And he came on to her? When he'd grown up with her and you were living right here?"

And considering what Lanny now knew about Meredith, she didn't doubt it for a second.

"From the age of about fourteen on my Marcia would tell me stories about the things he'd say." Sally slipped the pie into the hot oven and closed the door. "At first, I was frantic, knowing how Victor was with women, but my husband was alive then and, between the two of us, we impressed on Marcia what a louse Victor was. She'd seen it for herself so it wasn't hard to convince her to never let herself believe his lies."

"That shows remarkable maturity for such a young girl."

Sally poured herself a cup of coffee then poured Lanny a second one, slid another piece of pie on Lanny's plate and got one for herself. She sat heavily down across from Lanny at the ancient oak table.

"Yep, that's my Marcia. Smart as a whip. Heart as big as the Atlantic Ocean."

"So, what does she do that makes her a tumbleweed?"

Sally cut a piece of her pie then stared at her fork for a long time before laying it back on the plate uneaten. "Nothin' much. She just moves along, working where she can, never settling anywhere."

Lanny sat quietly. She knew there was more and she knew Sally would only tell her if she wanted to.

"With Victor dead there's no point in discussing him, but I would have told you this before you got on that boat with Victor."

"Told me what?"

"Well, I said Marcia gave him a run for his money. What I didn't say was in the end, she didn't...get away, you might say."

Lanny gripped her hands tightly around her coffee mug, afraid of Sally's bleak expression and the weight she gave each word.

"She ended up pregnant with Victor's baby."

Lanny's heart sank into her stomach and she wanted to drag Victor out of the morgue and kill him herself. "Does Grey know?"

Sally quietly answered, "No. Grey came and went a bit when he was a boy so he knew Marcia, but he was much younger than all of them. He didn't come to live here until later, until after Marcia was gone. No one knew for a long time. Not even me. It was right when she should be leaving for college. My husband died just after Marcia graduated from high school. I guess she was lonely and eager to believe in loving words from a man. She let Victor convince her she was special. He said he wanted her to be the mother of his children. He bought her expensive gifts and talked about how much he respected her for keeping herself pure."

"He said almost those exact words to me."

"He had it down pat, even back then. Marcia left here for college without me ever knowing anything had happened between them. Then the next thing I know she's quit school and moved without leaving an address."

"She went off somewhere to have the baby alone?"

"No, there was no baby. Victor dumped her after she told him she was pregnant. Marcia aborted the baby. Victor gave her the phone number."

"This must have happened years ago."

Sally nodded, "But I just found out about it. All I knew was that Marcia had cut me off. I thought it had something to do with her daddy dying. She'd call once in a while, but I couldn't ever seem to say the right thing to get her to come home. I didn't know at the time that her reasons had to do with Victor. Sometimes she'd call out of the blue and say she was in the area and I'd drive, it was always hours away, to see her. I'd get the occasional brief phone call late at night just to talk."

"How did you find out about it?"

"The last time Marcia called, she wanted to see me for the first time in two years. I drove to Houston and spent four days with her. It was the best I'd seen her acting in years. It all came out at that visit. Victor, the baby, the abortion. She'd hemorrhaged after the abortion and ended up with a hysterectomy so there were no more babies. It was all too much for her. She started drinking. When she called me she'd been sober for a year. She'd finally come to terms with what she'd been running away from and was ready to talk about it. I wanted to come back here and kill Victor."

Lanny heard the venom in Sally's voice and saw the hatred in her eyes. Lanny knew that Sally was angry enough at Victor that she could have killed him.

Sally continued, "Marcia helped me to understand that blaming Victor was what had kept her from healing all those years. It was only when she took responsibility for her own decisions that she could start to heal. I could see the truth in that because I was sitting there hating Victor for what he'd done and letting it build like acid in me when I had no business expecting a low down skunk like him to be anything other than what he is...was. The decision to stay and work here while my girl was growing up was mine and my husband's.

"Things didn't seem so dark when there were four children. Grey was in and out of the house and we loved him. Estella was married. She went out more and didn't spend so much time fixated on Pierre Devereau. When Grey's parents were alive, they'd come home and it was like a party the whole time they were here, lots of visitors and excitement. We should have gotten Marcia away the first time Victor made a pass at her, but the house just wasn't such a dark, foreboding place. Marcia seemed to be wise to Victor's ways. I thought we could cope with him. I was wrong. I needed to take responsibility for that.

"Then I came back here from visiting Marcia and found Clarinda had lost weight and never had a bath while I was gone. No one feeds her, no one helps her wash, no one keeps her clothes laundered or mended. I didn't know what to do, whether I should stay and not say anything, or dump this all on Grey, or leave Clarinda to survive on her own. It seemed too much like the way I'd let harm come to my Marcia by not doing anything. I couldn't bring myself to abandon the poor child. I'd decided to discuss things with Grey when he came home, but before we could talk, Victor was dead."

Lanny couldn't stop the image from crossing her mind of Sally so expertly wielding that paring knife. "You were going to tell me all of this before I left with Victor?"

"Yes, I knew he'd wait until the weekend because that's his way. I thought I'd give you a couple of days to come to your senses. But I'd have never let you go off with him, at least not without knowing what kind of scum he is...was."

Lanny reached her hand across the table top and rested it on Sally's. "Thank you, Sally. It's good to know someone was looking out for me. Just so you know, I'd come to my senses. I'd already found out Victor was lying."

"Good girl," Sally said firmly. "What's happening between you and Grey, well, I think it's a terrific idea."

"It's happening too fast, I know." Lanny said softly, tightening her hold on the housekeeper's talented hand. "But I can't regret it. He's...no one's ever..." Lanny lapsed into silence.

"You love him," Sally said simply.

"That's not possible, is it?"

Sally shrugged. "Not really, I suppose. A powerful attraction can feel like love and heaven knows that can happen in an instant. But love...real love...it takes time and commitment. The time should come first and the commitment second. You're doing things backward, but if the commitment is real, you'll grow into loving each other with no trouble at all. Both of you are good people, with good hearts."

"What it all boils down to is, even though I know it's crazy, I just can't resist the idea of marrying him. So, I'm going to."

A faint smile quirked Sally's lips. "I guess that's as good a reason as any."

They finished their dessert in companionable silence and Sally turned back to her dinner preparations. Lanny offered to help but Sally shooed her back to her chair. Lanny sat quietly for a while and into the silence another memory emerged.

A notebook.

The last one she'd written. By the time she'd begun writing in this last notebook she wasn't even satisfied with encoded notes. She'd carefully hidden the notebook every time she'd left her office. She'd written in it daily. Surely there were notes in there about that last day.

She had to get it. "There's a notebook in my office that I need to look at. I'm going to run up and get it."

"You're to stay here, missy," Sally said without looking up from the chicken she was spearing with whole garlic cloves.

"I know, Sally, but I'm going to just run up and grab the notebook and come right back. That notebook could clear up this whole mess. I have to get it. Put the kitchen timer on me. I'll be back in five minutes. If I'm not, you can pull the table cloths off the air duct and holler for Grey."

"This is a house of secrets. A house of evil. A nest for the devil if ever there was one." Sally reached for the kitchen timer and set it. "Five minutes. Not a second more."

"I'll be back in three." Lanny dashed out of the kitchen.

Grey stood, glaring at Estella and Allen. There was no avoiding this scene, but he couldn't enjoy it. Estella had aged ten years overnight. Her precious Victor was gone. All her dreams to restore the Devereau name died along with him.

She was a stubborn shrew, but he took no pleasure in piling more on her old shoulders.

Victor was little more than a modern day pirate. Estella's dream come true. But it would all play out publicly, and she would hate the attention of the press.

"What I'm going to tell you is just for courtesy's sake. I'm not debating it. The decision is made, and I've already talked to the police."

"What have you done now, Grey?" Estella sat, regally, in her chair in the sitting room. She did her best to slice and dice him with her words while she burned a hole in his hide with her eyes. "I've given the police all the evidence they need to prove Victor was stealing from me. From the Grey Trust."

Allen sat forward on the couch, his hands clenched between his knees, frowning. "He was stealing?"

"You had to bring the police into it, even with Victor dead?" Estella wasn't shocked, in fact it was possible she was proud. It was also possible that she knew. But she was unhappy with Grey, as usual. "You couldn't keep a scandal quiet when there's no point in talking of it?"

"Grey, I know the trust and your hard work have kept the house from having to be sold. I'm so sorry—"

"Stop, being a simpering fool, Allen." Estella slashed a hand at him.

Though he was far out of her reach, Allen flinched and his hands clutched more tightly.

"Yes, Mother."

"Get out, Allen. Now." Her voice had the command of a five star general. Allen rose and headed for the door.

"I'm not done, Allen." Grey didn't want anyone unaccounted for. In fact, he'd tried to get Trevor and Meredith in here, but Trevor was nowhere to be found and Meredith refused to come, claiming a headache.

Headache, another word for hangover.

Allen stopped at the door and glanced between Grey and Estella, his eyes shifted and Grey thought his weakling cousin had never looked more like a cornered rodent. Grey watched him, wondering who Allen would obey. Grey was, after all, his boss.

"Leave us. Grey and I need to clear a few things up once and for all."

"Allen," Grey employed a lot of men and he'd learned how to command a room. He had a five star general voice of his own and he used it. "I want the whole family together for dinner. I have a few things to say to every-one."

Allen gave him a nervous nod then opened the door and darted out. Grey didn't like letting him go but he seriously doubted Allen was capable of being dangerous.

He turned back to Estella. "Yes, once and for all is exactly right."

Instead of backing down, she stood and gave him the coldest smile he'd ever seen.

CHAPTER EIGHTEEN

L anny went straight to her office. She grabbed a pen off her desk and went straight to a heavy Victorian lantern to pull her notebook out from underneath it. She was ready to lift it when a motion in the murky corner of the room made her jump nearly out of her skin. The statue of Pan moved. But now Lanny didn't have amnesia, at least not *much* memory was lost. Just a few hours of that last day. She looked into the dimness behind the devilish beard and horns knowing what she'd find.

Clarinda.

Lanny immediately thought of Grey wanting to take Clarinda away. She forgot about the notebook for now, glad it was still hidden, and turned slowly toward Grey's cousin, not wanting to startle her. "Hi, Clarinda. I've been wanting to talk to you."

Clarinda didn't say anything. She peeked around the satyr but didn't come out. Lanny walked toward her slowly, mindful of how frightened the woman had been the last time they'd talked and how much Grey loved his cousin. "Sally made an apple pie. She's in the kitchen, let's see if she'll let us have a piece."

Come closer, Little Girl. That's right. Another few steps and I'll swallow you, one luscious bite at a time.

Clarinda inched out from the statue. When Lanny could just make out her face she couldn't control a gasp of horror. Clarinda's eyes were swollen nearly shut. The corner of her mouth was dark with dried blood. Her lips were bruised. A cut slashed through her eyebrow.

"Who did this to you?" Lanny charged toward her.

Clarinda ducked back behind the statue and Lanny stopped. Fighting back tears, Lanny decided she'd take Clarinda to the kitchen if she had to drag her there, but she hated to frighten the poor girl. Then she remembered how affectionately Sally had talked about Clarinda.

"Sally's waiting for us," Lanny murmured as gently as if she were trying to tame a wild animal.

Clarinda edged forward just an inch. "Sally?"

Lanny nodded and slipped along the wall behind the life-sized statue. The cold marble made her shudder. The wicked face of the lecherous demigod seemed to watch her, willing her to come to him. Lanny ignored the fanciful notion and stepped into the tight little corner. "Come with me, Clarinda. Be a good girl."

Clarinda cowered away from Lanny, shaking her head. "No, I'm bad."

Lanny could have kicked herself for the innocuous choice of words. She decided to quit talking. Slowly, she reached for Clarinda.

"You're bad!" Clarinda lashed out at Lanny, knocking her against the statue.

A sharp corner jabbed into Lanny's head and she whirled to see Pan had stabbed her with one of his horns. While she was glancing at the statue, she heard a hush of sound. She turned, expecting Clarinda to be trying to get away from her and faced a gaping black hole where the wall had been.

Clarinda yelled, "People die when they're bad!" She shoved Lanny into the yawning darkness.

Grey was glaring at Estella wondering where to start when Sally slammed open the door to the library. "Lanny ran up to her office and she never came back."

"How long ago?" Grey headed for Sally.

"Get back here, Devereau Grey." Estelle's voice could have frozen rain into hailstones. He ignored her without hesitation.

"Ten minutes ago." Sally was falling behind on the stairs but she could answer his question. "She said she'd be back in five. She was just running up to get one thing."

Grey clamped his mouth shut so he didn't start raging. It wouldn't do anyone any good. Instead he concentrated on running up the stairs.

"Lanny!" He charged into her office to find it empty. The lamp on her desk burned but she was gone. He rushed behind her desk just in case she'd passed out.

Fool. He should have insisted the doctor examine her. She might have fallen. But not in here. And not on the stairs he'd just come up. If she'd fainted she'd be easy to find, but there was nothing. No one was there. "I'll try her room."

He was sprinting by the time he got there. Empty. So was his room.

Grey thought of the attic. He'd found her up there once before. Struck with a chill of fear so cold it nearly froze him to death, he rushed up and spent fruitless minutes shoving his way behind everything big enough to hide a woman. Then he turned to the tower door, the only way out onto the Widow's Walk. Hating it, he opened the door to the empty tower room, then the one to the outside. There was no sign Lanny had been here but Grey was haunted by the memory of the brutal method the pirate Pierre had for divorcing his wives. The rain pelted him as he checked the roof. He even went out on the walk and circled the house, careful to never depend on the rickety wrought iron railing. No one was out there. When he came back into the attic, soaking wet and chilled to the bone, she'd been gone for nearly a half an hour.

Even though it hadn't been nearly long, Grey refused to wait. Sally had followed him up to the attic. "Call the police. Tell Case Garrison to send every spare man he's got. I'm going to tear this house apart if I have to. I think he'll jump at the chance to help." Sally left the attic at a run.

Grey rushed back down to Lanny's office. "Lanny!"

He'd look closer, see if she'd left anything behind that might point him somewhere.

A whimper sounded from beside Lanny. The crying grew louder...and closer.

Lanny lurched to a sitting position and raised her hands to deflect whatever approached in the inky darkness.

There was no breath of light. Nothing eased the pitch-black world. She had no idea how she'd gotten here. A soft brush of skin against her arm made her flinch away and cry out with fear.

The movement sent a lightning sharp bolt of pain through her ankle.

She cried out again, hating the weakness of the sound.

Fingers brushed her cheek.

"No, get away." She flailed her arms, slapping at cold, bony fingers. She imagined a skeleton, she was trapped with someone long dead who wanted her to join him in death.

Lanny hit at the caressing hand and the whimpering increased, but the crying came from farther back, not from whoever grabbed at her. The hand clutched her with a grip that cut into her skin.

"Stop," Lanny yelled. "Who are you?"

A second hand slid around her neck and Lanny clawed at the strangling, clawing fingers. A third hand tangled in her hair...or was it a third?

Lanny felt surrounded. Fingers tangled in her hair and pulled until Lanny's head bowed back. Lanny thought of Victor's slashed throat and caught at the hand on her arm to wrestle herself loose and run...where? She couldn't see an inch in front of her. Warm, fetid breath, released with a pant of exertion, flowed over her face on her right. She tried to shove herself away with her legs but her ankle didn't feel as if it would bear her weight.

Someone caught at her ankle and she cried out with pain. A hand clapped over her mouth. In the darkness she could imagine clinging demons sprung from the depths of The Devil's Nest.

Struggling, she couldn't move her legs or arms. The fingers enmeshed in her hair twisted deeper, winding her long hair tight and dragging her inexorably backward until her eyes watered with the pain of it. Something cut into her back. A board or a rock so she couldn't lay flat. Her spine bent under the force. She sucked in her breath to scream for Grey even though she felt the futility of it.

No rescuer could get to her here. She'd been plunged into the underworld. Drifting alone in the dark with a destroying phantom.

No sound escaped her covered mouth so she cried out to God from her heart.

Something rubbed her face, deepening the impression that she was surrounded. Another ghoul joining with the company that held her captive. Then she smelled the breath and knew whoever brushed against her was touching their cheek to hers. The whimper sounded from lips inches from her ear, sending dread crawling down her spine.

"You're bad."

Clarinda!

Lanny's world righted just a bit and she felt the terror of supernatural creatures ebb away.

This was Clarinda. Someone else, too, there were at least two people. The statue, the opening in the office wall. It was definitely Clarinda, and who else? Lanny tugged at the restraints on her legs and arm and now wasn't certain if hands held her or some other type of shackles. If she'd been bound it could be just Clarinda's hands.

Then that warm breath on her right again. But had Clarinda moved? She prayed for God to clear her thoughts of terror, to allow her to reason out what was happening.

Heated breath expelled against her ear, back on the left, too quickly for Clarinda to have leaned to that side. Barely audible Clarinda whispered, "People die when they're bad."

Grey wanted to single-handedly rip the house apart.

"Estella! Allen! Meredith! Trevor! Get out here!"

He stood in front of Lanny's office. Trevor surged out of his room.

"What is it?"

"Lanny's missing."

"Missing? Where was she last seen? How long ago did this happen?"

Again, with the sharp intelligence and observant eyes. Grey didn't have time to think about Trevor right now, but they were going to have a serious talk very soon.

"She came up here and said she'd be back in five minutes. That was almost an hour ago. I've been hunting for her and can't find her anywhere."

No one else came into the hall. Grey didn't have time to hunt down his family right now.

He rushed back into the office with Trevor on his heels.

"Have you checked her bedroom?"

Grey wanted to jam a fist through Trevor's face but it wasn't personal, he was just fighting mad. "Yes, I ran down there as soon as I saw she wasn't in here."

"I'll go check the other rooms up here."

"Get Meredith and Allen out of their rooms. I want everyone in this family accounted for." The reason? One of them was likely a murderer.

"Search this room more carefully. Look behind the couches and chairs, in the dark corners." Trevor rapped out orders and dashed out of the room.

Looking around the shrouded room, Grey realized he hadn't searched it thoroughly. Before he was done, he heard a car outside. The police were setting some kind of record getting to The Devil's Nest.

"Trevor, go down and let the police in!" Grey wondered at his willingness to trust his cousin. He hoped it wasn't an impulse he'd regret.

Bent nearly double against the sharp object under her back, Lanny couldn't believe the frail girl's strength. Clarinda had been her friend. Clarinda had come to her, depended on her to brush her hair. In someone with such shy ways as Clarinda, that was an act of supreme trust.

Lanny fought against the restraint on her legs. She couldn't pull with any force on the injured ankle but she struggled with the other. Tears spilled from her eyes at the pain and sobs wrenched themselves free from her throat behind the smothering hand on her mouth. In the ebony darkness she couldn't identify what held her. She had the sense of someone kneeling by her feet as well as someone on her right, and Clarinda on her left. But if they were there, the silence from them was profound, inhuman. Not even a heavy breath from the effort of holding her. Only Clarinda spoke.

"Victor was bad." Clarinda's hands began to tremble with the force of her grip and Lanny knew from the shaking in Clarinda's voice, so completely telegraphed down her arm, that Clarinda held her hair. Lanny's neck was in agony, bent backward to the breaking point.

"You came here because you're bad. Only bad happens in the passages." Clarinda spoke softly but sounded distraught to the point of madness. Her hands twitched, yanking and twisting Lanny's hair.

Lanny thought she heard something from the ominous presence at her feet. A flutter of laughter, quickly suppressed. Lanny began to think her tears would drown her as they flooded her eyes and clogged her breath. Had something pushed Clarinda beyond sanity? Was the frightened, gentle girl now capable of snapping Lanny's neck?

In an unearthly whisper Clarinda said, "I watch. I like to watch. I see everything. I have the key to The Devil's Nest."

"Key? What key?" Lanny spoke from behind the hand, hoping to distract Clarinda from her obsession with being bad, whatever that meant.

"The key." Clarinda jerked at her hair spasmodically. "The key everyone searches for."

There was a slackening in the grip on her mouth and she had a momentary hope that whoever held her was distracted. Lanny gathered herself to try to break free. She thought the talk of a key had deflected her captor.

"What key?" The muffled words were so garbled she didn't think Clarinda would understand them.

Clarinda's hands trembled with renewed strength. She hissed, "I saw you and Grey be bad!"

Lanny's legs jerked hurting her sprained or broken ankle. Lanny screamed under the lash of pain and the hand tightened on her mouth. Another sound near her feet, surely laughter this time.

"You know bad!" Clarinda's voice rose a notch and hysteria laced through it. "Bad is what you do with Grey!"

Suddenly Lanny thought of their feigned affair. If Clarinda was talking about that, it made sense. Lanny fought to control her rising panic. Think, she had to think, or Clarinda would see to it she died in this pit of blackness. When Clarinda had said before that Lanny was bad she had thought Clarinda was talking about Lanny and Grey telling lies. But an affair. Combine that with Victor and the ugly things he'd taught Clarinda to torment Grey, the message Clarinda had gotten had been pared down to 'it's bad'.

Clarinda hissed, "Victor taught me about bad."

Suddenly the hand was gone from her mouth and a sharp slap sounded in the air over her head. Clarinda cried out in pain. Clarinda had obviously been beaten earlier. Lanny could envision Estella administering the blow.

The grip shifted on her legs and Lanny cried out from the pain. Loudly this time because her mouth wasn't covered. Then the grip was back but colder. Lanny jerked at her legs and heard a chain rattle. Clarinda wept openly beside Lanny, jerking at Lanny's neck viciously when the tears wracked her body.

"You're bad," Clarinda's voice rose to a shriek. The back of her neck burned with the force of Clarinda's inhuman strength. Lanny felt her vertebrae grinding against each other and Lanny tried to lean back farther to lessen the force of Clarinda's grip but Clarinda twisted on her hair to renew the pressure. Clarinda whimpered when she inhaled then screamed, "You made Grey be bad and Grey is good! You're bad! People die when they're bad!"

"Shut up!" Case had joined in the search. Now he held an imperious hand up in Grey's face. "Did you hear that?"

"Hear what? I didn't hear anything!"

"Well, I did. It came...it came from..." Case looked doubtfully around the last room Lanny had been in.

The demon who held her feet faded away. Vanished as if he'd never been. But perhaps he never *had*. Her feet were still shackled to each other but nothing pinned them to the floor. She bent them under her and heard a metallic rattle. Some of the pressure came off her spine. Clarinda still held her hair in a vise.

Her mouth was no longer covered and Lanny shouted at Clarinda, trying to pierce Clarinda's obsession with punishing anyone who was bad. "Are you going to kill Grey?"

The grip faltered. The fingers relaxed slightly in her hair. Lanny silently apologized to Grey for possibly turning Clarinda's murderous fury on him. "If you kill everyone who is bad you have to kill Grey, too. If I was bad, so was he."

Clarinda froze as if she'd turned to stone. She could feel Clarinda's head shake, brushing Lanny's cheek each time. She said uncertainly, "I don't want to kill Grey."

"Like you killed Victor?" Lanny wanted to hear the girl say it. Even if Clarinda killed her, Lanny wanted to die knowing the truth.

"Victor was bad! I'm bad."

"You're not bad. Only Victor. Whoever said you were bad lied."

"No, not only Victor! Others are bad!" Clarinda's hand tightened again in Lanny's hair. Clarinda screamed, "I'm bad! People die when they're bad!" The solid grip on Lanny's hair relaxed and slid to her throat. "You're bad."

Grey's eyes landed on a pen. It was on the floor behind the statue of the Greek god. He went to pick it up and this time he heard the sound. His eyes went to the blank wall behind the statue.

Lanny brought both hands up hard, knocking Clarinda's grasp loose regretting that she was going to have to fight the distraught woman who had been hurt so much already. But Lanny wasn't about to lay here and die either.

She shoved Clarinda, who fell backward mewling and crying like a whipped animal.

Sobbing moans of pain washed over Lanny in the darkness as she rolled off whatever was gouging her in the back. She leapt to her feet and her ankle folded. She stumbled backward trying to keep the weight off her left leg. The chains tripped her. She flailed her arms out for something to grab hold of and touched only empty space. As she teetered backward something in front of her exploded. Light blinded her from a source Lanny couldn't identify, then Grey was there. His arms wrapped around her.

"Angel, are you all right?"

"Clarinda," Lanny babbled and clung to Grey. "Someone else was in here, too. I think."

Grey lifted her into his arms. "Get more light in here."

In the swirl of motion and blinding light, Lanny recognized the police detective. A flashlight cut its beam into the narrow room. Lanny looked around and saw a steep flight of stairs plunging down behind her. Another flight went up. She and Clarinda had been sitting on a landing about three feet square. Lanny had been inches from pitching down the stairs into the black abyss, falling into the bowels of The Devil's Nest.

Clarinda had vanished.

Uniformed policemen split up on the stairs. Grey lifted Lanny and carried her out of the passageway and into the shadowy light of Lanny's office, directly behind the statue of Pan which had been shoved over on its side. The wall had been battered open by Grey but now Lanny could see a door mechanism. She thought of all the times she'd been frightened by Clarinda and how often she'd wondered at the girl's ability to slip so silently into the office. Now she knew how Clarinda had done it. And now she knew that if she'd wanted to, Clarinda, almost supernaturally strong, could easily have knocked her cold and dragged her to Victor's room.

I had her! How did I let her slip away?

I wanted to revel in the power, that's where I went wrong. I should have swallowed her whole. The appetizer only did what appetizers are supposed to do, awakened my belly. I can't endure one more night.

CHAPTER NINETEEN

Grey carried Lanny down the long hallway to his bedroom. It wasn't until he rested her on his bed and her foot brushed against the mattress that the pain cut through her haze of fear.

"My ankle!"

His worried eyes sharpened as he lay her down with exquisite care. Case said, "We brought every available officer to search, and I called a doctor."

A quiet man in a hastily donned suit, carrying a doctor's bag came past him. "You shouldn't have moved her."

"Grey, don't let them touch me. Don't leave me." Lanny heard the hysteria in her voice and fought to control herself before she started shrieking. Grey was back, leaning over her. The man shouldered his way past Grey and came quickly to the bedside.

"I won't hurt you. I'm a doctor. I need to check you over."

Lanny wanted to scratch the eyes out of the man who separated her from the only anchor that existed for her—Grey. She stared at the ceiling and stopped the words of panic that clamored to escape from her throat. Her chest heaved with the strain of controlling herself. "I'm not hurt, except for my ankle."

Grey, hovering like a storm cloud behind the doctor, she saw Grey's tension threatening to unleash thunder at any available target and increased her effort to gain mastery of her emotions for his sake. She said, "I don't think it's broken."

The doctor turned to check her ankle. "What is this?" He sounded shocked.

Lanny felt the tug on her legs and remembered the chains. She lifted her head and looked down to see a pair of handcuffs snapped onto her ankles. She remembered the weird impression of more people being around her and wondered if, in her fear, she'd created monsters in the dark. Her whole body began to tremble in reaction to the terror she'd just lived through. Her legs shook until the chains rattled. Her teeth chattered as if she was freezing to death.

"Get a policeman in here and see if he can get these off," the doctor ordered Grey.

Grey said fiercely, "I'm not leaving her."

With barely contained fury the doctor said, "Just go to the doorway and call someone. I'm not here to hurt her."

Grey's eyes flashed with rage. "I'm not leaving her alone again. Never again."

The doctor growled in disgust and jogged to the door. He swung the door wide and yelled,

"I need a key for a pair of handcuffs." He immediately returned to examine Lanny's ankle.

A uniformed officer came in, took in the situation at a glance and moved toward Lanny's brutally tight shackles.

Case stepped into the room. "Don't smudge any fingerprints. Have any of the rest of you touched them?" His sharp, cynical eyes shifted from the doctor to Grey.

Both men said, "No."

Case nodded. "Let me know when I can talk to her."

"It's going to take a while to calm her down. I may need to give her a sedative before I can treat her." The doctor fidgeted as he waited for the policeman to remove the cuffs.

"I want her head clear." Case looked at Lanny.

"She won't be able to answer your questions in her current state," the doctor said. "The sedative might make it easier if she doesn't fall asleep."

"I'll leave medicine to you, Doc. I've got plenty to do in the meantime. We can't find your cousin anywhere, Grey. Can you tell us where the passage leads?"

Grey shook his head. "I didn't even know it existed. Heaven knows how many miles of hallway run behind the walls of this house."

The uniformed officer pulled on a pair of gloves, unlocked the handcuffs and dropped them into a paper bag. He left the room with Case. There were deep red creases around her ankles from the cuffs.

The doctor bent over Lanny's head, lifting her eyelids. Then he ran firm, gentle hands over her ankle.

Grey paced back and forth at the foot of the bed with his eyes always on Lanny, shifting from the man working over her to her leg, then back to her face. He felt like a caged tiger as he watched and waited to pounce on anyone who hurt her.

The doctor wouldn't let up until he'd examined her thoroughly despite Grey's threatening presence, or maybe because of it. As the minutes ticked by, Lanny's shuddering fear eased.

Finally, the doc wrapped an Ace bandage around her leg. "No break, just a mild sprain. There isn't much swelling, most of the damage is because of how tightly the cuff was clipped on. I'd keep her off of her leg at least overnight. I hate to haul her down this mountain if we don't need to. The road is so treacherous and of course we can't bring an ambulance over from the mainland. And it had just started raining again when we drove up here. There's a hurricane whipping up a storm in the Gulf. It's not supposed to hit right here, but it'll be close enough. Bring her in tomorrow for an x-ray if you want to double check."

He looked with kind eyes down at Lanny. "I thought you were going into shock there for a while but it seems to be passing." The doctor pulled a vial of pills from his bag and shook two out onto his hand. "I think you'll need to take these to have much hope of sleeping." He handed them to Lanny. Grey came with a glass of water. Lanny took them without hesitation.

The doctor asked, "How did you get that bump on your head? It looks like it was a beaut. It looks like it's been there a while. How long were you trapped in there?"

"Well—" Lanny stumbled over an excuse.

"Did you fall in the dark?" Grey interjected.

Lanny met his eyes, then said weakly, "I did fall. I don't remember bumping my head, but things are pretty mixed up once I was shoved through that panel. It was pitch dark."

The doctor didn't pursue the subject. He finally packed up his supplies.

As soon as the doctor stepped out of the room Grey moved to her side. Taking one hand with aching gentleness, Grey lifted it to his lips and, between kisses, murmured, "I couldn't find you. I thought this house swallowed you."

Grey quit kissing her hand and roared, "Why didn't you stay with Sally like I told you to?"

He grabbed her shoulders and thought he'd shake an answer out of her. Instead he yanked her into his arms and hugged her.

Wrapping her arms tightly around him, she broke down and cried.

Case came in while Lanny was crying. Grey growled and Case, probably because he could see Lanny wasn't up to questioning, backed out again.

The storm turned violent. Lightning slashed, driving rain buffeted the house, gusting wind rattled the windows. Thunder shook the eaves. Every light in the room blazed. Lanny's tears finally eased and she fell asleep in Grey's arms.

He'd have willingly held her forever, but knowing she'd rest better, Grey let go and covered her securely, then sat in a chair to keep watch.

Tears occasionally slipped from under her closed eyelids. Her lips shone as if they were bee stung. Her skin, always fair, was ashen. She stirred in her sleep every few minutes as if she was awakening, then she'd shudder and cry out. He rose from his chair, sat on the side of the bed and held her until she calmed.

Now, an hour later, he watched her and wanted to cry himself. Because the soft emotion was unthinkable, he got mad. He raged internally at himself. He was supposed to keep her safe. He hadn't even been worried, not just because he'd left her with Sally but because he'd been planning to talk to Estella, Allen and Meredith in the library. He'd thought any danger in the house came from one of them.

The only other person in the house was Trevor, who had been accounted for during the search. Grey had never for an instant considered Clarinda a threat.

Lanny moved in her sleep and muttered, "I'm bad."

Her sleep was so tormented that he wondered if it wasn't a form of torture to let her endure it. But he couldn't bear to put her through another bout of the gut wrenching tears.

The thunder which she hated, adding to the persecutions of the night.

Grey could feel the blood dried on the back of his shirt where several times she'd clawed at him in her panic. The storm passed over at last and, with the fading of the thunder, she finally began breathing more deeply.

A sharp rap sounded at the door. "This is Case. I have to talk to you, Miss Cole."

Grey knew Case had been more patient than any lawman alive. Now the time had come. Grey reached the door just as the knocking began again.

He jerked open the door and whispered gruffly, "She's finally sleeping."

Grey saw genuine regret in Case's eyes. "I have to talk to her, Grey. I need to know what exactly happened before any more time passes."

In an adamant whisper, Grey said, "She told me about it. She repeated herself several times. Clarinda opened the door behind the statue. She pushed Lanny through it. The two of them were trapped in the room for quite a while. Clarinda whispered threats and tried to strangle Lanny. Then Clarinda started screaming and we busted in on them. End of story."

"Grey, I need to know more. I need to know exactly what Clarinda said. We can't find her. We've searched every inch of that passage but in the dark, we could be missing something. In this old mausoleum there may be secret passages off your secret passages. Lanny may know where she went."

"She doesn't."

"I get it, you're protecting her from any more trauma. But under expert questioning sometimes information comes out that's helpful. I have to talk to her."

"No, I won't allow it. She was terrorized tonight, and I let it happen." Grey's fists raised in impotent fury. "I never considered that Clarinda might have been the one who killed Victor."

"Did Clarinda actually confess?"

Grey hesitated. "It sounds like she did."

Case looked at Grey, then looked over Grey's shoulder at Lanny for a long moment. He said with dissatisfaction, "She can sleep a while longer. Step out into the hall and tell me everything she said and what went on around here before you called us."

Grey nodded slightly. "I appreciate it. She's in terrible shape." He switched the lights off, hoping Lanny would sleep better and swung the door so a bit of the hallway light shone on Lanny's face. He stood guard while he talked. A loud clap of thunder made him look in at Lanny, who slept on.

"This rain will never end."

"Tell me what happened. Start at the beginning."

"I was in the library with Estella when Sally came in and said Lanny hadn't come back from going to her office..." Grey took another step away from Lanny's door so his voice wouldn't disturb her.

Lanny jerked awake. Her eyes flickered open and she silently searched the room, sensing danger. She heard the muted sound of male voices on the other side of the doorway. She looked toward the door and saw Grey standing like a sentry, his arms folded. As her eyes scanned the darkened room, a shadowy form emerged with ghost-like silence from a darkened corner.

Lanny gasped but the noise was cut off when a bony hand clamped over her mouth. Was it the same hand that had covered her mouth in the passage? The form lunged forward until a face took shape in the darkness. Estella.

Her eyes snapping with fury, Estella leaned down and hissed in a menacing voice only loud enough to reach Lanny's ears, "Don't try to call Grey."

Rivers of ice-cold fear coursed through Lanny's veins. She grabbed Estella's wrist but Estella's hold never slipped and Lanny's strength was heavily compromised by the sedative. She held Lanny as much by the force of her will and the coldness of her eyes as she did with her strength.

"In each generation the blood of Pierre Devereau flows thick in one of us. Pierre's spirit was too strong to kill."

The thunder rolled. It invaded Lanny's body with its force and Estella's words invaded her along with it until everything Estella said became like a chant of witchcraft, casting a spell of terror on Lanny's soul.

"Victor was the incarnation of Pierre and you have destroyed him."

Estella gripped harder until Lanny's jaw ached. Estella's eyes burned, and Lanny felt herself being utterly dominated by Estella's evil will.

"Bringing out Pierre's soul in this generation fell to me because I possessed it in the last. I had my chance with Victor."

An explosion of thunder cracked through the room. Estella seemed to bring it with her and Lanny had the impression of Estella with her arm raised, preparing to strike her. Lanny mewled behind Estella's grip and her vision cleared and she realized Estella was just as she had been before. Leaning over her, not drawing back to strike.

"Only Victor had the strength to carry on the family name. Only Victor had me as his teacher."

Lanny tried to pull Estella's hand away. The old woman was immovable.

"Victor was our only hope for the future. Now he's dead. And you killed him."

Lanny saw murder in Estella's eyes. She saw a hatred so strong Lanny knew Estella was capable of murder. Estella leaned forward. Thunder crashed against the house as if it wanted inside to have a turn at Lanny.

"I want you to go away, Miss Cole." Estella said with brutal simplicity. "I'm giving you one last chance to walk away from The Devil's Nest. There are others who can be molded in Pierre's image. Trevor has already started down the path. Victor has sons who could be molded. This is your last warning. Leave here with the dawn. Turn your back on Grey and say nothing of this to him or I promise you..." thunder streaked across the sky and exploded over their heads. "...your beloved Grey will be dragged into the bowels of The Devil's Nest and never be seen again. And your grandmother won't live to see another day."

Estella pulled away so that Lanny could see the lightning blaze in the window. In the instant the light blinded her, Estella was gone.

Lanny lay there, quaking with fear.

Estella's voice sounded in her ears like an incantation. It flowed in her blood, enhanced by the drug. The thunder rolled until the room rocked under its assault and again, she saw Estella raise her arm to strike. Then the lightning flashed and Lanny was alone. Lanny didn't know what was real and what was fear. She believed Estella would do exactly what she said she'd do. She had to protect Grey. She had to protect her grandmother.

With a whimper of despair, she pulled the blankets up until they covered her head and cowered away from the terror of The Devil's Nest.

My chance. Right now. Push the door slowly so it doesn't creak. Slide in like a ghost, like a pirate and approach her bed. The knife gleams in my hand like a pirate's treasure. I have time for one quick slash, just like Victor.

There was only a quivering mass under the covers.

At least she knows terror before she dies. I want more. I want to have her in my clutched for a long time, but I can't wait.

CHAPTER TWENTY

Grey opened the door to his bedroom and saw Lanny sleeping under the covers.

He'd finished talking with Case, never stepping more than five feet from Lanny's door. The look of stark terror on her face when he'd finally gotten to her in that hidden stairway would be something he'd carry with him until the day he died.

Case and his men were done with their search and the detective agreed to let Lanny sleep.

He promised, or threatened, Grey wasn't sure which, to return the next day to interview her.

Something scratched in the corner and Grey whirled to look in the absolute darkness. A rat maybe, or a noise that came from the wind? Grey realized how wild the storm had gotten and how fierce the thunder. He breathed a sigh of relief that it hadn't wakened her.

Then he sensed the tension in Lanny and touched her shoulder. She must be caught in a nightmare again. He sat beside her to awaken her and slid an arm under her shoulders. At first, she resisted him. He must have entered her dream somehow. She never spoke and after a few caresses and murmured words of comfort she quit struggling and clung to him with trembling hands as if she thought it was the last time they'd ever touch.

Grey held her tight and thought about Clarinda. It nearly overwhelmed him with rage and guilt to think of what his cousin had become. He wanted to strike back at Clarinda for terrorizing Lanny, but he should have gotten Clarinda out of here years ago. Instead he had turned his back on her. He wouldn't give himself a pass. The responsibility was his because no one else had both the power and the inclination to get her away from The Devil's Nest.

But he'd caved in the face of all the opposition. And now his cousin had become a monster.

He'd often thought that when a child was being abused by one parent and another parent stood by and let it happen, the truly evil one was the one who stood by. Grey had known how Estella was. He had no excuse.

But he'd never seen even a hint of violence in Clarinda. He couldn't reconcile her innocence with the brute who had slit Victor's throat. Grey shuddered when he imagined Clarinda wielding a knife. His guilt made him pull Lanny closer until he surrounded her.

His tight grasp must have disturbed her because she began to make agitated movements.

She was so tense Grey wondered for a moment if she was awake. But she didn't speak to him so the torture must be in her dreams. He knew her sleep wasn't peaceful. He thought again about waking her.

The thunder sounded directly over their heads and Lanny flinched and clung to him. He whispered comfort and massaged her rigid muscles and prayed for this night to end and tomorrow to come so they could leave here and begin their life together somewhere in the sunlight.

Lanny watched the dawn change the sky from charcoal to sullen gray.

She hadn't slept after Estella left, although she feigned sleep in the hopes she could hide her terror from Grey. As surely as thunder would come again, Estella would carry out her threats.

Lanny might have tried to slip away and found a ride down the mountain with the police if Grey hadn't held her hand through the night. Even when he finally slept in his chair, he'd hung on. If she had run, he would've come after her. If that got Grey to safety, Lanny would have risked telling him the truth—except for Grandma Millie.

Grey had said how influential Estella was. Lanny could picture, right now, a nurse, ready to act. It would take a single phone call. Lanny couldn't shake the image of someone holding a pillow over Grandma's face, or dosing her with a powerful drug, or lacing a drink with poison. Grandma was utterly defenseless.

But for all her terror that Estella would hurt Grandma Millie, the deepest fear was for Grey. A vision of Victor with his throat slit wouldn't leave. He'd been a strong man and he was dead.

Estella had gotten in this room somehow. She could get into Grey's. Attack while he was sleeping.

Lanny had to protect him. To do that, she had to end things with Grey in a way that would make him not only let her go, but want her out of his life forever. The need to do it fast was an internal scream that she fought to keep from uttering aloud.

The crepuscular gray of dawn gave way begrudgingly to a smoldering, gloomy, mistshrouded morning. The first distant rumble of thunder gave its warning that the rain planned to come again. Grey sat beside her, in a chair pulled close to the bed. An involuntary movement on her part brought his head up. Half awake, he straightened and leaned closer, studying her, worried.

Lanny loved his touch. She loved him.

Then she thought of Estella.

Not just the visit of the night before and the threats, although that alone chilled her blood. But also the possibility that she might be not only *listening* but watching right this moment. Lanny knew Estella had gotten in last night by some secret means.

Clarinda had said, 'I like to watch. I see everything.'

Estella and Clarinda could both be standing just a few feet away watching them this very instant!

"Let go of me." Lanny pulled away from Grey's grip and climbed out of the bed on the side away from him.

"You're awake." Grey stood from his chair.

She swiped several times as the wrinkled mess of the clothes she'd slept in but it was useless so she ignored her appearance as she gathered her strength for what she must do.

Her ankle buckled but she caught herself before she fell. Carefully putting her weight on her other foot, she tested her ankle gingerly and found it would hold.

To save Grandma Millie, to save Grey, it was time to give Estella what she wanted. Lanny thought of Victor. She forced herself to see that ugly sight of him dead. Someone in this house had the strength and the murderous temperament required to slit his throat. Her heart lurched at what she was about to do, but she never wavered from her certainty that she must do it. She glanced at the air duct and saw that they had never covered it the night before. Then even if Estella weren't watching she would hear everything.

Good!

Smiling, Grey came around the bed and reached for her. She stepped back, wincing at her tender ankle.

The smile vanished from Grey's face. "You're supposed to stay off of that. Here lean on me."

"Don't touch me!" Lanny backed farther away from him, thinking wildly of what she could say that would make him believe she was serious after the way she'd acted the last few days. It was almost too easy. In many ways it was exactly what she wanted to say, except she didn't include Grey in any of her horror at the people who lived in this house.

"Angel, I know you're upset..."

"Upset?" she screeched. Yes, far too easy. "After what this family put me through last night you think *upset* covers it? I don't know what I've been thinking of these last few days. I wanted out of here while Victor was still alive. I must have been out of my mind to even consider tying myself to you and this family. I'm leaving, and I don't ever want to see you or any of your sick, nasty relatives again."

Lanny turned her back on him so she could nurture her anger without looking at his compassionate expression.

"Don't get my family mixed up with me." Grey's hands settled on her shoulders. She wrenched them away and cautiously moved. Her ankle bore her weight just fine now that she was ready for the pain.

She headed for the door that connected their rooms. "I'm packing my bags and getting out of here. The only reason I let myself get caught up in your ludicrous wedding plans was because that crack on the head scrambled my brains for awhile. I was feeling weak, and like a weakling I put my fate in someone else's hands."

Grey got in front of her and blocked her way out of the room. His expression was pure compassion. How could she make him give up on her, on the idea of them being together if he just kept being kind and understanding?

"I'll accept that you want to get out of here. I'll even accept that you dread the idea of joining yourself to this family. But I won't accept that you don't have feelings for me. I know it hasn't been long enough. But what's between us is special. It's real. I'll find a safe place for you this morning and come back alone for Clarinda. Then we'll spend time together, the way two people should, rather than this rushed business. When you're healed and the fear is behind us and our feelings have had a chance to grow, we'll be together."

Lanny knew Estella was listening. She knew Estella wouldn't believe anything other than a total break. And Estella had heard that Grey would take Lanny away, then come back alone. She might even now be planning his death.

She didn't know what it would take but she thought of an attack that would have devastated her. "You may or may not be part of this insanity, Grey, but the thought of Devereau blood in my children's veins is disgusting. I want children someday with a man I can *respect*. A man I can trust all the way to his soul, not someone doing his best to deny his true nature. I can never have that kind of faith in you. I'll always know that the day will come when something scratches you too deep and the blood of a ghoul will come gushing out. The same blood that made Victor and Clarinda evil and your aunt into a twisted old fiend." *Take that Estella.* "I won't have that for my children. I couldn't love children who had such evil in them."

Grey's face had gone pale as she slashed at him with her vicious tongue. "Lanny, don't make a decision when you're hysterical."

"I'm not hysterical. I'm making sense for the first time since we've met. I want out of this house and I want you out of my life. Forever!"

"Lanny..." Grey still had that expression on his face that said she just needed time and safety and everything would go on as before. Lanny needed to find in Grey that part of who he was, the descendant of a murdering pirate.

Suddenly she thought of a way. "Do you remember when I got my memory back...?" Lanny wondered if Estella had realized Lanny had amnesia. It didn't matter now. "...you said, 'this is the real you isn't it?' At the time I didn't know what you meant except that I was giving you some opposition to your domineering treatment of me for the first time."

"Domineering? I saved you. Covered for you. When have I..."

Lanny thought of Estella and didn't want Grey to say anything incriminating out loud so she cut him off. "You were half right. That was about half of the real me."

"Half?" Grey's brow was furrowed with confusion.

"Today I'm all the way back. This me, the real me. And I'm not interested in what you're offering. You had feelings for an illusion, Grey. You found a real live damsel in distress in your house and planned to protect her for the rest of your life while we lived happily ever after. And when I was feeling so vulnerable, I wanted a knight in shining armor to protect me from the world." And she still did desperately.

"But that's not who I am. I'm self-sufficient." That was true so why did she depend on Grey and trust him so completely? "I'd suffocate with you. You think you're better than Victor but you're the same kind of man. He manipulated me with lies and you've been doing the same thing while I was too injured to think clearly. Well, no thanks. I don't need some overbearing man running my life."

She didn't need him, that was true. She'd always taken care of herself. But she *wanted* him so badly she felt her heart breaking even as she saw his sweet concern alter into something hard and cruel. A pirate's face.

As she tried to hurt the man she loved, she realized that a lot of what she said had a grain of truth to it. She was angry at this whole family and she did have serious doubts about being tied to it.

She even had doubts about Grey. She'd seen enough evidence of his family's indecent behavior. How did he escape without being touched by it? Had he? How could she think she was in love after so short a time?

The whole thing was irrational and she suddenly didn't want any part of it and she put real venom into it when she twisted the knife deeper. "In your own way you treat women just as shabbily as Victor. You think any decent woman would tie herself to a man whose blood runs thick with the madness of his ancestors? If you had any respect or true feelings for me, you'd get away from me and stay away forever. If there's no one here to drive me to town, I'll just wait until the next time the police have to come up here for something you or your twisted family does. Then as soon as I can clear it with the police I'm going home to try and remember how normal people live. I don't ever want to see you again."

Lanny walked around him as he stood blocking her way.

He never moved—as if he were the loser in a life and death game of freeze tag. She opened the door to her bedroom and shut it crisply.

He never left her side again all night. And I can't wait. My knife, so shiny, so sharp. I can't let it go to waste. Maybe there's someone else...

CHAPTER TWENTY-ONE

G rey heard the door slam behind him and the noise jerked him out of his rigid fury.

He whirled to barge into the room and scald her, then her words came back to him and he stopped.

"I couldn't love children who had such evil in them."

"I'd suffocate with you."

Who was he really going after? He was staggered by the sudden change in her. Was it possible that the woman he'd been falling in love with the last—what? Three days? Had it only been that long? What kind of fool binds himself to a woman he's only known that long?

Was this insulting, arrogant woman the real Lanny? He stared at the door and said in a hoarse whisper, "Who are you?"

The bald fact was, he didn't know. He stumbled as he backed the few steps toward his chair and sank down on it. He hadn't known her long enough to tell if this cruel, spiteful woman was the real her. Or had the vulnerable nymphet in the shower been her? Or the frightened, intelligent woman he'd been protecting?

He didn't know.

He balled his hands into fists that still shook with the anger she'd stirred in him. You were supposed to spend time, a year or two, getting to know someone before you married them, so you would be able to judge situations like this. He still believed that at least part of her cruelty this morning sprang out of fear. She was driven by trauma until getting away from The Devil's Nest, and from everyone associated with it, was more important that any feelings she had for him.

But whatever her reasons, she'd said awful, ugly things. She couldn't love a child they had together. Those words burned into his heart and burned away his feelings for her. Just as simply as that those feelings were gone.

With sudden purpose he stood from the bed and walked to her door. He banged on it twice with the side of his fist. Lanny came to the door and yanked it open with the same taut, angry expression she'd had before. His first instinct was to drag her into his room and kiss her until she begged his forgiveness and pleaded with him to let her stay. That might have worked with his Angel, but not with the cold, insulting Miss Cole. She'd already pulled on another boring outfit. Grey looked past her and saw an open suitcase on her bed.

"I'll be ready to drive you to town in half an hour," he said through clenched teeth. "Anything you leave behind gets thrown in the garbage."

He slammed the door in her face and started changing into fresh clothes. He couldn't wait to be rid of her. But as he dressed, he was struck by a sudden pang of longing for his Angel. He wondered if he'd spend the rest of his life loving a woman who didn't exist.

Grey walked out into the stormy morning and got a car out of the garage, noticing another car was already gone. Grey pulled his up to the front door. As he entered the house, Estella appeared in the hallway beside the stairs and watched in brooding silence. Grey stared at her, hating her and everything about this house that had spawned him. The malevolence in her gaze reflected his own feelings.

Lanny appeared and set two suitcases and an overnight bag at the top of the stairs. She went back to her room as Grey, suddenly in a rush to be rid of her, jogged up the stairs to bring her things down. He carried them out to the car to the sound of approaching thunder.

Lanny made two more trips bringing out boxes, carrying the last one down herself. She passed Grey on the stairway but they never made eye contact. He picked up the remaining boxes and turned in time to see Lanny reenter the front door, soaked from the pouring rain. Then Lanny caught sight of Estella and froze under her frigid stare.

Grey read such fear in Lanny's eyes that he almost charged to her rescue.

'I couldn't love any child we had together.'

Those weren't words a man could forgive. He simply brought the boxes down. As he came abreast of her she turned away from Estella and looked at him for the first time. He saw pure contempt for him in her eyes as if her dislike for Estella had been fully settled on his shoulders. Her jaw was so rigid he didn't think she was capable of speech.

Grey had battled his whole life to be separate from his family. He'd carved out a life almost completely divorced from theirs. To find a woman he thought he could care for who couldn't judge him apart from the blood he shared with his ancestors, struck him in the most vulnerable part of his heart. No, this wasn't something a man could forgive.

Tension, taut like a wire quivering under an immense strain, stretched between them. He was furious at her yet drawn to her, like a wolf to a poisoned carcass. All he could think of was to get her away from him. Get her out of his life and never set eyes on her again before the rage that simmered inside of him erupted into violence. He had never laid his hands on a woman in anger. He'd never thought he could. But right now, his control was so shaky he couldn't risk being near her much longer.

"If this is everything let's get going."

She jerked her head in one hard nod of agreement and followed him out the door into the relentless gusting rain.

They drove away from The Devil's Nest in a silence broken only by the rumble of thunder.

Halfway to The Overhang, Grey had the windshield wipers going on full speed in a futile attempt to push aside the sheeting rain. In the gloom ahead Grey saw a lone figure rushing toward them. He recognized a very bedraggled Allen slipping and sliding up the road. Grey had been creeping along and pulled to a stop almost instantly. He saw the look of desperation on Allen's face, opened his door and stepped out into the lashing rain just as Allen staggered and fell against Grey, soaking Grey's clothes with mud.

Allen clawed at Grey and panted heavily. "The road...my car almost went over the edge. The Overhang collapsed." Allen caught Grey's shirt front in his filthy hands and broke into desperate sobs, "Meredith...she's inside. My car is buried in mud. I couldn't get to her. It's hanging...she's hanging right on the cliff!"

Grey grabbed Allen without a second's hesitation and thrust him into the back seat of the Jeep. "No emergency vehicles can get up here. We'll use my tow chain to hook your car to mine and get her out."

Grey started the car forward with increased speed, mindful of the treacherous road. "Tell me what we're up against, Allen. How did you get out and not her? How buried is the car?"

Allen slid onto his side and sobbed brokenly. He didn't respond to Grey's questions.

"Allen," Grey yelled. "You've got to pull yourself together. I'm going to need your help."

Grey glanced sideways at Lanny and saw the sharp, determined look in her eye. She might be fed up with him but he knew he could count on her in an emergency.

They rounded the last snakelike curve of the road and saw the devastation. The Overhang had collapsed completely. Thousands of tons of mud and rock covered the road in front of them. The car was buried until little more than its trunk showed. Its hood was steeply canted downward, front tires hanging over the drop off. Shocked by the sight, he fought his car to a full stop.

Lanny gasped, "She can't have survived."

Allen wailed in the back seat.

Lanny shoved her door open, running for Allen's car.

Grey roared, "Come back here." He started driving forward again.

Lanny's ankle threatened to give out as she neared the mudslide and stopped within inches of the black bumper of Allen's car. She started scooping at the mud with her hands.

Grey pulled to a stop within a few yards of the buried car. Its trunk angled upward slightly. He jumped out of the car and shouted over the wind and the rush of the pouring rain, "If you want to help get out of the way."

Lanny had uncovered the back windshield. It was half broken out. Lanny pulled a shred of cloth away from the glass. "Allen must have climbed out this way, then more rock and mud caved off onto the car. I'm going in for Meredith!"

She climbed up on the trunk. A sudden shudder took the heavy car a foot farther over the edge. Grey grabbed her around the waist and pulled her off the trunk. "Don't be a fool. If that car slides off the cliff and you're inside it you'll never get out. You'll die right alongside her."

Lanny wrenched herself away from Grey and his diabolical protective streak. It tempted her to lean against him and let him take care of everything. But turning to him could mean asking him to sacrifice his own life.

"I'll only be inside a second. Give me that towing chain. I'll take it in and wrap it around her. We'll pull her out!"

"I'm hooking it to Allen's car!" Grey shouted over the whipping wind and slashing rain.

Lanny shook her head. She wiped her wrist across her eyes, at the soaking rain that blinded her and yelled over the shrieking wind, "You can't. It's too deeply buried. There's no way we can pull it out from under that mud. If the car goes over yours isn't heavy enough to hold it. But if I'm inside the car hanging on to the chain, with it wrapped around Meredith, we'll swing free even if the car goes."

"Unless it gets hung up on something."

"Give it to me."

"I'll go in," Grey said. "I'll hook the chain to my car and go in myself."

"We need your strength to pull me back. I can't hold your weight." Lanny backed away from him and held out her mud coated hands for the chain. The car slipped another inch. "We don't have time. Give me the chain."

Grey ground his teeth together in barely suppressed rage. He swiped at his face. The car moved again and the metal groaned under the weight of the avalanche. Lanny took the decision out of his hands. She snatched the chain from him and climbed gingerly onto the trunk of the car. The nose of the car eased upward with her weight.

"Lanny, no," Grey cried out.

She didn't look back. She lay on her belly on the trunk and wriggled into the jagged hole.

The front seat was completely buried. Lanny couldn't see any sign of Meredith.

The mud muted Lanny's shouting. Grey heard her calling Meredith's name, nothing else. No response from Meredith. Seconds ticked by. Then a minute. Then five minutes.

He wrapped the chain around his wrists. Bending, he watched fiercely through the shattered back window and watched her feet, he couldn't see much more. The chain vibrated as she manipulated it. Once she seemed to be backing out and he almost dared to breathe again, but she went back in farther. The car front began tipping forward again.

Oozing mud and rocks had filled most of the back seat. The roof, partially caved pressed down from above. Lanny wormed her way forward, shoving mud aside to gain every inch of forward progress. She realized after she started that she didn't know if Meredith was the driver or a passenger. Following her instincts about Meredith and Allen's marriage, Lanny began digging on the driver's side. Within seconds she found a hand extended backward. Lanny kept digging.

"Can you hear me?" Mud slithered in from the driver's side window and splattered her in the face as she yelled. She choked and spit even as she dug. As she uncovered the arm, she realized it led to the passenger's side. She turned her attention to uncovering the smothering mud from the woman's face in hopes she'd be in time before Meredith drowned. Lanny dug frantically as she felt the car shift.

Another sudden gush of mud spated through from the side. It knocked her sideways. She swallowed some of the grit and gagged on it even as she fought her way to the woman. The chain she held in one hand was in her way so she spared a few precious seconds to wrap it under her arms and snap the heavy metal hook so she wouldn't lose it. She tore her hands against the jagged rocks salted through the crushing mud.

She kept on and on, digging and shouting and begging Meredith for some sign that she was still alive. Her arms were exhausted. Breathing hurt. Rivers of filthy water gushed around the thick mud and rocks, soaking her and weighing her down. She pushed mud aside only to have it replaced by more. The car roof bowed farther downward, narrowing the space Lanny had to work and the passenger's side window shattered and mud flooded out, lowering the level of it. With grim determination Lanny kept battling the collapsing mountain. At last she uncovered a shoulder.

"Lanny, get out of there." He couldn't drag on the chain because he might pull it right out of her hands. Standing on the rear bumper, he tilted it back to a more level keel.

Then, even with him on it, the car began slowly, inch by inch, tipping.

"Lanny, right now. Get out of there. The car's going over." The car continued a steady tilt that sent the trunk higher.

"Just a little more," she muttered tersely to herself. "Just a few more inches. Please God, please just give me those inches."

The car began tilting forward as if God was warning her that time was up. Lanny knew she only had seconds to pull the woman free. The tilting car sent mud raining through the front seat and out the broken window on the passenger's side. It lowered the level of mud until Lanny could see without doubt that it was Meredith in the car. As the muck rained away uncovering more of Meredith, Lanny knew she had her miracle.

Then she knew it was all for nothing.

"I'm pulling you out now." He gripped the chain, prayed she had a firm enough hold that he'd not tear it out of her hands, and tensed to pull just as Lanny screamed.

It was a bloodcurdling cry of pure unadulterated horror.

"Pull!" Lanny screamed again. "Pull! Pull! Now Grey! Now!"

Grey reeled that chain as the buried car's trunk tipped up and up, lifting Grey into the air. He had seconds to get off this car or he was going over the cliff with it. But he'd go rather than abandon Lanny.

Legs came out the window. She was frantically shoving herself out backward.

Allen's car lurched forward. The chain caught on something and the car slid instead of tilting.

Grey dragged on the chain, watching as Lanny floundered trying to back up. Had she fastened the chain to Meredith or herself or both?

He had no chance against the weight of Allen's car and all those tons of mud. They were all going over the cliff.

With a sudden snap the chain broke free of whatever it was hung up on. Grey fell backward off the car and landed with a splashing thud in the soaked road. Someone was yanked roughly out of the window and landed beside him. She was so coated with mud Grey wasn't sure who he pulled from the car.

The car tilted until its tail pointed straight up in the air, hung for a second in the slashing, blinding rain as Grey battled the ankle-deep mud to get to it and hold it on the cliff with his bare hands.

With a shriek of tearing metal, the car dropped out of sight. With a cry of defeat Grey crawled toward the ledge. He got there, dropping to his belly to look over the cliff at the plunging, rolling wreckage of the car. The woman he'd saved rolled onto her back beside him and Grey recognized Lanny.

"Dead," Lanny gasped. "She's dead." Lanny, oblivious to the pounding rain and the mud coating her from head to toe, rolled onto her stomach to look over the ledge. Grey shoved to his knees beside her. Together they watched the car tumble down the jagged mountainside whirling, rolling over a dozen times. For a moment it was flying free, airborne, then it hit another outcropping and bursting into flames.

At last it hurled itself into the angry, greedy sea with a thunderous splash. The car floated belly up for a few seconds, fire on water. Rain, sea, land, fire...God's great gifts. God's great destroyers. Then with a hiss that Grey could hear even from far above, the flames extinguished and the car sank out of sight.

The sea swallowed up a life.

Lanny muttered, "She's dead. Dead."

Grey untwisted the chain from his wrists and staggered to his feet, watching Lanny drag breath into her lungs. She pushed herself up on her elbows and leaned away from the brink and began to heave and choke as she vomited into the soaked ground. Every time she found a breath to spare, she whispered, "Dead."

Their fight completely forgotten, Grey dropped to his knees beside her and held her hair back through her retching, then pulled her into his arms to comfort her.

"Meredith," Allen screamed as if he were dying himself. Grey jumped up and grabbed Allen when it looked like he might cast himself off the cliff after his wife. Allen fought with him.

"Let me go. I don't want to live without...Meredith...Meredith."

Grey hung on tight. He hadn't noticed Lanny get up until she caught an arm Allen was using to strike at Grey.

"Allen," Grey roared, "Allen, stop. She's gone. There's nothing we can do. I'm sorry but she's gone."

The fight went out of Allen. Grey's voice dropped to a whisper, "She's gone."

Allen sank to his knees and began to sob. He leaned forward until his forehead was on the muddy ground.

Grey caught Allen's weight and virtually lifted him into his arms. He half carried, half dragged his grief-stricken cousin away from the ledge. "I'm sorry, Allen. I know you loved her."

Grey tucked him into the back seat. "We have to get you home."

He turned to help Lanny but she'd already limped to Grey's car and climbed into the passenger's seat, a dejected mud-soaked waif who trembled under the assault of the last few minutes. And still she held up, she kept moving. Grey wanted to help her. He wanted to be her strength, but she never looked at him. Instead she sat huddled against the door and stared at her hands tightly clenched in her lap.

Every few seconds she'd say, "Dead." She wasn't talking to anyone.

She'd just escaped death by inches herself. Still battered from last night, heaven knew how many times she'd been hit being dragged out of that car. Of *course* she was trembling. Of *course* she was withdrawn. Grey sank back onto the seat and, after gathering his strength for a moment, he stared at the road ahead of him.

Gone.

There was no road. There was no way out of here.

He was trapped with a woman he might love who hated him for the blood that flowed in his veins.

With a family that hated him for having a moral code.

With a murderer.

With one long look at Lanny, he stretched his arm across the back of the seat and turned to see Allen, laying on his side, coated in mud, sobbing. The weight of it threatened to crush Grey like a mountain's worth of mud and stone. Then he looked at the road behind him. Nothing would change what he had to do.

Go home. To The Devil's Nest.

Grimly, he started the car. The vehicle inched along backward, sliding and sputtering as it clawed its way up the hill. There was no place on the earth that he more passionately did *not* want to be.

Another family member dead. Another senseless tragedy to add to centuries of misery for the Devereaus. His backing on the slippery road took concentration but he had time to spare for one thought.

Lanny was right. She shouldn't get involved with the Devereaus.

They were almost gone now. The bloodline nearly extinct. Allen had no children and, with the love of his life dead, most likely never would. Victor had died without ever acknowledging any of his children, beyond Grey sending them money. Those children would be raised away from the legacy of evil. Clarinda was unlikely to ever give birth. Grey could cut Trevor off, kick him out. It would be the greatest favor one man had ever done for another.

Grey had always seen himself with a family someday but now he decided never to let that happen. It could all end with him. Estella would die. He would grow old alone and die. The legacy would die.

The Devil's Nest would be left empty. The family would be erased from the face of the earth. He'd worked hard to restore the Grey Trust Estella had drained. He'd nurtured the few remaining investments until he'd rebuilt an empire. He'd paid all the debts on The Devil's Nest mainly for reasons of honor, because the people who held that debt needed to be repaid. Now he saw that his greatest accomplishment wouldn't be career or money. It would be to not have children. It would make the world a better place if no Devereau blood coursed through the veins of anyone on this earth. It was within Grey's power to end it.

It would be his epitaph.

CHAPTER TWENTY-TWO

Lanny shuddered and tried to recreate what she'd seen in that car. She focused on it, then she shied away and tried to wipe it from her mind. Then she focused again.

"Dead." She couldn't talk about it now. Not with Allen in the car. Not with Grey hating her and wanting her gone, with his life in the balance as long as she stayed here. Meredith. Dead. Not from drowning in mud or being crushed under rock.

Meredith. With her throat slashed.

Lanny felt her stomach heave again but her belly was empty. She swallowed the bile and tried to remember.

And tried to forget.

Allen sobbed brokenly. "My Meredith."

Maybe Lanny had misread what she'd seen. Yes, she'd seen a gaping wound in Meredith's neck. But she'd been in a car wreck. Maybe she'd been hit by flying glass or a sharp rock. There was mud everywhere. Maybe what had looked like a wound was really...something else. Maybe Lanny misunderstood.

Allen's sobs cut across the fragile hold she had on herself. She wanted to scream at him— ask him if he'd done something to cause the avalanche to cover up the crime. Did that mean Allen had killed Victor, too? For a stunning moment Lanny was very sure it meant exactly that. But his grief seemed so genuine.

Then she had another sickening thought, maybe if Meredith's throat had been cut, it had happened after Allen left her in the car. He might not even know it had happened. He'd walked a long way trudging in deep mud, driving rain and high winds. Someone would have had time. If Clarinda prowled the hidden passageways of The Devil's Nest maybe she also knew back trails and shortcuts down the mountainside. Grey had said there were underground caverns and caves all across the face of the cliff where he'd explored as a child. Maybe one of those reached around to The Overhang. Maybe Clarinda had come upon Meredith trapped in the car and, with a new taste for killing whetted by Victor's murder, slit her throat.

Lanny thought of Estella. It was unthinkable that an eighty-year-old woman could reach this remote part of the road and climb into the car and hurt Meredith. But maybe Meredith had already been dead when Allen had put her in the car. Maybe he was just under his mother's control... Lanny could attest to how Estella could wield power. Even if he knew she'd been murdered, Allen's grief could still be real. It just didn't override the chains that bound him to the Devereaus.

She thought of Sally and her hatred of the Devereaus and the handy way she wielded her paring knife. And Trevor, he was the one with the strength and youth to best do this.

Lanny's head spun from the possibilities and dry convulsions heaved in her stomach again.

She still had flashbacks of Victor's deathly white skin awash in a river of flowing crimson. If she hadn't seen that so few days ago, she'd have never imagined Meredith's muddy throat was cut. Maybe this was simple exhaustion and emotional collapse. Maybe she was making it all up.

Maybe.

"Allen, try and get a hold of yourself." Grey cut into her terrible thoughts and she was grateful for it. He came to a wider spot in the road and made an expert three point turn.

He drove toward The Devil's Nest. "We have to call the police. We have to report this. Maybe if there's a let-up in the rain, they can get a crew up here and open the road. We're completely cut off now. No way in or out. But we'll find a way even if we have to climb a mountain to do it. And once we get out, we have to abandon The Devil's Nest and do it now—all of us, I don't care if it kills Clarinda or makes Estella foam at the mouth. We have to leave before anything else happens."

Lanny had almost convinced herself that she'd made up Meredith's murder. She had nearly stopped trembling. That was the only reason she caught the thread of anxiety in Grey's determined voice. What did he expect to happen? Could he possibly think Meredith's death was other than an accident? Why else would he be so determined to get everyone away from The Devil's Nest?

Lanny tried to pull herself together and ask him. She said with faltering speech, "No one can get in here. The road can't be opened in this weather. We have to wait out the hurricane."

Grey didn't even look at her. Lanny was grateful because she wasn't ready to deal with his anger yet.

"And since the storm seems to never end," he said, "we're trapped in The Devil's Nest."

"That about sums it up."

They drove the rest of the way with the only human sound being Allen's sobbing.

Lanny got out of the car the minute it pulled to a stop. She grabbed one of her suitcases, left Grey to deal with his cousin and headed through the downpour toward the house. She had to make it clear to Estella that she was only back because of the avalanche. Things were still over between her and Grey.

She pulled open one of the heavy front doors and stepped inside. There was no one in sight. With a determined squaring of her shoulders Lanny turned toward her old room. She wasn't going to face Estella at such a disadvantage. She'd wash the muck away. Climb into one of her boring outfits and go make certain Estella knew Lanny had broken things off with Grey even though she was trapped in the house for now.

Lanny trotted up the stairs not even bothering to turn around when the door opened behind her, and she heard Allen whimpering. She listened for her name. She wished for her name on Grey's lips even while she was terrified he would call her back and—already weakened from what she'd seen—what she thought she'd seen—she'd cling and beg his forgiveness.

He didn't speak.

She didn't linger.

She scrubbed for what seemed like forever before the water stopped flowing brown off her body and out of her hair. She uncovered a hundred tiny cuts and scrapes from digging in the rocky mud. They started to sting as the soap cleaned them. Pain fit her mood so she didn't mind it much. She stepped out of the shower, dressed quickly and headed for her showdown.

She went straight to Estella's rooms on the ground floor, knocked sharply twice and barged in. Just because she was letting Grey go for his own safety, didn't mean Lanny meant to cower. Estella wasn't in the room. Trevor was.

He jumped to his feet from the place he'd been kneeling beside a closet door. He quickly swung shut a panel that vanished when it was closed.

"Another entrance to the passageway?" Lanny said tightly. She knew, from Estella's appearance in her room last night, that the house must be riddled with them.

Trevor stammered as he stepped toward her. He looked uncertain... no...guilty. Lanny was suddenly sure Estella had no idea Trevor was poking around in her sitting room. Trevor wiped at a cobweb that dangled from his hair and brushed at the dirt on his knees. He'd been in that passageway. Lanny wondered what he was up to.

His face lost its guilty expression and it was replaced with the slightly oily smirk of the overgrown adolescent that had been there each time he hit on her. "We really shouldn't be in here, sweetheart. How about my room instead?"

"This time I'm not buying it, Trevor. Why the act?"

His eyes hardened slightly but otherwise his attitude didn't change. "You think I'm lying when I say I want you?"

"I think everything you do is a lie," Lanny retorted, sure even as she said it, that it was the truth. "Including, I would imagine, that you're any relation to the Devereaus."

"Come with me to my bedroom, and I'll prove how honest I am about my interest in you." Trevor smiled as he walked toward her. Lanny had to will herself to remain where she was.

Just as he reached out to stroke her arm Lanny said pointedly, "How about instead we wait here for Estella, and I tell her that you were snooping through her room?"

Trevor's hand tightened on her arm and he pulled her full against him. "You really think Estella would take your word over mine? Estella and I are very close. I'm her next project. I'm going to replace Victor in her affections and in her will."

Lanny watched his eyes. He said the words just right but his eyes were too calculated. Too cold. She knew in that second that Trevor had an agenda of his own and, while it might be tapping into the Grey Trust, Lanny thought it was something else.

"I don't know what you're up to, Trevor, and I have to tell you, I really don't care. I need to have a talk with Estella and since she's not here I'm going to go looking somewhere else. If you'll let go of my arm, I'll leave you to your hunting."

Trevor's eyes were cold. Lanny knew he didn't want to let her go, but while she saw definite signs that Trevor could be a dangerous man, she didn't think she was looking into the eyes of a cold-blooded murderer. Just to experiment she said blandly, "Have you heard that Meredith is dead?"

"Yes, I've heard Allen crying in the hallway."

No outward reaction. "Did you know she'd had her throat slashed before she went over the cliff?"

Stunned amazement made him jerk back a step from her. He dropped her arm. His eyebrows slammed down until they almost met. His gray eyes narrowed until they glinted fire. With steel underlying his voice he asked rapidly, "Are you sure? You saw it? No one said anything about her being murdered!"

Lanny had her evidence. No one could fake those reactions. Which meant Trevor hadn't killed her, if she'd been killed.

"To answer your first question, no, I'm not sure. There was so much mud and I didn't have much time but I saw something. There was glass and sharp rocks. I don't know. I couldn't swear to it but it looked like what happened to..." Lanny clamped her mouth shut. She couldn't say it looked like Victor. She wasn't supposed to have ever seen Victor. "...it made me think of what happened to Victor."

Trevor's eyes looked sharp and calculating as he studied her. Lanny's mind flickered to something, a lost memory maybe. There was something familiar about Trevor's remote intensity. Lanny remembered Trevor lurking in the upstairs alcove. And he knew about the passageway. He probably knew every secret in this house and she was wasting her time lying to him. For some reason she was briefly tempted to tell him what had happened the night of Victor's murder. What she'd seen in Allen's car. Spill her guts about everything just because this Trevor was so much different than the shallow, slutty man who'd been hounding her since she'd arrived at The Devil's Nest.

She quashed the impulse.

"I've enjoyed our talk but I have to find Estella." Lanny turned to leave the room.

"What could you possibly have to discuss with me?" Estella's voice could have frozen Mt. Vesuvius and saved Pompeii. Lanny stared in those dagger eyes and wished like crazy one of them had been born back then so they didn't have to talk now.

"I believe," Estella said acidly, "I've instructed you to call me Mrs. Devereau."

Lanny stared at her and tried not to quake. Estella was one scary old bat. "I need to talk to you, Mrs. Devereau. Will you please ask Trevor to leave us alone for a moment?"

Estella held Lanny's gaze for a long minute then, when Lanny didn't back down, Estella's eyes shifted ever so definitely to Trevor. "Leave us," she ordered.

Lanny glanced quickly at Trevor who was slightly behind her. He had that lapdog look on his face again.

"Yes, Ma'am." Trevor was so obedient and obliging he almost trotted out of the room.

Lanny waited a minute to see if he'd return with Estella's slippers in his mouth.

"You're supposed to be gone from here I believe, Miss Cole?" Estella said turning her attention back to Lanny.

"You know why I'm not," Lanny said evenly. "You had to have heard about the road collapsing. Everything is over between Grey and me. I can't get away from here, but I didn't defy you. I want you to know I'll do anything...anything to keep..." To beg for Grey's life right now gave Estella too much power. Let Estella think it was Grandma Millie who most worried her. "...my grandma safe."

Estella's eyes never wavered as they tried to freeze Lanny to death. At last she said, "I want you to move down here. There is an unused bedroom at the far end of my suite. You'll stay there. You'll have nothing to do with Grey or anyone else in this house. Any food you eat, I'll have Sally bring to you. The avalanche tore out the phone lines."

And Lanny remembered that there was no cell service at this house and no internet. Even the power was such a low voltage it was hard to keep a computer charged. It was why she'd taken all her notes by hand.

"None of us can call anyone."

"Like the people who are caring for my grandmother? To warn them she might be in danger?" Lanny would obey Estella but the awful old woman would know Lanny held her in contempt.

"And you'll have no visitors—certainly not Grey. And no more work."

The last order was too strident. She overplayed her hand. Lanny knew in that minute that her work was what all this was about. Estella wanted it stopped. But Estella had started it. If she wanted the research to cease why hadn't she just fired Lanny? The answer lay in that last hidden notebook.

Lanny did her best to keep her thoughts from showing on her face. "I'll do just as you say, Mrs. Devereau."

"And you'll be the first one out of here when we find a way."

"I will leave as soon as possible, and I'd *prefer* to be left alone until I go." That was no more than the truth. If only this family would leave her alone.

Estella commanded, "Follow me."

Estella led Lanny to a minuscule back room about twice as wide as the lone twin bed in it.

There was one side table bearing a lamp.

"The power is out, too. There is a lantern and matches." Estella seemed to revel in telling Lanny just how gloomy this little room would become with only a single weak lantern.

Stepping aside, Estella gesture for Lanny to enter. Once inside Lanny sank onto the bed.

Estella stood in the open doorway. "I'm not going to lock you in. I'm not going to issue any threats. If Grey comes to see you, I'll let him in. But rest assured Miss Cole, the details of your grandmother's pathetic life are well known to me and arrangements have been made. So, think very carefully about each word you speak."

Estella closed the door with a definite click, no histrionics for the lady of the house. Lanny looked around the barren little cell. A servant's room most likely. Perfect. Mrs. Devereau had assured her she was the help on numerous occasions. Lanny sighed and realized she ought to be grateful. It's a wonder she hadn't been sleeping in here right along.

Trevor eased himself away from the wall inside the passageway when Estella left. He muttered to himself, "Lanny girl, how did you ever get yourself mixed up with this bunch of loons?"

He was tempted to go in and talk to her again. He'd enjoyed having Lanny here. He was really rooting for the kid to make it out alive.

Following the passageway up to Lanny's office, he stepped out from behind Pan. Once he'd found the entrance in here, he'd kept busy exploring the honeycomb of secret hallways. He had only scratched the surface of the web of walkways and rooms. And just before Lanny had come into Estella's room, he'd stumbled onto an entrance to an underground cavern that looked as if it went all the way to sea level.

He decided to have a more thorough look in this office. He made of point of keeping up with Lanny's research and he knew she wrote every day, but the last few days were missing. He went to her desk just as a deafening bolt of thunder slammed into the house.

Clicking on the lamp, he got nothing. He clicked it again, then realized there was no light from the hallway, hadn't been since he'd come out of the passageway.

The electricity had gone out. He went down to his rooms, knowing there was a hurricane lantern stored there. Standing in his room, lit by the miserable gray light of the storm, he heard a woman crying. He neither ran toward the sound of distress, nor ran for his life. He'd been in this rock pile long enough to recognize the sound.

Silver Girl.

He wasn't a man who believed in ghosts but he was seriously considering making an exception for The Devil's Nest.

Grey slammed down the phone. "The lines are down." He tried his cell but it never worked up here.

There was no way to call out.

He turned to look at Allen, huddled in the chair, soaked with mud, sobbing into his hands.

"It doesn't matter." Grey thought of the avalanche. "No one can get up that road anyway."

It would take days. Why did they live in this wretched house perched up here on top of a mountain? What kind of fool built his house hanging off a cliff? What kind of stupid family kept living in it, when the most humble little bungalow would be warmer and more comfortable?

Grey tried to commiserate with Allen, but all he could do was feel contempt. Grey was torn between comforting him and slapping his face.

He'd stayed until now, afraid to leave the distraught man alone, but Grey finally couldn't bear being in the same room with him anymore. "Allen, I'm going to wash up. You'd better do the same."

Allen didn't respond, unless maybe he cried a little harder.

There was water but it was stone cold. Grey emerged from the shower wondering what had become of Lanny. As he dressed in his warmest clothes to fight the frigid chill of the water, he tried to quell the protective streak that kept nudging him to find her and take care of her.

He decided he could at least tell her there was no way off this mountain for the foreseeable future. He checked in her room—empty except for a single open suitcase on her bed. Next, he tried her office—deserted. Standing there, where Lanny worked, he studied the gaping hole he'd kicked in the wall.

Clarinda had known about it and he hadn't. She'd always disappeared. Even as a small child they'd accepted that peculiar habit of hers and learned she'd turn up eventually. If he found Clarinda, then Lanny would be safe. High time he began searching out the secrets of The Devil's Nest.

He never came home without a flashlight and plenty of batteries, power outages were too common. He got the light out of his luggage and went into the dark passageway.

It would keep him busy so he wouldn't go crawling to Lanny and beg her to overlook his family and come back to him.

Now it's not the hunger, it's revenge. It's safety. Before, I just wanted her to die because her neck was so long and I wanted to put my hands on her. I wanted to watch the blood spill. But now Meredith is dead and it's all Lanny's fault.

CHAPTER TWENTY-THREE

Sitting in the little cell of a room, Lanny could think again, and she started to get mad.

Who was in this house anyway? Yes, Clarinda was surprisingly strong, but Lanny was ready for her now and that included being ready for her to walk through walls.

Estella's main strength was being terrifying, but after dangling off a cliff with a murdered woman, not to mention waking up in bed with a murdered man, Lanny was almost getting used to living with terror. And with the phone out, no orders could be sent to hurt Grandma.

Allen was curled up crying last time Lanny had seen him.

And Sally was wicked with her knife, but Lanny could outrun her, and besides she didn't think Sally had a thing to do with any of this.

Grey might have managed to kill Victor, but why conk Lanny in the head to set her up for the murder, then provide her with an alibi…and his alibi for Meredith's murder was unshakable. Only Trevor was at full strength, and Lanny's little talk with him had convinced her that whatever his plans for the Devereaus, he was no murderer.

"I'm sick of being afraid." Her voice echoed in the little room. If someone heard her, well, fine. She could handle whatever came her way.

"It's time to kick over a few rocks and see what crawls out." The stupid monstrosity of a house was apparently riddled with secret passageways, so maybe it was time to find out just where they led. She knew for a fact that at least one of them led to her office and she wanted her notebook.

Something in that notebook, something she'd discovered that last day, had set this into motion.

Estella's eyes had flashed cold fire when she'd said, "And no more work." But there was more behind it than being fired. Estella didn't want Lanny digging up any more secrets about Pierre Devereau. She didn't want one more sentence read from Giselle's diary. But what in the world could Lanny have found that so upset Estella? Pierre was pure evil. He didn't just commit every possible sin, he reveled in them, boasted of them. No diary page exposing the Devereau dirty linen would have so much as turned one of Estella's perfectly controlled hairs.

No way to know what had upset Estella so much without looking at that notebook. Lanny wrote daily and knew where she hid her notebooks, but she couldn't remember what that last notebook contained.

Clenching her fists, Lanny decided the Devereaus had pushed her around and tormented her for the last time. She carefully examined the walls of her Spartan room. Nothing here. Why would anyone put a secret passage in this wretched little room anyway?

Lanny listened to Estella moving around. The old bat always sat in the library reading for an hour before dinner. Then she insisted on at least four courses, almost always eaten alone.

Victor's death hadn't disrupted her routine, why would Meredith's?

Right on schedule, Estella quietly opened and closed her door. Lanny waited until her footsteps faded. Slipping out of the little cell she'd been stashed in, Lanny entered Estella's room.

She needed to use the passageway Trevor had come out of so no one could see her in the hallway.

Without electricity, she'd be in total darkness. Lanny remembered being trapped in that passageway with Clarinda and shuddered. The lantern in her room. Lanny ran and got it and after a few fumbling minutes, found the lever that opened the panel Trevor had come through.

Feeling as if Estella was nearly breathing down her neck, Lanny took a step to duck into the opening and her eyes landed on a long, silver candlestick on Estella's cluttered mantle. It made a likely weapon. She snatched it up and hoped there were so many things jammed onto the mantle the missing candle and its holder would probably go unnoticed, but Lanny was beyond caring.

With her lantern in one hand and the candlestick in the other, Lanny headed into the passageway.

She took a moment to study the latch so she could let herself back out, then closed the door. She listened for a footstep or a voice or the presence of the family ghost. All she heard was her own accelerated breathing. There seemed to be the presence of salty air, dank but not smothering. Lanny wondered if this passage opened into a cave so someone could get outside unseen.

Inching her way along, she stayed in contact with the wall with the hand carrying the candlestick. There was a low ceiling overhead that made the space tight enough she felt almost as if she'd locked herself into a crypt. She slid each foot forward carefully, testing the floor, mindful of that stairway she'd almost fallen down when Clarinda had attacked her. She held her lantern as high as possible but it seemed to only light up the small space in which she stood, what lay behind or ahead was shrouded in darkness.

Something moved under her fingers and she jumped and squeaked. A bug maybe. Shaken she realized no cobwebs brushed against her face. There was enough activity in this passageway to keep them down. Estella and Clarinda for sure. Trevor too, obviously.

Grey had been surprised by them so not every member of this family slipped along back here. Not much point in having a secret passageway if everyone knew about it.

Her toe hit something and she nearly pitched forward. Lowering her lantern, she illuminated a staircase going up.

The passage was wide enough she could go around the stairs and stay on this level. She wondered where it would lead? The kitchen? Sally's room? Outside?

But up would most likely take her to her office, as Estella's rooms were right below it.

The steps creaked like tormented souls. There was a wall on her right and nothing but empty space on her left. The lantern didn't light the stairwell enough for her to see over the edge. It couldn't fall any farther than the level she'd been on but it felt like a drop into a bottomless black pit. Staying close to the wall, she raised her lantern and saw the steps end as her head emerged to a new level. And there in front of her was that hole Grey had kicked in the wall. To save her. To hold her.

All she needed in here was her notebook. Her last entry might tell her enough to awaken her memory. She could find out what had happened that last day. Maybe there would be a clue to what brought on the attack on her and Victor. She knew she included personal observations in her notes but the memory seemed permanently blocked by the blow to her head.

She needed that notebook. It held the answers to the slumbering evil that had broken free.

Stepping into her office, she looked around, relieved to find herself alone, then rushed to the ornate Victorian lantern and lifted it off its base.

Her notebook lay there, untouched. She snatched it and rushed out of the room.

She hurried back down the stairs. She should be in plenty of time to get into her room before Estella returned. She'd find a place to tuck it out of sight, then read it and maybe finally figure out what had happened.

Footsteps echoed from below.

"Well, you wanted to be brave," she muttered. "Here's your chance."

She whirled and went back toward the opening in her office but ignored it. There was no place to hide in there. She passed the gaping hole and found another flight of stairs. This one would take her to the attic, and she could get out of this maze and go back downstairs, and even walking boldly through the halls, she'd probably still not see anyone. Though if she did, she'd handle it.

But she needed time with this notebook before someone took it from her.

Boldly she began to climb.

The footsteps behind her continued upward.

She reached the next level and found a blank wall with no passage to lead in any direction.

Remembering the lever in Estella's room, it was the work of seconds to slide her fingers along until she found it and, with a rusty squeak, a door swung open.

The attic tower.

It reminded her of the noise she'd heard that day in the attic when Grey had found her. There had been someone up here. Clarinda most likely. Lanny wondered how close she'd come to being dragged into the passageway that day.

Closing the door, Lanny stood for a moment in the tower room. The circular room was small, probably fifteen feet in diameter and there was no furniture jammed in here, unlike every other room in the house. The walls were mostly glass. Windows looking out in all directions. If the day hadn't been so shrouded from the storm, Lanny would've been able to see the crashing ocean to the east and the steep road down to town on the west. Trees and mountains descended sharply to the north and south.

But today, instead of a view she suddenly remembered was spectacular, she saw only windows opaque and gray, sheeted with heavy rain.

The room was circled by several short benches evenly spaced along the walls. There were doors in three sides, one to the roof, one to the attic and the one she'd just come through. She clicked the secret door shut, set her lantern and notebook aside and dragged the closest bench over to block the passageway entrance.

She went to the door that opened into the attic, opened it and looked around. Her eyes went to the heavy silver candlestick she held in her hand and thought, "Come for me now, Estella."

Lanny stepped back into her little fortress. "Let's see you shove me through a doorway now, Clarinda."

She went to the bench on the wall that didn't have a door and sat down. In here, with her back pressed to the window, she could see someone coming.

It was still daylight, though the heavily clouded day was ending.

She sat down to do some light reading that provoked murder. Flipping open the notebook, she saw the front had a pocket, which contained several sheets of paper yellowed with age. Lifting the first one gently, mindful of the fragile paper, she held it close to the flickering lantern and read.

August—1769

Poltron renamed SeaCliff
The Devil's Nest.

Lanny, startled, looked closer at the paper. Hadn't Pierre named it The Devil's Nest?

I thought it suited him perfectly. Poltron let me live because I was the only one who knew where the treasure was. But he enjoyed his power over me.

My son's life hung in the balance every second. The coward has been stripping SeaCliff of all its finery since he killed Pierre and took over his life.

Lanny stopped and read the sentence again. Since Poltron killed Pierre? But Poltron was Pierre. Or was he?

Yet Poltron knows there is more. He threatened my life, my little Pierre's life, he caused me unspeakable pain. But I knew, despite his threats, that I'd be dead the hour he got his hands on Pierre's jewels. And the coward knew if he killed my son, it would end any hope he had of shaking the truth from my lips.

The coward introduces himself as Pierre Devereau and has been accepted as my beloved Pierre. Pierre had been gone more than home since we arrived here. And when he was home we spent the time in each other's arms. He has never met anyone from the small settlement across the narrow waters at the bottom of our mountain because he came and went through the caves.

The visitor knew me and insisted on seeing my son. I knew Poltron wouldn't kill me, but he might well kill the visitor. When he'd left, the coward started laughing. He said, "From this day forward I'll only answer to the name Pierre, my sweet."

The coward indeed became Pierre. He went out among the people and became one of them. He began training 'his' son in the way of lies and cruelty and spoke greedily of the child I would one day bear him.

But Poltron leaves often enough, though his men don't allow me to flee. While Poltron is gone, I teach my son the way of a Christian, like his father and I.

Lanny flashed on finding Giselle's notes lying on her desk. Like all of the notes from Giselle's diary it had been given to her by some unknown inhabitant of this house.

Thrilled at this new piece of the puzzle, Lanny had gone to Estella with the news that Pierre had died young, all the stories of evil passed down were the work of Poltron, whom Giselle loathed.

Then Lanny remembered the blow.

And as she'd staggered around, she'd seen her attacker.

Lanny stood to run to Grey, tell him she knew who'd attacked her when she heard the creaking of approaching footsteps. She shoved her notes inside her sweater. To hide it, but also to keep it with her and let her hands be free.

The door to the attic slammed open. Estella came straight for her wielding a fireplace poker in one hand and a lantern in the other.

Jumping up, Lanny grabbed her own weapon, noting with some satisfaction that her candlestick was longer than Estella's poker.

"You're not sneaking up behind me again, Estella. Let's see how you do when you attack someone face to face."

"So, you finally remembered." Estella stopped advancing.

"I did. I remembered that all your history of the rogue pirate Pierre Devereau wasn't true.

He was a decent man. A Christian man. He wasn't even a pirate. He was a man who would have had contempt for the way you live, the way you've treated Victor. The legend you love so much belonged to the man who killed him."

"You work for me." The old woman's bitterly cold expression turned lethal and her face darkened to an unhealthy shade of florid red. "That makes anything you find mine."

"I do work for you. I'm researching the family history. And I found a really big part of it that you didn't like." Lanny tested her grip on the candlestick. She didn't want to whack some old lady, but she wasn't going to stand here and let Estella batter her, either.

"Give Giselle's letter to me. I've been searching for it ever since you told me you found it. If you hand it over, we can just walk out of here, no one needs to get hurt."

"By *no one* do you mean you? I don't see myself losing a fight between us and neither do you. That's the only reason you want to make a deal."

Lanny wished Grey was here. Estella didn't look inclined to back down, which seemed suddenly odd. Why wouldn't Estella be at least wary of a candlestick-toting researcher a fraction her age?

The door behind Lanny blew open as if the storm had battered it down. Allen stepped in from the Widow's Walk and wrapped an arm around Lanny's neck before she could raise her weapon. Allen choked her until she couldn't breathe and laughed in a way that didn't match a grieving husband.

Lanny hadn't planned on fighting a team. But so what?

She swung the candlestick down and back and slammed it between Allen's legs. He inhaled so hard it turned into an inverted scream. He stumbled back until he hit the door out to the Widow's Walk, but didn't let her go.

His flailing knocked Lanny's candlestick forward and it smashed Estella's lantern. The lantern flew to the side and crashed into the lantern Lanny brought, both shattered. Kerosene splattered the walls. Flames raced to follow the path of the fuel.

"Allen, hang onto her." Estella ignored the fire and came toward Lanny.

Lanny raised her candlestick and hammered it straight back into Allen's stomach. The blow staggered him into the door. The window broke and the door shattered its rotten hinges and fell drunkenly outward.

Icy rain lashed Lanny and Allen. He pulled her with him as he fell. She flung her arms wide to catch at the door. Thunder exploded around her, ripping a scream from Lanny's throat. Her hand hit the doorframe and knocked the candlestick free. She landed hard on top of Allen. Her eyes followed her only weapon as it rattled across the narrow Widow's Walk. It went through the railings but stopped on the edge of the roof.

Lanny rolled aside, free of Allen, intent on retrieving her club. Soaked by the storm, she regained her feet in time to see Estella rushing for her with her poker raised. As Estella came, Lanny saw it happening before. Finally, completely. Estella coming at her just this way the night Victor died.

Fire flashed out of the tower cutting off Lanny's only way down should she survive this madness.

Lanny dodged back. The poker caught her shoulder and knocked her flat on her back. Estella charged for her in the bitter, soaking rain. Lanny tried to get her feet under her but another swing made her fall. She scuttled backwards. Her candlestick was nearly within reach, just outside the railing.

"You'll destroy the Devereau legacy." Estella raised the weapon again.

The Widow's Walk surrounded the whole house. On the sea side it hung over the crashing ocean. Here it looked down three stories onto the stony soil of The Devil's Nest. Either fall would kill.

"You killed Victor!" Estella swung. Lanny flung her right hand up, taking a hard blow to her forearm.

"You lied your way out of that!" Estella pulled back for another blow.

The pain in Lanny's arm was excruciating. It went numb and wouldn't function. She was within grabbing distance of her candlestick but it was on her right. To reach it with her left she'd have to roll over, exposing herself to Estella's vicious assault. The silver object stuck out over the eaves, tantalizingly close. If Lanny could just get it, block a blow or two until she regained her feet and could fight this awful woman.

Thunder exploded all around her. Lightning lit up the gray and Lanny saw Allen behind Estella, his expression murderous.

Estella, soaked, skeletally thin, powerful with rage, raised her arm for one final blow. Lanny dove under the rickety railing. The poker clanked as it hit iron.

"Another Silver Girl." Estella laughed madly. "Jump, Silver Girl. Leap to your death."

Lanny felt the edge of the roof crumble and the candlestick plummeted out of her reach, dropping, its silver lost in the gray of the rain. Clawing at the roof, Lanny grabbed something solid with her left hand as she fell over the edge. She tried to force her right hand to work but it wouldn't bear weight.

Her legs dangling, the thunder slammed at her, battered her. Estella laughed and Lanny looked up to see the old witch shaking the railing of the Widow's Walk. It broke away, putting Lanny within reach of Estella's iron. The club raised.

Thunder threatened to break what was left of Lanny's hold on sanity. Her grip on the eaves slipped.

Lightning surrounded Estella. Her weapon swung down for Lanny's hand. Suddenly Estella jumped straight for Lanny. Then flew past her with a bloodcurdling scream.

Lanny followed her descent with horror. Estella vanished into the storm but a distant thud told Lanny the woman had met her fate.

Lanny shook her head at the nightmare that surrounded her and forced her wounded right hand to work. Getting a firm grip on the slippery roof, she looked up. No, not fell. Estella didn't fall.

Allen stood inches from Lanny's clinging hands. Smiling. Grotesque.

"Your days of making a fool of me are over." He spoke to the storm, to the ground far below.

Lanny knew in a split second.

Estella wasn't lying when she accused Lanny of killing Victor. Estella truly believed that. But it wasn't true. Allen uttered words that he could have said now three times. To Estella, to Victor and to Meredith, as he killed each of them.

The trio that had conspired to cuckold him in his own home. And he'd used Lanny as a scapegoat when he'd found her unconscious from Estella's attack.

A crackle that wasn't the storm drew Lanny's attention. Flames engulfed the tower and crept out onto the roof. Even the pouring rain wasn't enough to stop it.

She clung, afraid to draw Allen's attention by moving. But maybe in whatever madness gripped him, he had finished his rampage.

Then his eyes lowered to her and he smiled and Lanny knew the truth. He wasn't done.

"One more to go. The witness to it all."

He bent, clearly intending to shove her off the roof. Lanny looked wildly around and saw a window ledge only a foot or so below the roof line. With no choice, she let go with her stronger hand, caught at the window and, hating the precarious hold, she released her grip on the eaves and dropped out of Allen's reach.

Praying for strength, she held on.

"It won't save you." Allen knelt above her. Fire lit up the night behind him. He lay flat on the roof and stretched out murderous hands. Lanny dangled from the ledge and searched for something better. There was no purchase for her feet but she heard the rattle when she kicked and knew it was glass. She lashed out a foot and smashed a window. Kicking again and again, she fought to widen her opening enough to get inside without cutting herself to ribbons. Allen's hand suddenly gripped her injured wrist and yanked it free.

"No! Allen, stop. Help. Please God. Help me!!!"

"God abandoned this house when we named it The Devil's Nest," Allen roared over the storm.

Lanny clutched at the window ledge. Her grip was solid. The glass in front of her broke fully away. Even in the rain, fire lit up the roof.

"Allen! The house is burning!"

"It's mine. All mine. Clarinda doesn't care. Grey will leave. I've got money enough from the Trust and my smuggling. And I was smart enough to point the finger at Victor." Allen pulled hard at her hand, lifting her until she was almost shaken loose.

Her fingers slipped. If she was torn free, he'd drop her into the mist, following Estella to her death. Following Silver Girl.

Her grip broke.

Allen laughed and let her dangle. "You saw Meredith, didn't you? You know I killed all three of them."

"Allen no. Please."

He raised her just an inch, enjoying his power, then let go.

In that instant her legs were caught in an unbreakable hold.

Lanny looked down into Grey's furious eyes. He dragged her in through the shattered, slashing edges of the window.

Grey had been tearing through the house searching for everyone—anyone—since he'd smelled the fire. He'd found no one. Then he'd heard the scream. He'd charged in here to see Lanny's legs dangling in front of the broken window.

"What is going on?"

Allen's furious scream drew Grey's attention. He looked out to see Allen's arm come around holding a gun. A sharp crack cut through the thunder, the fire, the screams.

Grey whirled away from the window with Lanny caught tight against him as bullets blasted into the room, peppering the floors and walls. Another shout from Allen, this one laced with pain.

The gunfire stopped.

Grey saw the gun fall past the window. He let Lanny go and stuck his head out to see Allen rise, his feet teetering on the roof's edge. His clothes flaming in the sleeting rain.

Allen staggered sideways, flailing for balance, a human torch. Then, with a cry of agony, he pitched forward, plunging, the ugly male scream fading as he was swallowed up by the fog shrouded dusk.

The scream cut off with sickening suddenness.

With a cry of horror, Lanny turned and buried her face in Grey's neck.

His arms tightened for seconds, then he shoved her away, his hands bruising where he gripped her upper arms. "We've got to get out of here. This house is burning to the ground." A door opened into the hall and Grey saw smoke billow in.

"We might already be cut off from the stairs." Grey caught her arm and propelled her toward the door just as a whoosh of fire flashed in.

Grey changed course. "This is a suite. We can get closer to the stairs through Allen's kitchen."

He nearly dragged her. He'd pick her up and carry her if she didn't keep up.

Grey stormed through a door into a living area, then on into a kitchen. He headed for the door and skidded to a stop. Reaching down he touched the knob.

"It's hot, but not burning hot. The fire hasn't gotten to the door yet." He looked down at her. "When I open the door, keep down, wait until I say go, then run for the stairs. Stay low and keep going no matter what happens."

"Clarinda? Trevor? Sally?"

"Sally's looking for Clarinda. I don't know where Trevor is. I couldn't find Estella, either."

"She's dead."

Grey froze for a split second, then shook away the questions that bombarded his mind. No time now. "I have to get you out first. Then I'll see to the others."

He looked around and found a pair of white hand towels hanging from a hook in the kitchen. He grabbed them, soaked them in water, and shoved one into her hands. "Are you ready?"

Lanny nodded.

"Take a deep breath. Then cover your mouth with this. Try not to take a breath once we're in the hall, but if you have to, breathe through the towel."

Lanny filled her lungs and clapped the towel over her mouth and nose. Grey stood so the door would swing back pinning them away from whatever was in the hall. He wrenched the door open. Flames exploded inward. Pausing for a second to let them die back, Grey looked around the door into the hallway, then yelled, "Move!"

Like passing through a corridor to Hades, flames licked the walls around them. Overhead, fire crawled along the ceiling. The house groaned like a dying monster. Grey had a sense that he now truly knew what the devil's nest would be like.

With his face mostly covered, he reached the stairs just as a beam cracked and swung down splintering the stairs. Grey staggered back and fell to dodge the cascading fire from above. He grabbed Lanny as he fell, sheltering her with his body.

One look told him the stairway was impassable.

"Crawl." He tugged on Lanny but she was already moving, helping save herself.

"There's a passageway in your room." Lanny shouted over the snarl of fire. "Estella came in through it last night."

Grey had never seen the passageway and he hadn't known about Estella's visit. More to talk about once they got out of this miserable house.

Grey's door was just ahead. He scrambled to his feet and, with a firm hold on Lanny, he ran inside and slammed the door shut. The room was murky from smoke but no fire had ignited in here yet. "Where is it? Where's the passage entry?"

Lanny gave him a wide-eyed look. "I don't know. I only know she got in here somehow." Grey felt a tremor of fear so strong he almost lost control. But that was a waste of time.

"Start searching."

The room was dim from the storm and approaching night. Smoke was thick and getting thicker all the time.

Grey ran his hands long the wall, trying to picture the layout of the house and figure where a few feet of extra space could be hidden.

Suddenly a shape appeared in the murky room. Someone wearing a dark dress, her face shrouded by the smoke. She had dark hair. Clarinda.

He saw a dark rectangle in the wall that separated his room from Lanny's. Clarinda had to have come in through it. She lifted a hand that glittered around the wrist. Clarinda beckoned with a single sweep, then turned and headed for the opening.

"Lanny!" Grey fumbled through the smoke until he found her. "The door. Come on!"

They raced for the blackness just as a gust of fire blasted under the door to the hallway and began eating its way through. Grey saw the dim form of Clarinda vanish into the gaping passageway entrance, then she was swallowed up by smoke. He was only a few feet behind with Lanny's hand firmly gripped in his.

When they got into the passage Clarinda had vanished. Grey inched along until he found a stairway going down. "Be careful on these steps. They'll be narrow."

They started down in the stygian darkness. "Thank God you found this so quickly."

"Clarinda came in through it. Didn't you see her?"

"No, but that means she's all right. We're all going to make it out, Grey."

"We're not safe yet."

They reached the bottom of the stairs and a door stood open to the night air.

"I thought we'd have to fight our way through the main floor but there's a door out. Clarinda opened it. She must've known this was here for years." Grey rushed out into the cold rain with Lanny a step behind him. The rain battered them as they put space between themselves and The Devil's Nest.

"Where is Clarinda? I thought you said she led you?"

"I can't see five feet ahead of me out here. The car we drove is sitting out. Let's get you inside and I'll find everyone else."

Lanny threw herself in front of Grey. "You're not going back in there."

Their eyes met. Then they both turned to look at the house. It was completely engulfed. Fire licked out of every window. The front door was gone, a rectangle of fire licking upward. The heavy rain pelted them but the fire raged on, as if the devil had created something unquenchable.

"Where is everyone? Where is Sally?" Grey took a step toward the house, staring at the black rectangle they'd just emerged from. "I can get in there. Get to Sally's room." An explosion rocked the house and the tower began to tilt straight for them.

"Run!" Lanny screamed, pulling on Grey. He had no choice.

He and Lanny ran, slipping in the mud. The tower slammed into the ground covering the door they'd emerged from. Stones and splinters of flaming wood knocked them to the ground and they slid to a stop only a few paces from the crumbled tower. A massive stone block smashed through the windshield of the car and ripped the roof most of the way off.

Grey dragged her to her feet and put more space between them and the fire. Grey turned to study the nightmare they'd just escaped. Flaming remnants of the tower blocked anyone from entering the house. Lanny leaned her head against Grey's shoulder. "We know Clarinda got out, right? She led you."

Nodding, Grey realized he didn't know anything of the sort. Clarinda wasn't normal. She might have gone up instead of down. In his explorations of the afternoon, he'd found the passageway leading into the heart of this cliff.

"If she's out here, we need to find her and get her under shelter."

"I think the rain is ending." A deep rumble of thunder sounded inland, carried along by the storm. The house howled as the roof collapsed. The ancient wood burned like gasoline.

"There's no way anyone left inside can still be alive." Grey spoke the words out loud, thinking of Sally. Had she stayed to search for Clarinda? Had she given her life to save the poor woman who'd been like a daughter to her? Grey knew Sally would have done it if asked. But maybe Sally had gotten out. Clarinda, too.

The rain began winning its fight with the fire as the flames consumed wood and left only blackened stone behind.

Grey couldn't think where to begin searching for Clarinda. If she'd gotten out, had she made it into the woods? Could she be in a cave in the heart of the cliff? She'd seemed unafraid when she gestured for him to follow her.

Grey slipped his arm around Lanny. "Will you pray with me for Clarinda's safety, for everyone?"

"Yes, and I need to tell you about Estella and Victor."

"What went on up there?"

Lanny told him swiftly as the fire ebbed and the rain slowed.

By the time she was done the rain had ended and the clouds overhead were thinning. "So, all that you said about leaving me, not wanting my family's blood flowing in your children's veins—"

"Hush!" Lanny threw her arms around his neck and kissed him. Long moments later, she said, "I'm so sorry I said all that. I just had to think of something so awful you'd believe me. Estella said she'd kill you. I couldn't put you in danger. Not when I love you so much."

Grey cut her off with a ruthless kiss as his heart lifted so high it almost made him laugh. Only the grim day kept him from feeling true joy.

"Will you marry me, Lanny? Will you let my blood flow in the veins of your children?"

"Please, yes. Oh, Grey, I'm so in love with you."

He silenced her with another kiss. When next he raised his head, he realized a bit of sun peeked through clouds to the west. There was still some daylight left to them.

As he opened his mouth to suggest they begin a search, he saw movement to his left.

Turning, he tucked Lanny behind him. His instincts to fight were still on full alert. Sally came out of the woods, her arms wrapped around her plump waist.

"Sally!" Grey took Lanny with him as he hurried over to the housekeeper.

Sally's face was drenched with tears. She was bedraggled, muddy. Her no-nonsense walking shoes were caked in mud. The normally fine lines in her face were cut deep.

"I couldn't find her, Grey." Sally stumbled and nearly fell.

"Clarinda?" Grey slid an arm around Sally's waist.

"She came to me in the fire and led me out."

"She saved us, too." Lanny clutched Grey's shirt as if she was holding herself up.

He bore the weight of both women, but their strength held him up, too. "She was ahead of us. Why would she have gone back into the fire?"

"Maybe she led me out and went back for you?" Sally wiped a shaking hand across her eyes.

"And then went back for Trevor?" Grey fumbled for the handkerchief he kept in his back pocket. He had Lanny in his right arm, but she was holding on tight enough he dared to release her for a second. He pressed it into Sally's hands.

"And Allen and Estella." Sally took the drenched handkerchief and held it over her face as her shoulders trembled. "She was trying to save all of us. Didn't anyone else get out?"

Grey exchanged a long look with Lanny. The sight of her dangling in front of that window would haunt him forever.

"Estella and Allen are dead." Lanny said it with calm that sounded almost irrational. No one could be calm after what she'd gone through.

Sally shook her head as she studied the flames.

"I remembered everything from that last day." Lanny looked from the smoldering ruins of The Devil's Nest to Grey. Then she looked past Grey's shoulder and followed the line of her vision to see Trevor running up the driveway, coming from the direction of the washed-out road.

"One more alive." Grey quietly studied the young man who approached them at a brisk pace. "Good old cousin Trevor."

"What happened here?" Trevor met his eyes and even from this distance, Grey knew Trevor was up to something. As always.

"We had a fire." When he closed in, Grey asked, "Road open yet?"

"They're working on it. The road crew is digging a path big enough for us to walk out on." Trevor's gaze went to the wreckage of the house. "I don't know if they'll be willing to dig it wide enough to get a car out though, not with the house gone."

"The only car left up here is destroyed so I'm not worried about it." Grey was struck by the maturity in Trevor's tone. He wasn't acting like Victor anymore.

"Who are you?" Grey knew it was long past time to ask. Trevor's sharp gaze went to Lanny and Sally before he spoke. "My name is Trevor Romo. Agent Trevor Romo, FBI."

Lanny gasped. Sally shifted away from Grey to stand without support. Grey wondered if she wasn't giving Grey room to throw a fist. "What brings you to The Devil's Nest?" Grey kept his arm firmly around Lanny.

"Your company is under investigation for smuggling. We've managed to narrow our search and today I found tunnels that reach all the way down to the bottom of the cliff. Under the auspices of the importing companies that are part of the Grey Trust, someone has been bringing contraband into the United States."

"Victor." Grey knew Victor had been up to no good.

"No, Allen was behind it," Trevor said.

Grey's eyes narrowed. "I turned evidence over to the local police. I came up here to put a stop to money laundering. I found a financial trail that was sending stolen money through the Grey Trust and that trail led me back to Victor."

Shaking his head, Trevor said, "It was always Allen. He's the money man. I have no doubt Allen made any evidence he couldn't completely bury, point to Victor. But I ran around with Victor long enough to know he couldn't stay sober long enough to make a scheme like this work."

"I can imagine Victor doing it, but not doing it well." Grey nodded. "And this was done very well. There was a little corner of the Trust I didn't even know existed. It was all shrouded with the legitimacy of my company, but the money came in and went out without my knowledge."

"I've seen what you turned over to Detective Garrison."

"He knew what you were up to?"

"I only introduced myself after Victor was murdered. But Garrison is a former FBI agent so he's been very willing to work together. I told him, from what I'd seen, Lanny wasn't the type to kill anyone, but then Victor had been badgering her until I couldn't rule her out."

"Allen killed Victor." Lanny crossed her arms and Grey felt her shudder. "He admitted it to me along with the smuggling. Estella is the one who hit me, knocked me out. She was furious about the journal I'd found and she wanted me to stop my work. She fired me and, when I told her I would make public what I'd learned, she hit me. Then Allen found me unconscious and arranged things so I'd look like a murderer."

"Where are those two?" Trevor gave the incinerated house a grim look.

"Neither Allen nor Estella made it out of the fire alive." Grey offered no explanation beyond that. Trevor's eyes narrowed but his next question wasn't about them.

"And Clarinda?" Trevor's sharply intelligent eyes took on the first real softness Grey had seen. Maybe Trevor wasn't a pure cynic.

"She led me out." Sally's voice broke.

"She saved us, too." Tears welled in Lanny's eyes. "But she must have gone back." Lanny's face was smudged with soot and tears rolled down.

"She got all three of you out?" Trevor asked.

"She guided us to a door we didn't know existed," Grey turned from watching the smoking hulk of The Devil's Nest. "I wonder if she went back for you?"

Trevor's solemn expression turned dark with regret. "I saw her earlier."

"When you were in the passageway?" Lanny asked.

"Yes. I've been exploring it ever since we found you inside, Lanny. I'd been trying to figure out how Estella seemed to know everything that went on in this house. And Victor had a talent for disappearing, and reappearing. I never knew why until I found that passage."

"Do we just give up on Clarinda, then?" Lanny looked at Grey with sad eyes.

Grey stared at the ruin. "Judging by the way she led us, she probably knows the passageways in there better than anyone. There's a very good chance she got down into the caves below the level of the house and took cover from the fire. She could be alive."

"But it's red hot." Sally took an uncertain step toward the smoking remains. "How do we begin to find a way in to search for her?"

As Sally spoke movement from the south side of the wreckage drew Grey's attention. He said with awe, "Look at that. We don't have to search at all. She got out."

Clarinda appeared wearing a thin, flowered dress, much like she wore all the time. She clutched a large rectangular object in her arms.

"She had on a black dress earlier," Grey said. "I've never seen it before. A floor length black dress. There were wide cuffs. She gestured with her arms, waved me to follow her and in the dim, smoky filled room, those light-colored cuffs shone like she was holding a lantern."

"Clarinda doesn't own such a thing," Sally started for Clarinda as the woman approached them.

"Maybe she found it in the attic." Grey watched Clarinda and Sally hug.

Lanny rubbed her arms as if she was chilled to the bone. "The dress Giselle is wearing in her portrait in the library has a gold collar and cuffs." Grey wished Lanny hadn't said that.

Trevor had more to add. "So, Clarinda found a dress, hundreds of years old."

"I didn't say it was Giselle's dress," Grey didn't like where this was going.

"She put it on," Trevor continued doggedly. "Then led you all to safety, even though you two and Sally were on different floors, far from each other."

"Someone did that." Lanny's hand settled on Grey's forearm and clung so tightly it hurt.

"Then went back into the passageway. In spite of the fire." Trevor had more to say. "And changed back into her regular clothes. And she did all of this while the house collapsed over her head?"

Lanny looked from Clarinda to Grey. "Why would she do that?"

"Giselle said I wasn't bad." Clarinda approached Grey, lifting the small box she carried.

A chill went up Grey's spine and he focused on the box to keep from asking Clarinda what made her quote—in present tense—a woman who'd been dead for centuries. Changing the subject was in order. "What did you find?"

Clarinda held a black chest, very old with ornate carving on all sides. It was about the size of a shoe box with a latched, domed lid on top. Grey urged Lanny forward, he wasn't about to let her out of his sight again, not even out of his reach. Grimly he remembered making that promise to himself before.

They met Clarinda just as she extended the small chest toward Grey. "This is yours. It belongs to the children of Pierre Devereau. And you're the only one. Giselle says you're safe now, all the Poltrons are dead. The bad ones. I'm not bad."

"Of course, you're not bad, my girl." Sally went to Clarinda's side. "It's heavy, take it." Clarinda's arms shook as she held the chest out.

Grey took it and the weight surprised him. He didn't know much about precious metals but he suspected this is what silver looked like. Very old, tarnished silver.

Though the box looked ancient, Grey lifted a complex little latch and it slid easily, as if it was kept oiled and was used regularly. He swung the domed lid up to find...

"Pierre's treasure." Lanny gasped.

Gems. Gold coins. Necklaces studded with diamonds and emeralds and rubies. Pearls laced through the pile of glittering wealth like a river of priceless cream.

A king's ransom.

Lanny reached for it. But she didn't grab a jewel, she reached for the lid.

That's when Grey noticed the lid was lined with brittle, yellowed paper lined with words. With a tiny laugh, he realized that of course Lanny, the historian, was more interested in old words than gems.

She carefully pulled the papers free and whispered, "Giselle's writing. I recognize it. It's dated, look."

Lanny tore her gaze from the paper and said to Clarinda, "You've been bringing me the letters she wrote, haven't you?"

"You needed to read the papers. You needed to protect Grey so Giselle could rest."

"Uh…Giselle?" Lanny exchanged a long look with Grey. He saw her swallow hard but she didn't ask Clarinda any questions.

Grey wondered if maybe it was because Lanny, who was always searching for knowledge, didn't want to know.

Poltron is back.

He hasn't come to me yet. But he is done waiting, I can sense it. I believe this will be the last time I write.

The precious child I bore with Pierre is grown and gone. Safely set free. What Pierre's son makes of himself is between him and God now. I've done all I can to preserve Poltron's son's life and teach him right from wrong, good from evil. But his father was a powerful influence, and I could only be seen by my beloved child as a weakling and a coward.

If Pierre had come one more time, without Poltron at hand, I'd have told him everything.

The truth. He is old enough now to protect himself. Old enough to know who his father really was.

Old enough to understand the danger my words would place on his shoulders.

I'd have given him the treasure and perhaps my son could have found a way for me to escape. But he has tarried.

Perhaps he will never return. I understand fully if he has rid himself of his family.

I have prayed. I have prayed until my knees are worn and bruised. And I feel the hand of God holding me up when I had not the strength to do it myself. The one unshakable truth that stays in my heart is that it is wrong to choose the time and place for my own death.

But my only choice now is to tell Poltron of the treasure and die quickly or not tell him and let him do his worst. I don't believe I have the strength to withstand his cruel hands another time. I can think of only one way to leave this to God.

Poltron's harsh blows are not measured. Not when I defy him as I fully intend to do. And he is desperate, which he clearly is, for the treasure is all the money that is left. I will go to the Widow's Walk and let him find me there. If he strikes me, he won't have a care. Falling to my death will be the end result. It will end things and I welcome that.

Poltron will make his home here, for himself and his own son. But my son will come here, too and be part of Poltron's life.

And when Pierre comes, there will always be danger.

I can think of only one way to protect my son, so I end this letter with a vow before God.

I have read of ghosts in the Bible. It is written that on occasion people come back after shaking off this mortal coil.

If there is a way to protect my son and his descendents from beyond the grave, I will find it. I solemnly vow that until the bad have died and the good are safe, I will be here if God allows.

Until The Devil's Nest is destroyed, I will stand guardian over you, my son. You and all your descendants.

And though God is not a respecter of earthly wealth, if He wills it, I will find a way to give you the treasure of Pierre Devereau.

Giselle Fontaine Devereau

Lanny looked up from the diary page. "I've...I've..." She fell silent with a helpless shrug.

Grey looked at Clarinda, hoping she'd fess up to being the one who'd led them out. "Where did you find the black dress you were wearing earlier?"

Clarinda didn't answer. Instead she was looking at the house, her eyes calm, serene. "She can rest now."

"So, it's all yours, Grey." Sally gestured at the smoldering pile of rubble. "You're the only true descendent of Pierre and Giselle Devereau."

A smile quirked one corner of Grey's mouth. "All mine. Great. I own a ruin."

"You also own a fortune in gems." Trevor gestured at the little chest.

"There are a lot more pages here and I got one of my notebooks out, the last one." Lanny tapped on the front of her sweater to reassure herself the notebook was still there, then thumbed through the pages from the chest, reading bits. "I can finally write a true history of the Devereau family with what I'd found before and what's here. A history that you'll be proud of, Grey. Pierre and Giselle were noble, Christian people."

"Hey!" The shout turned them all around.

Detective Garrison trudged up the driveway toward them, coated in mud, looking exhausted. "We've finally got a path cleared, wide enough to walk is all."

Several more men followed, dressed in work clothes, equally grimy.

Grey balanced the chest in one hand and touched Clarinda's arm. "We have to go. You know that, don't you? We have to leave The Devil's Nest."

"I'm ready. I can be happy anywhere."

Sally rested one arm around Clarinda's waist. "And where ever you go, I'll go too. We'll find a place where we can be happy together."

They began walking down the driveway to meet Garrison. Lanny slid her hand into the bend of Grey's elbow. He squeezed it between his arm and his body and slowed to let the others get ahead. "So, you're sure you're okay with my blood flowing in your children's veins?" Lanny smiled. "I'm looking forward to it."

"Me too."

Lanny rested her head on Grey's strong arm and added, "You know, having a great heritage is a wonderful thing, but in the end, we make our own choices in life. Faith or the lack of it shapes us far more than our fore-fathers."

"We can be married immediately."

"I would very much like to marry you immediately. And we can take all the time we need to make sure Clarinda is settled somewhere. She and Sally can live with us if they want. In some nice modern house with no secret passages."

"As a matter of fact, I own a nice house in Houston." One handed, Grey hoisted the chest up to draw her attention. "And our real treasure will be one that can never be lost or stolen."

Thunder cracked in the distance, and Lanny jerked her head around to face yet another oncoming storm.

"Let's hurry, so we can get you out of the worst of it. You're going to be even more afraid of storms after what we've been through today." Grey looked solemnly at her. "But I'll be with you to weather every storm."

"I know you will, and I'm so glad to not be alone anymore. But the reason I turned so suddenly wasn't fear, it was realizing that the terrible fear isn't there. I think I've finally learned that the noise is just God sending the gift of rain. Just like he sent me to The Devil's Nest—of all terrible places—to find you."

EPILOGUE

Clarinda's sweet laughter turned Lanny from her paperwork to look out the window. A sea breeze wafted in. Sally sat drinking tea on the patio while Clarinda knelt in the grass and tickled the belly of a golden retriever puppy. A tray of cookies sat on a table at Sally's side. Chocolate chip if Lanny was smelling right.

"Come on out. You need a break." Grey came in, tanned and rested, his hair a bit fly-away.

"We're all having fun and you're working."

Delighted to leave her work behind, Lanny stood. She rested one hand on her aching lower back and squeaked.

Grey was at her side instantly, steadying her. "Are you all right?"

"My back has been sore all day but I think maybe it's more than being a big old round woman. I think it's time we headed to the hospital."

The grip Grey had on her arm went from gentle and supportive to terror induced strangulation.

"Ouch!"

"How bad is it? How much pain? Is the baby coming now?"

"You're crushing my arm!"

Grey let go instantly, looking so guilty Lanny was sorry she'd mentioned it, though it was nice to have the vice off her arm.

Leaning close, she whispered. "I'm done."

"No, you're not. You're just getting started. Babies can take hours." Grey looked a little pale and his knees might have wobbled a bit.

Laughing, Lanny said, "Done with the *book*. The history I've been writing about the real Pierre Devereau. He's an honorable man whose legacy was stolen from him by a coward. I've written the book telling the truth, that he is a man to be proud of as an ancestor."

"We don't have time to talk about that now." Grey slid his arm around her waist as if he was planning to carry her all the way to the car.

"Just hold on a second. We've probably, unfortunately, got plenty of time."

"I want you in the hospital. This baby is *not* going to be born in the car."

"Just let me send the manuscript to my agent." Lanny sat back down and pecked quickly at the computer keys.

"Leave that until later." Grey reached for her but Lanny dodged him. She was pretty sure he only let her keep typing because he didn't want to get into a wrestling match with a woman in labor. And anyway, it was the honest truth that he had trouble denying her anything.

"I should really write to my editor too, and send her a copy. Though I told my agent I'd leave it to her. Still, the editor would like to get the book as soon as possible."

"Lanny, for heaven's sake. Let's go."

She pointed at the suitcase, already packed. "You can carry that." She gave him a smug smile.

"Of course I'll carry your suitcase." He sounded outraged. "If you don't come right now, I'm going to carry you."

Since they'd left the ancient mansion, Lanny had lured Grey back up there several times. They'd sifted through rubble and found a lot of artifacts that Lanny had restored and researched.

She'd done the work out of a love for history and to resurrect the good name of Devereau. They'd also found the passageway down to a honeycomb of caves that reached all the way to sea level. The FBI had arrested the entire highly organized smuggling ring.

When a publisher had shown interest in Lanny's book, it had turned into a race to get the book done before the baby came.

Grandma Millie had died peacefully. Lanny had spent time at her side, and felt peace knowing Grey and Grandma had met. Grandma was confused, but whoever the nice young man named Grey was, she loved him.

The tumult of giving birth ran its usual course. Lanny came through it wonderfully and when Grey escorted her home with their little bundle, Lanny tried one more time to convince Grey he owed it to his destiny to claim the family name for his son.

"His name is Robert Leland Grey. You agreed to stop nagging me. We already filed the birth certificate papers."

"It's not *nagging* to tell you what I want." Grey snorted. "You know I hate that name."

Lanny liked to keep up the *not*-nagging just a bit because, even though she was dead certain Grey was never going to stick their child with the name Devereau, it would help her get her way the next time they disagreed. Even the struggle, which Lanny had to admit she'd lost, didn't mar her happiness.

They hurried inside, the baby buckled in the car seat and carried in Grey's strong hands, to beat the oncoming spring rain. Thunder cracked and clouds boiled and grew dark overhead. High noon turned to dusk.

Lanny paid it scant attention beyond not wanting to let her precious baby get wet. When they rushed inside, they met the rest of their family, waiting and eager.

"Can I see him?" Clarinda smiled, no fear left in her eyes. She and Sally lived nearby and came over often. They were both here now, along with Sally's daughter, Marcia. The three women had a noon meal simmering that smelled wonderful.

And the Garrison's, Grey's family of the heart, would be here, in fact Hangin' Judge Janet was flying in. The rest of them would spread out their visits so they wouldn't be overwhelming.

Garrison grandbabies were showing up regularly now and the Hangin' Judge was turning out to be a softy. And she'd already declared little Robert Leland to be one of hers.

Before the onslaught of company, Lanny took a few moments to enjoy the peace. She pulled back the blanket on the little car seat, to show Clarinda her newest cousin while Grey urged Lanny forward into a chair. Lanny was surprised he hadn't carried her in as well as the baby.

The storm unleashed it's violent, pounding rain while lightning cut through the overcast sky. Thunder seemed to hammer on the house, wanting in.

Lanny rocked her baby, prayed for wisdom to be the best mom who'd ever lived and gave thanks.

She looked up at Grey and it was all there between them. How they'd met. Overcoming all that stood between them. Defeating evil so thoroughly that what was once a terrible fear of thunder, was now a bond between them.

Grey took his sleeping son and kissed Lanny thoroughly.

"We met in a thunderstorm, Grey."

He gave her an exasperated look. "I don't want to discuss the night we met."

"The first time I told you I loved you, it was during a thunderstorm."

"Well, it was raining pretty much non-stop that week."

"And our son came home in a thunderstorm." Lanny smile. "I've come to love rainy days."

Grey kissed her again, gently this time. "Are we ever going to tell this story to our children?" Lanny had thought this over a few times. "Maybe a condensed, sanitized version, no dead bodies for sure. And certainly not with me in bed with one. We'd better get our story straight."

"Let's tell him we met while we were singing in the church choir."

Lanny grinned. "I might not change it quite that much. A treasure, a haunted house, a raging inferno, hidden passages. We don't want to leave that out."

"You write it up and we can study it together, memorize the details."

A loud motor roared outside and they both turned to look out the window. The Hangin' Judge was here.

More Books by Mary Connealy

Garrison's Law

Loving the Texas Lawman

Loving Her Texas Protector

Loving the Texas Negotiator

Loving the Texas Stranger

Loving the Mysterious Texan

Sierra Nevada Sweethearts

The Accidental Guardian

The Reluctant Warrior

The Unexpected Champion – April 2019

Cimarron Legacy Series

No Way Up

Long Time Gone

Too Far Down

Wild at Heart Series

Tried and True

Now and Forever

Fire and Ice

Trouble in Texas Series

Swept Away

Fired Up

Stuck Together

Kincaid Brides Series

Out of Control

In Too Deep

Too Far Down